Of Woe *or* Wonder

Tony J. Stafford

Of Woe or Wonder

Copyright © 2022 by Tony J. Stafford.

Paperback ISBN: 978-1-63812-357-6
Ebook ISBN: 978-1-63812-358-3

All rights reserved. No part in this book may be produced and transmitted in any form or by any means, electronic, or mechanical, including photocopying, recording, or by any information storage and retrieval system, without permission in writing from the copyright owner.

The views expressed in this work are solely those of the author and do not necessarily reflect the views of the publisher hereby disclaims any responsibility for them.

Published by Pen Culture Solutions   06/11/2022

Pen Culture Solutions
1-888-727-7204 (USA)
1-800-950-458 (Australia)
support@penculturesolutions.com

Inscriptions

Horatio, Hamlet's friend, says, standing amidst four dead bodies at the end, including Hamlet's, says, "What is it you would see? If aught of woe or wonder, cease your search." *Hamlet* 5. 2. 401-2

"But at my back I always hear
Time's winged chariot hurrying near;
And all before us lie,
Deserts of vast eternity. . . .
The grave's a fine and private place,
But none, I think, do there embrace."
Andrew Marvel, "To His Coy Mistress"

Prologue

A weak female voice squeaked on the hall side of his slightly ajar, and beckoning, office door to which was attached the sign, "I AM HERE" and another sign which informed the observer, "Bienvenidos. You are always welcome." "*In the room the women come and go, talking of Michelangelo. . . No, wrong poem.*" He regarded his office door as the poetical portal into his life and beyond, in some cases way beyond.

"Dr. Sandberg?"

Justin reeled in his feet from the top of his desk and launched himself out of his swivel chair with, "Come in."

The door tremulously opened to reveal Paloma Garcia standing in the doorway, which Justin sometimes called *Cerberus's domain* (Cerberus being the many headed dog that guarded the gates of Hades to keep victims from escaping; Justin had numerous names for his office door, depending on the visitor). Paloma, who was a student in Justin's course in "Shakespeare's Plays and Poetry," seemed to be about nineteen or twenty years old, came from working-class heritage, as did most of the university's student body, was brown in skin tone (Shakespeare's favorite color for many of his heroines) and praise-worthy black hair (as was most of the University of Texas at Mountain Pass's student body), and would qualify to be labelled as fetching. Unlike many of the undergraduate female students who, this time of year, wore cut-off shorts and T-shirts, Paloma was adorned in a frilly, flowery spring dress, cut above the knees and a low swoop across her chest, with sexy sandals and painted toenails. It occurred to Justin that she had on an unusual amount of make-up with lots of lipstick and eye-liner, a bow in her hair, and a cloud of perfume. *She must be going to work,* was Justin's silent assumption, which was usually the case for hordes of their students. A student in high heels in a classroom usually communicated that she was on her way to work after class.

"Paloma," Dr. Sandberg welcomed her by gesturing at a chair in front of his desk, "have a seat."

"Thank you." She seemed shy, tentative, and hesitant. Paloma was of medium height with a smallish body type, but sufficiently curvy and sensuous looking, *just the type I would go for were I a college student,* he daydreamed and immediately booted it out of his consciousness, never permitting such notions to linger over a co-ed. She crossed and uncrossed and re-crossed her exposed legs with her hem riding farther up with each shift before proclaiming her business. She blinked her eyes rapidly and cocked her head to one side as though to make him notice her by such an unorthodox pose.

"What's happening?" Justin tried to communicate with hip, collegiate lingo and student-body language.

"I didn't do too well on my midterm," she modestly offered.

"Let me see," he saw himself survey his desktop and extract his grade book from under a pile of paper rubble. He flipped the pages, stopped to consider a certain spot, and moved his finger down the roster, stopping at "Garcia, Paloma."

"Well, it's not all that bad." He consoled both of them.

"It's not acceptable to me," she explained.

"Your cause is not a totally hopeless one."

"Dr. Sandberg, you don't understand," she stated.

"What?" He popped his head up from his gradebook. "What don't I understand?"

"I'm an English major. I need to make an A in this class. I plan to get a teaching certificate, to be a high school English teacher, I can't have grades like that on my record." She revealed her plight as a desperate one and her dress's hem travelled a centimeter up her thigh.

"Well, you're doing pretty well on the reading quizzes; that'll help some."

"Dr. Sandberg—"

Justin was inside his grade book considering her overall record and then looked up on command. "Yes?"

A seemingly interminable pause hung between them while she spoke to him with her big brown eyes, and then the moment seemed to fall to the floor as her eyes followed it down and rasped, "I'll do anything for an A." Her eyes remained fixed on the floor as though she were embarrassed by what she had just rapidly tumbled out and did not want responsibility for.

Justin mentally ducked.

"Well—" He straightened up his wits. "There is still the term paper—"

"Do you understand what I am saying?" she proceeded.

"—and there's the out-of-class projects—"

"I mean anything."

"—and don't forget the final exam—"

"Anything you ask of me, I'll do for an A." She brought the moment back up into the space between them and latched onto his eyes again.

"Yours is not a totally hopeless cause, if you'll—just—you know—"

"What?"

"Study harder."

"I studied hard for the midterm, and look what happened. I can't take any chances. I mean, I do plan to study harder, but—" She halted.

"But, what?"

"I need to guarantee myself that I'll get an A, and there is only one way I know to do that," she spoke shyly.

"Which is?"

"Look," she spoke with her eyes again, "we both know that it is completely in your hands what I make in this class. That's just the way it is. And the way I see it, I need to please you—somehow. I am at your mercy." She bowed her head to play the humble act again--and perhaps a little discomforted by her offer. Justin wistfully wished that he was thirty years younger, that she was not a student, that he was not her professor, that the moon was made out of coconut cream pie, that he was a millionaire playboy, and that they were in a hotel room somewhere on a Mexican playa.

"No. *I* don't give grades"

"What?" She looked up to question him.

"My calculator does."

"Oh." She batted her eyelashes at him and then ran her tongue slowly around her lips. "Aren't you even tempted—?"

"I have to go to class now."

"—just a little bit?" she asked

"Yes." He let his affirmative answer hover in the air between them for dramatic effect, not to raise her hopes, and repeated, "I've got to go to class now."

"Don't you find me attractive—somewhat?" She continued her interrogation.

"I cannot afford to answer that question," and added, "Do you know what would happen to me?

"What?"

"They would have my head on the chopping block so fast I wouldn't have time to even say a prayer. I would be tried, hung, boiled in oil, tarred and feathered, and castrated all within one hour."

"Nobody would know," she argued.

"I would. And—I would then be at your mercy."

"Seems fair," she said.

"Look, I'm no saint. I am very human. But, in my profession, there are some boundaries one just does not cross. What you're suggesting is one of them."

"Will you think about it?" she asked as she stood.

"I just did. I have to get to class. Close the sacred door as you leave, please," and she did after stopping at the door, turning to him, blowing him a kiss, pushing up her bra/breast, and throwing her hip at him. *Poor baby,* he thought as he stood contemplating his desk. Little did Professor Justin Sandberg intuit that he and Paloma Garcia were destined to cross paths again under very different circumstances.

1

Justin Sandberg, giving sway to recollections such as Paloma Garcia, sat in his office during the last week of August and the first week of the fall semester, the blessed, sacred, and hallowed, as he deemed it, time of the year. While the desert seemed wiltingly hot to the newest faculty members and easterners who cursed and condemned the arid landscape, Justin, having sojourned in the desert for some thirty years and well acclimated to it, could sense that underneath the ninety-degree thermometer reading something had furtively crept into the air, a farewell to summer and a prelude to an autumn assault of abundant beauty; the sun still persisted in warmth but the air was changing its mind. This present August, he thought, known in the desert as the monsoon season, had successfully soaked sand dunes and city alike, cooling things by an infinitesimal fraction, and, in Justin's mind, escorting in the preamble to a promising fall. Little did he suspect what lay ahead. Very few persons, looking only at the glazing sun, were as attuned to desert nuances (or in the minds of non-natives, nuisances) as Justin was. It excited him in the extreme, anticipating meeting his new classes and fresh faces, initiating a new season of "happy hour" with his colleagues, resurrecting the academic rituals of convocation and committee meetings (even the boring ones which accomplished little), and escorting in a new football season (always begun with such great hopes of success only to be met in November by the cold reality of another failed season). It did not matter; it was the anticipation of fresh starts that buoyed him. Everyone can always benefit from neo-natalism. *Ahhh, the seasonal deaths and resurrections*, he thought, *the diurnal wobbling of the ole planet*, the same faith which sustained Shakespeare in the eternal renewal of life as seen in his Last Romances, especially spelled out in his *The Winter's Tale* which celebrates the arrival of spring. "Apprehend nothing by jollity," says

Florizell to the shepherd lass Perdita who is welcoming guests to the sheep shearing festival. "See, your guests approach. Address yourself to entertain them sprightly, and let's be red with mirth," instructs her adopted father, the shepherd. Perdita then offers flowers to the two new guests with "grace and remembrance be to you both, and welcome to our shearing." "Well you fit our ages with flowers of winter," says King Polixenes, disguised as a shepherd in order to spy on his son Florizell. Perdita then blesses them with gifts of flowers, especially "the marigold, that goes to bed with th' sun and with him rises weeping. These are flowers of middle summer," given to men of middle age," Perdita diplomatically adds.

Sitting at his desk on which his feet were claiming authority by right of being on top of it, in spite of the important papers they were subjugating, Professor Sandberg let his eyes linger out the window, which looked out over the perfectly and meticulously trimmed university campus. Before him lay the Centennial Plaza, created in honor of the one hundredth anniversary of the university, with its ample green surface (being defaced at the present by a student-led pickup soccer game and dominated by an aggressive co-ed), with its array of ambitious mimosa, palm, Arizona ash, Mondale pines (yep, expressly bred, believe it or not, for the desert), and Italian cypresses (which sometimes attain the height of fifty or sixty feet), its persistent and wildly colorful desert flora (Birds of Paradise being the most dominant), without a single cactus among them (a fact that the east-coasters shamelessly misunderstand about the desert), and the Bhutanese motif of the campus architecture, adorned with prayer wheels, prayer flags, and a Bhutanese temple in the middle of the plaza, gifted by the ambassador from Bhutan after its exhibit on the National Mall in DC during a folk festival. The scene inspired a kind of silent awe and contentment in Justin, as he relished the uniqueness of the campus, the ancient western academic heritage of which he felt a part (harking back to Socrates), the lofty challenge of enlightenment, learning, and higher education, the satisfaction of acquiring intellectual questions and development, and the excitement spawned by pursuing and birthing worthy thoughts in reluctant and sometimes resistant youth. All was gently nestled in timelessness, even eternity. Beyond the verdant campus lay the brown desert merging into a brown mountain which reigned over illimitable spaciousness.

"How can one describe space? It is nothingness, as far as the eyes can see. It feels like eternity, like forever, like immortality, like endlessness, like vast blue skies that peer off into the universe and bring peace. The only colors are blue and brown, blue vastness above, blue everlastingness, blue space, interfered with by enormous bulging brown mountains, which this border town wraps itself around at its feet into a fading distance on each side of its hulking, barren brownness. Space fills the heart with the feeling of freedom, it uplifts, it carries aloft, it soars beyond thoughts and emotions. It is liberating, licensing, loftiness, languid, lazy, luxurious, lustrous, bestowing enlightenment."

So meandered Justin Sandberg's mental stream as he gave it license.

The first time Justin Sandberg experienced the southwest desert, he was stunned by his liberation from the claustrophobic choking, crowding vegetation of the South, to which he would never permanently return. He was pleased with his discovery and recovery. Andrew Marvel suddenly made his presence known:

But at my back I always hear
Time's winged chariot hurrying near:
And yonder all before us lie
Deserts of vast Eternity. . ."

"Deserts of vast eternity," he repeated, relishing the thought and the feel on his tongue, and then the magnificent ending,

Thus, though we cannot make our sun
*Stand still, yet we will ma*ke *him run*

The bitter irony pleased him as he came back to the present pleasure

His eyes returned from the lush desert-scape outside of his window to the office-scape inside, also brimming with memories and emotions. His office walls were laden with numerous book shelves and his auto-academic history. Every book contained a memory and a confession. There were countless copies of the complete works of Shakespeare (one volume, which he carried to class for over twenty years, was so worn that it had no bookbindings to enclose it); there were volumes of Elizabethan and Jacobean plays, numerous anthologies of the mighty tradition of western drama (from Sophocles and Aristophanes to Ibsen, Strindberg, and Shaw to *Waiting for* Godot), to individual plays and playwrights such as Williams, Miller, Albee and countless others lost to the voracious appetite of time and history. It filled Justin with an immense satisfaction and the warm glow of belonging, of being a part of, and a unity with the accomplishment of western learning and erudition.

The birth of a new academic year for Justin was always a time for nostalgic reflection and analysis, glancing backward, assessing the present, peering forward, and anticipating the future, which unbeknownst to him on this afternoon contained a few surprises ahead, and he always found sustaining satisfaction and pleasure in examining how far in life he had come. Justin Sandberg, originally from North Carolina, derived from poor dirt farmers on both sides of his family, germinated from working class parents who knew only the wearying grind of hard labor, exhaustion, frustration, and hopelessness, finding comfort only in the Southern Baptist church and the hope of an ameliorated life in the hereafter. He sprouted in a village with a poor, blue-collar, textile factory soil, barren and bleak, which was without fertility, nourishment, or fecundity, and he rose above it, with the help of his poor but aspiring parents and his own drive for self-actualization, which, in spite of poverty, drove him to seek a college education, his only hope for growth and escape into a wider realm. In college, he budded into the full flowering of his personhood. A college education exposed him to exactly what a college education is intended to do, ushered him into a broader awareness of a kingdom which had been totally unknown to him and into which he became an immigrant, an interloper, but soon became a resident, a naturalized citizen, and a civil contributor, inside the borders of illumination. He became entranced by the new universe he found himself standing in and regarded it as more sacred than the Baptist church itself. He had attended a small, liberal arts college, which his parents could not afford, with extremely high academic standards and discovered a pride in his intellect. He majored in philosophy, with the thought of perhaps going after college to a Baptist theological seminary, and spotted himself in the company of some extremely bright young fellow students and made his light glow among them through the sheer passion and zeal which was midwifed by labor, endurance, passion, and discipline.

And then he switched lanes. He discovered that philosophy, with all its questions, had no answers, but the conflagration for learning had been kindled. And he had a pellucidly unclouded sighting of the path he would travel down. From the time he was a senior in high school, in spite of his football playing enthusiasm, and even further back to his pre-puberty yearnings, he had a powerful romance with reading, which was engendered again by college literature courses. "This above all: to thine own self be true, and it must follow, as the night the day, thou canst not then be false to any man," so says the pontificating Polonius in Shakespeare's *Hamlet*. In spite of Polonius's superficiality, the words always adhered to Justin. And then he added Polonius's further caution to his son Laertes, the wisdom of, "give every man thy ear, but few thy voice." (Justin understood the irony in the scene and Polonius's loquacious propensity but chose a literal reading of some of the lines.) Wisdom: that is what resonated from literature for Justin, human wisdom, not abstract philosophical debates that led up *cul de sacs*. Even as a philosophy major, Justin practiced the exercise of writing down memorable, poetical passages and deposited them in the file cabinet of his memory. One summer, inserted between his junior and senior years in college, he served as a swimming pool lifeguard and spent countless hours on his lifeguard perch memorizing passages he had scribbled down each day and brought with him to work. Turning away from philosophy, he made the effortless, natural leap into literature. It was as natural as a heartbeat, and his destiny was set.

After a two-year sojourn in the military after college, during which hiatus he spent blissful hours in the post library reading the classics of Western society, from the Russians to the French to the English and Americans, everything from *War and Peace* and *The Brothers Karamazov* to *The Red and the Black*, *Lady Chatterly's Lover*, and *The Scarlet Letter* to *Catcher in the Rye* and *Lord of the Flies*, he entered graduate study in English and American Literature, served as a Teaching Assistant, and honed his career in literary studies. After he finished his doctoral residency, the University of Texas at Mountain Pass touched his telephone and welcomed him back to the university from which he had earned his Master's degree. While thinking about his newly chosen career, Chaucer's *Canterbury Tales* came to mind, and especially the Clerk of Oxford who had also chosen an academic career. The passage reaches its soaring and touching conclusion with

> *Of study took he most care and most heed.*
> *Not one word spoke he more than was need,*
> *And that was said in form and reverence,*

> *And short and quick, and full of high sentence.*
> *Resounding in moral virtue was his speech,*
> ***And gladly would he learn and gladly teach!***

That's me, thought Justin, even though he was cognizant, as was the Clerk, that he would always be monetarily handicapped ("*Yet had he but little of gold in coffers; But all that from his friends he might get, On books and learning he spent*"). Monetary considerations could not compete with his need for self-exploration.

These were Justin's mental meanderings on this first day of classes as he sat in his office. It was a liturgy he practiced annually upon his assault on a fresh academic year, and, out of the bountiful supply of memories, as he sat inventorying his memory, a particular incident snagged his attention from the previous spring semester, which occurred in the middle of the semester one spectacular day, when boundless space filled the biosphere, the week before Easter (or the Feast of the Lupercal, as he liked to call it, the Roman celebration of springtime, fertility, and primal procreative stirrings). Thus the memory of Paloma Garcia's visit to his office from the previous spring semester came to him as fresh as yesterday. It was a common practice of his to be afflicted by bizarre episodes in his career.

Justin re-lived that memory of himself, after Paloma had left, standing behind his desk for a moment in order to clear his head and to think about Shaw's *Mrs. Warren's Profession*, which he would be lecturing on in a matter of minutes, bent over to put his hands on his desk while bowing his head, and thought about Jake Barnes in Hemingway's *The Sun Also Rises* who compares life to a huge market place with all these beautiful objects which are available to us, which, upon closer inspection, one realizes, every wondrous object comes with a price tag on it, that nothing is free in this world, and, Jake realizes, that in his relationship with Brett that sooner or later "he would have to pay the bill," which he did. "*Paloma is a very desirable commodity*," Justin thought, "*but there is an enormous price tag on her.*" He eradicated Paloma from his consciousness and turned his thoughts to Kitty Warren, Shaw's prostitute, who also carried, like all prostitutes, a price tag, gathered up his notes and textbook, and rushed off to class to present to the world the lesson to be learned about price tags. He relished recalling those intoxicating moments in the class room from the past.

2

Justin vividly recollected his lecture that day, especially because of the affliction of the preceding event in his office behind a private portal:

"Who is the greatest playwright in the English language?" Dr. Sandberg tossed a question up into the classroom ether in order for someone to lob it back to him. He had long ago surrendered on the straight lecture approach—during which students were dreamily free to review last weekend's party or the one coming up next weekend or sleep with their eyes open, an art which some students had perfected—in favor of the interrogation (or Socratic) method, not that it was much more effective but students paid partial attention because of the potential for embarrassing themselves.

"Shakespeare," returned an ace from the back row by the name of Marcus.

"Very good," the professor encouraged the young player. "And now, Marcus, who is the second greatest playwright in the English language?"

"Well," Marcus continued the match, "since we are studying George Bernard Shaw right now, I'd guess it would be Shaw."

"And you would be correct. However, Shaw claimed that he was a better playwright than Shakespeare. What would be the basis for such a claim?"

"An enormous ego," mumbled a member on the second row.

"That too," Justin snapped back a volley.

"Because he wrote more plays than Shakespeare did?" Marcus continued to play the game.

"That is a fine guess, Marcus." Dr. Sandberg gave a hydraulic pump to the timid Marcus. After giving others a chance to enter the tournament, the Herr Doctor Professor, having gotten everyone's mind in the rankings, brought it to the last stroke with, "Shakespeare had no social conscious, so asserts Shaw, but my plays, he claimed, have the purpose of correcting the ills of society, they deal with real social problems, such as prostitution, which, when he could not get *Mrs. Warren's Profession* approved by the censor for a production, argued that a good production of his play would keep the men in the audience out of the houses of ill-repute for at least two weeks. What is he suggesting?"

"The hypocrisy in society." Marcus was on a roll.

"Very good, Marcus. Remember the character Sir George Crofts who says, 'There are no secrets better kept than the secrets everybody guesses.' No one is willing to pay the price for their behavior, everything has a price tag, all actions have consequences." The good professor could not help but be aware of the subject of Paloma Garcia and the price she would cost him should he relent, unbeknownst to the class. That day was still dwelling in his memory.

3

Justin retrieved the scene of how he executed his return to his office that day to keep his office hours before his next class and to erase the memory of Paloma's spring-semester offer which had been made to him. He saw himself disencumber himself of his class folder and texts, retrieve the class folder and textbook for his next class from the same shelf and deposit them on his desk, check his watch without really seeing what time it was (his mind absorbed by other matters), glanced out the window by rote without registering anything on his consciousness, and, stimulated as usual by cerebral contact with his students, sat down in his desk swivel chair with a great exhalation. He was in another reality, one of his own making in which he saw himself as the dreamer in a dream.

"Was I tempted?" he recalled querying himself and let his imagination indulge itself for a moment or two in unfathomable pleasure, even though he knew what the decision would be. "Darn right, I was," he auto-answered. "God knows I'm no saint, not perfect. Just an ole flawed human being trying to do the best I can without screwing up too badly." It was not a matter of morality or righteousness or ethics or sanctimoniousness—it was a matter of practicality, a pragmatic stance, not an ethical one: he needed his job—and his self-respect.

On the day that Paloma had come to his office, his mind was reflecting on his earlier days when he had just finished his PhD residency and accepted the position at Mountain Pass at the age of twenty-nine. The doctoral program had been one of three years of laborious torture, even though he found exciting satisfaction in his studies, but it was a 24/7 routine of studying, researching, writing, cramming, memorizing, outlining, note-taking, concentrating, reading and reading and reading and constantly underlining, (while also teaching, lecturing, and grading papers), with no time for rest, recreation, nor renewal, even though he had a wife and small daughter. Some grad students did not reach the other shore with their wits still intact. It was a period of searing purgatory, the survival of which he credited in part to the tenacity he learned from blistering August days of football practice ("I knew there was a purpose somewhere in all that torture"). Upon arriving at Mountain Pass, he felt liberated, relieved, freed, unshackled, unchained, let loose, and like being released from prison, even though he still had to finish his dissertation, which would be as easy as eating coconut cake and ice cream, after what he had been through the three previous years. It was time to have a little fun, take it easy, slow down, and maybe even mess-around a little bit—and still be able to publish enough to keep the administration off his derriere.

As far as Paloma's offer, or any other co-ed's, was concerned, there was no question about what he would do: the answer would remain a permanent "no," but he had not arrived at such a capability without a fierce fight over the years. He had grown in many ways from his "salad green days [Cleopatra]," but it was not without a struggle. In the early days of his professorship, he was subjected to numerous temptations, some of which he succumbed to, **but never as long as a student was enrolled in his class.**

His brain in the present tense seemed to be in a nostalgic mode, as was often the case in the initial days of a new semester, provoking him to an awareness of the continuity of, and responsibility to, his life, and he resumed, and exhumed, mining nuggets farther into the past. His memory was operating like Matryoshka dolls, Russian nesting dolls or stacking dolls, a memory inside of a memory inside of a memory, ad infinitum.

He recalled his first class meeting of his embryonic year, an Introduction to the Forms of Literature wherein he would teach fiction, poetry, and dramatic literature, the kind of class that he as a novice delighted in, instead of teaching freshman composition, a perk that was awarded to him by virtue of being a PhD candidate. At the inceptive class hour, he went through the usual ritual of verifying the roster by calling the names of each student who would then raise a hand for identification purposes. When he came to the name of Eva Diaz, he looked up, saw no raised hand, repeated the name several times, and moved on to the remainder of the roster. After laying out the academic landscape for the coming semester and about a half hour into the class hour, the door, which was off to Justin's left from where he stood at the front of the class, timidly began to push back and then stopped. *"A magical door, just like my office portal,"* he thought.

"Come in," the young professor raised his voice to the door to demonstrate his command of his territory. The door stopped. *I didn't mean to scare anybody,* he reflected.

"Are you coming in or not," he again tried to sound authoritative. The door began to back off as though to shut itself. *Maybe Cerberus is tending the door and keeping my students in Hades.*

"What the--?" He looked at the class, strode to the door, yanked it open, and hauled in a young lady who was holding on to the doorknob. She smiled a weak grin. Justin noticed that she was not a teenager, maybe a little more his own age, with thickly smeared on make-up, heavy black mascara which hyper-outlined her eyes (and totally missing her eyes in some places), and dark red lipstick which was smudged away from her lips in places (*does she not own a mirror,* Justin wondered). Her blouse was cut low, revealing a deep cleavage, of which she had plenty, and her skirt was cut high, exposing lots of thigh. *Not a thing of beauty,* Justin thought, *but absolutely fetching. Looks very sensuous. Hummm.* She did have a voluptuous body, well-proportioned and just the right amount of abundance of white flesh, relatively rare for the border culture.

"I—I—I'm so sorry. I'm a little lost." She was very tentative.

"What are you looking for?" Justin asked. She squinted at a crumpled piece of paper in her hand.

"Uh--?" her words stumbled as she read slowly, "Introduction to Forms of"

"Who is the professor?"

"Uh—" again haltingly, "Sand—Sandberg—?" She seemed almost inoperable with fright.

"This is it," he quipped, "what's your name?"

"Eva Diaz."

"Find a seat anywhere you can, Eva, [he prided himself on learning students' names early in a new semester] and see me after class." Justin wanted everyone to be clear about who was in charge of his classroom while keeping a deadly stern facial feature.

After the finalizing bell and a small congregation of inquisitive students had evaporated from around him, Eva Diaz stepped up to the professor's podium with "you wanted to see me?"

"I wanted to make sure I marked you as present." He picked up his roster, found her name, and crossed out the absence. "Since we are mainly a commuter school, I just want you to know that I take roll at every class meeting and enforce a strict attendance policy. Did you get a syllabus?"

"No sir."

"Read over this very carefully," he relayed to her a small sheaf of stapled printed matter, "if you have any questions, you can come see me during my office hours. They are listed on the syllabus, along with my office location."

"Thank you sir." She turned to walk toward the classroom entrance.

"Eva?" She turned away from the entry and back to his desk.

"Have you been out of school for a while?

"Ten years."

"Do you have any college credits?" He was following a hunch about her.

"No sir."

"Maybe you should come talk to me," he said.

"Yes sir.

4

Justin sat in his office ruminating on the fact that it was this very office that Eva Diaz, several weeks into his fledgling year as a fulltime faculty member and feeling completely legitimate as such, softly knocked on his slightly opened office door (the portal to his destiny) to which beckoning he responded with, "come in." "Here's a knocking indeed! If a man were porter of hellgate, he should have old turning the key. Knock, knock, knock! Who's there, i' the name of Beelzebub," Justin was thinking of the drunken Porter's scene in *Macbeth* where the Porter imagines himself to be answering Hell's gate. He always delighted in the hilarity of the scene and the wit and drunkenness of Shakespeare's Porter, complaining of "never at quiet," interrupting his drinking and snoozing. *Some porter*, thought Justin.

Eva seemed paralyzed at first, and then shyly took several hesitant steps through her professor's portal, her shoulders scrunched up in order to fill as little space as possible. . "May I come in," she spoke softly and respectfully. He signaled with an open hand toward the chair in front of his desk. It seemed like a geological age for her to reach the chair. Her make-up was as thickly applied as ever, her mascara making even wider circles around her brown eyes, her lipstick smudged ever more so, and with, the new look, peroxided hair. She had a pleasant face, even when plastered with make-up, a ready smile, and a heart-fetching shyness about her.

"What's up?" Justin reverted to student slang as a bonding move.

She stared in front of herself at vacuity for a moment, and then found the bravado to mumble, "I think I'm in over my head."

"How so?"

"I have been out of school for a long time—and I never was much of a student."

"That doesn't matter."
"I am scared to death. I feel so out of place—"
"It just takes a little time."
"I feel like the other students are laughing at me—"
"To hell with'im—you're better than they are."
"I'm afraid to say anything in class—"
"What brings you back to school?"
"I've got two little girls—which I am raising all by myself."
"Where's the fa--?
"My husband left me for another woman, and he's not even paying child support. I—I—"
"Yes?"
"I just want to be a good role model for my girls—and—"
"Admirable. Very."
"I am really struggling. I have to work late at nights. I don't even have time to study—and when I do, I am so exhausted I can't stay awake," she went on to explain.
"Where do you work?"
She bowed her peroxided, blondish, streaked head while Justin waited. He felt thermal compassion for her, wished to accommodate her need for support, visualized rendering a warm pat on the shoulder, and remained seated.
"You don't have to answer that, if you don't want to."
She contemplated going any further and then confessed:
"At a lounge down on Texas Street—Chuy's, it's called," she elaborated.
Justin hesitated, giving her the platform he felt she needed and to be someone to listen sympathetically to her plight.
"I think I am going to drop out," she said reflectively.
"NO!" He checked his firm stance, and then finished reasonably with "no," "Don't do that. Education is your only way out." Justin believed passionately about the platium worth of an education, even though he was acutely attentive to the pedestrian, nay, corny, quality of his beliefs. Regardless, it was a deeply held position that reached to the smallest cell in his being, to the core of his existence, to his very personhood and identity.
"I don't want to do poorly—for my girls' sake. I want to be a good example," she said.

"You're doing the right thing." Justin was touched by her aspiration and her struggle. "I'll help you." It was not uncharacteristic of him to toss out such an offer, for he had done it often with the purest of motives, and with some success. He recalled one incident when he had an older female in his class, who was divorced with a battered and inglorious self-image and who did not attend the final exam. He called her during the exam to hear her say that she was not worthy of taking the final exam, that her life was a miserable failure, and that she was only deceiving herself about her audacity to be taking college courses. In short, Justin sermonized her with a fiery harangue and finally convinced her to get in her car and come to the university to take the final. He would be waiting for her after the exam when everyone had left. This lady went on to get her degree and eventually became the principle of an elementary school, with renowned success. She always endowed Justin with her gratitude and he filed it with a cache of such life examples. Some persons may be unable to accept Justin's hokey enthusiasm toward education, but he held his subjective tenets in pure sanctity.

Eva lifted her head to him, straightening up for the first time since entering his office, with watery eyes.

"I don't want your pity," she declared.

"It's my job. It is what I do." If Justin had a hidden agenda, he was unaware of it—at the moment.

5

"We have a basketball game tonight," Justin, now into basketball season, remembered telling Eva after a number of tutoring sessions with her, during which time she had begun to plume up in her literary efforts. "It's a good excuse to get out of the house."

She, confused, waited.

"I thought I might drop in at Chuy's and have a drink."

"Oh. You have a wife?" she asked. It propelled their relationship into another sphere, a more personal arena.

"Yes. Much to my--." He checked himself from sounding like a bastard.

Her facial expression changed as she frowned, furrowed her forehead a little, and became warily distant.

"Is that all right?" He pushed the idea forward.

"I have to tell you something." He waited for her to sojourn on.

"Go ahead."

"I am more than just a cocktail waitress."

My god, thought the professor, *don't tell me she's a prostitute. That would be too much of a cliché*"

"It's all right, whatever you are."

"I'm a Gogo dancer." She paraded it out for his consideration.

"What's wrong with that?" He tried to seem nonplussed.

"I am also the Girl on the Swing."

"After all, you're just trying to work your way through col—" He stopped.

"A what?"

"Girl on the Swing."

"How does that work?"

"You see, there's this swing over the bar, with velvet ropes, and I get on it, in this skimpy outfit, with nothing on underneath—well, you get the picture," she concluded.

"Let's take a look at Robert Frost's "Stopping by Woods on a Snowy Evening."

And they proceeded to dissect Frost's amazing poem and concluded with,

> *"But I have promises to keep,*
> *And miles to go before I sleep,*
> *And miles to go before I sleep."*

"I'll see you about eight o'clock this evening." He closed the book.

6

"I want to see you swing," he was reliving the moment, thinking back to that first night, as he said to Eva when she served him his gin-and-tonic while he was sitting at the bar. He had located Chuy's after traversing Texas Avenue several times, neighbored by pawn shops, ropa usada (used clothes) tiendas (stores), unappetizing cafes, taco stands and various street vendors, used car lots, and an assortment of broken down retailers. It was in the south part of town, not far from the Mexican border, unfamiliar territory for Justin, but curiously alive to him. Over the years, he would become acclimated to a culture which was at first unknown to him but which he slowly became a part of, adopting it as his own through his identification with his students.

He was now in her country and felt conspicuous in his collegiate garb, a UTMP sweater (to convince his wife that he was actually going to a basketball game), tasseled loafers, and fresh jeans. He may as well have been wearing an incongruous priest's smock and collar, which might have been more appropriate and less conspicuous than his own attire.

The swing with the red velvet ropes was pulled back to the opposite wall behind the bar with a smallish step ladder beneath it, which Eva approached to comply with Justin's request. Her Gogo outfit was about the length of a tutu, red in color of course, just barely covering her Business. She stood on the top step of the ladder, unlatched the swing from its mooring, sat on it facing outward, and let go. Her first glide came out over the bar and Justin had to duck to keep from getting a foot in his mouth. He moved over one stool and looked up as the second arc of the swing came by him during which he saw everything. Her pubic hair was also dyed blond and her thighs looked like whitish marble in the dimly lit bar. She continued to pump and swing while Justin continued to ogle, feeling a rising sensation in his lower parts and a creeping guilt spawning in his chest. The battle was on. *She's my student, for gosh sakes,* he thought, *a violation of everything sacred in my profession. I've got to restrain myself.*

"Did you like that," Eva asked him after the completion of her demonstration.

"Whatta you think," was his rhetorical reply. "Where's the tip jar?"

"Over there."

Justin handed her a folded up ten spot with "you keep that."

"Thank you."

"Would you like to get together sometime?" Justin was now moving at mach speed.

"Sure," was her compliant response.

"The semester will be over in two weeks. You won't be my student any longer." Even in the days of his novitiate professorship, he devoutly adhered to the principle of separation of student and teacher, adapted from the Southern Baptist tenet of separation of church and state. It was an inviolate principle with him.

After basketball season was over in the early spring of the following semester, Justin remembered, he had a difficult time finding excuses for his absences from home with no basketball games to attend, but he remained very creative, until his marriage crashed and burned, an inevitable ending in consonance with his conduct in the marriage. He blamed no one but himself.

7

Paloma Garcia's proffered courtesy, of "I'll do anything for an A," from the previous semester, ignited sepia-colored old memories of his earlier days in his professorship as he returned to the present moment in his office between classes on this inaugural day of the present fall semester. He was more than a little embarrassed by the memory. While he was philandering with Eva, he had begun his climb up the academic ladder, and, after several years, due to some political infighting in his department, he found himself the preferred young faculty member (by the older, scholarly, wiser heads of the department, who wielded a lot of political punch but no desire to serve as the Head) to escort the department out of the desert, or lead them through the desert. They christened him to be the next departmental "Head" (which he quickly changed to the title of "Chair" to make it sound more democratic because he had new ideas with new approaches as opposed to the old autocratic power of Heads). As the Chair, Justin taught only one class each semester and soon realized that his passion for teaching and scholarship was more powerful than his desire to be an administrator. This administrative interlude became a valuable lesson to him, for he discovered that being an administrator devoured his time with desk work: making out class schedules, hiring, firing, and studying resumes, squeezing pennies out of budgets, entertaining student complaints, mollifying disgruntled faculty, refereeing faculty squabbles, maintaining the happiness of secretaries, chairing committees eternally and everlastingly, keeping faculty's sordid and questionable behavior and information out of the public scrutiny, and all such mundane activities. It became luminously clear to him that he had no appetite to be a college president, provost, dean or dust collector. *No thank you,* he politely excused himself *if I am going to spend my days sitting at a desk full of headaches and aggravations, I may as well go into the business world and make real money, which is not of my inclining.* He thereupon re-affirmed his primal passion, "gladly would he learn, and gladly teach," *Chaucer again,* he thought.

One would assume that as Chair, he remembered, he would, being in a position of serious duties amidst the magnet of attention, from faculty and the general public alike, would make him morally behave himself—which he did as best he could at that time in his life. As he continued to perform his annual reminiscence of surveying his career, it was a different fresh academic year that arose in his mind as he rumbled through the past in the present, memory inside of memory (Russian doll inside Russian doll), an episode that occurred during his term as departmental chair.

He remembered that he was returning to the Chair's office after class one new semester when his eye picked out a young lady standing in the hall, amidst the throng of students between class bells, buried in all the clamor, obviously in great distress, perhaps to the point of tears. She was holding in her hand, which seemed palsy-like, what appeared to be her class schedule.

"Can I help you with something," he offered as he emerged near her.

"I am so confused." Her voice quivered.

"Relax. It's not that bad. Let me see your schedule."

"It is my first time on a college campus, I can't make heads or tails out of the schedule, and I don't know where anything is. I just feel like going home."

"Ok, Norma," he had noticed her name on her schedule, Norma Montoya. "The next period you have Mr. Penfield. I'll take you to his classroom." Moses-like, he led her out of the wilderness and to the promised-classroom-land. "After this class is over, you have a class on the fourth floor, 405, which will be the floor above Mr. Penfield's class. My office is located right where you were standing when I met you. Anytime you need help with anything, just come see me. I'll let my secretary know that you have my permission to see me anytime. Just ask for Dr. Sandberg."

She was not what one would call beautiful or even attractive, but she was cute as a butterfly, Justin thought, average height, shapely understated figure, short wavy black hair, crooked but pleasant teeth, boots up her calves—shy, appreciative, and vulnerable—the kind your heart goes out to and wants to protect in a world of lurking dangers, he being one of them at times. She was darkish in skin tone, had strong chin lines, dependable cheek bones beneath her eyes, an average forehead and humble eyes, often casting them down when attention was given to her. For some strange reason, his heart was snagged. Maybe it was her helpless vulnerability which beckoned him.

"This is your classroom here," the department chair turned to her, "let me know if you need any more help."

"You are so kind. Thank you so much," she said as she passed by him into the classroom.

"What's my name?"

"Er—"

"Don't forget—Dr. Sandberg." He looked back over his shoulder as her perfect rear-end dissolved into the body of students.

Professor Sandberg pondered about himself as he made his way back to the Chair's office. *I have had my fill of beauty queens and lookers. They are so into themselves that they can't get outside of themselves. I really like the cute, humble sort who know how to*—he stopped. *What am I thinking—except that she seemed so available, but not in a sexual way. Let it go. You can't go around chasing after every cute undergraduate that comes across your path. Time to put on my academic regalia.*

Back in the Chair's chair, he remembered the moment so sharply, his secretary Mary Lou, a tall, weighty figure of backwater origins, enlightened him to the fact that Professor Gilda Glenn had requested an appointment with him for the upcoming hour. Professor Glenn was an African-American, newly acquired, faculty member, whose specialty was African-American literature. She brought herself up to about six-feet-four-inches, weighed in past two hundred-and-something whatevers (matching his secretary Mary Lou's dimensions), and had a trumpet-like, clarion voice. She also had a lot of unsuppressed anger, not surprising considering the times in the backwash of the civil rights movement of an earlier era, which did in fact endow her with greater freedom to speak her thoughts. She was not one of a timid mind.

"Professor Sandberg!" Her voice was laced with rancor as she stood in the doorway, an ingress portal not an egress (which he urgently wished it was) leading into his inner office.

"Gilda, come on in," he offered.

She stepped in and then slammed the door behind her, (*a real slammer,* **he** thought) blocking his escape through the only exit, except for the locked windows from which it was too high to jump anyway. She had on adequate black boots, (*like storm troopers,* the Chair thought), stood momentarily against the guarded and guardian door, and glared at him with fierce eyes, as though the door, dark behind her dark skin, had eyes and he thought of Porta Bella, the gateway of war. Her mood was as black as her skin, her eyes had fiery crescent shapes (*Shakespeare, Lear*), the corners of her mouth sagged toward her ample bosom, her hands, balled into two fists, shook with rage, and she stomped the floor with every step so that the shelves rattled. *Apparently she's not here for cocktail hour,* he tried to amuse himself with wane humor.

"I need to talk to you," she initiated. She lumbered to the chair in front of his desk and tossed herself into it. He could feel the floor shaking, as much as he was, figuratively. Justin Sandberg could have sworn that he saw his life pass before him.

"What's on your mind, Gilda?' He tried to create a calm approach, which didn't work. He was determined to assuage her anger and aggression with tranquility and the gentlest voice possible, being barely audible. *She is not going to intimidate me or dominate this romantic rendezvous,* he entertained himself again.

"I feel that I am being discriminated against in this department," she led off.

"Oh, now—"

"Don't 'oh now' me," she severed his retort. "I know discrimination when I see it, and I'm not going to take it."

"Talk to me." He tried to fumigate the air with reasonableness and imperturbability.

"I've seen the spring schedule. I've got three classes of freshman composition and one literature class. AND, there is no African-American literature class scheduled—"

"Courses are scheduled on a rotating bas—"

"The other faculty are criticizing me to their students—"

"That's not tru—"

"I invite faculty to my house and they make excuses not to come—"

"I came—"

"and left after a half hour—"

"I had another—"

"--the faculty give parties for each other in their homes but never invite me." [*It's her monologue, let her have at it,* he reasoned.] I am snubbed and alienated and nobody sits with me in the faculty lounge. This place is full of racism. I'm thinking about a law suit."

"Oh, jeez—" Justin sighed under his breath.

Justin blocked out the remainder of the painful one-on-one, but remembered her parting shot:

"I've already talked to a lawyer. You'll hear from him next." She lifted off from her chair, galumphed to the door, [*doors can also provide relief when they are used in an egressive way,* he thought], turned back to him as she opened it, "this department is in deeeep shi-et. You'll also be interested to know that I am looking for another position at a better institution," and exited.

I hope she finds one, he thought. He sat in befuddled silence until his phone buzzed.

"There is a student here to see you, that girl you mentioned, Norma," his secretary informed him with sharp-edged, judgmental condemnation.

"Send her in." He raised an eyebrow. *Well now.*

"Am I intruding?" she spoke from his office door [*a door can also provide pleasure when the right person uses it as an ingress and maybe a portal to a novel future*].

"Nono. Come on it. Have a seat."

"I just wanted to thank you for what you did for me. I was so scared and confused, I really was on the verge of just quitting and going back home."

"I'm not going to let that happen."

"What?"

"I'm not going to let you quit." Justin wondered if his heart was pure. Superficially, it was.

"Why would you do that for me?" she asked.

"Because I believe education is the golden path, the promised land, the holy grail, the high heaven—"

"Wow," she uttered.

"It's my religion. It's the entryway to a fulfilled and meaningful life. It was for me. I believe it is for everybody." He was teasing her and not teasing her.

She glared at him, wondering if he was making fun of her, patronizing her, or being sincere and straight with her. *Maybe it's how he really feels* and gave him a little allowance for all her dubiousness.

"Pretty corny, hunh?"

"But it may not be for everybody," she counter punched.

"All human beings have a brain. You just have to believe in yourself and never quit. That's all there is to it."

"I could never do that."

"Do what?"

"Believe in my self—" Her assertion was weak and it moved him to concern.

Justin remembered that she had an extremely negative image of herself, felt compassion for her, and wanted to lift her up.

"Are you leaving campus right now?" he led off.

"No. I was going to the bookstore and look for the textbooks I need."

"Listen, I have a faculty carrel in the library. I plan to go to it around one o'clock to do some research. Why don't you meet me there."

"What's a ca—car--"

"It's a cubicle in the library. Mine is on the third floor, number thirty-five. Can you come?"

"If I can find it."

"Just take the elevator to the third floor, turn right when you get off the elevator and come over to the stacks. You'll see the carrels are numbered consecutively. It is easy to find."

"Yes, I'll come."

He recalled walking Norma to the front office to show her out of the door.

"So if you ever have any academic problems, feel free to make an appointment with my secretary." Justin, standing in front of his secretary's desk, remembered trying to cover up what appeared to be a suspicious-looking tete-a-tete while his secretary lobed a vile look at him and slowly shook her head. Mary Lou had suspicions about her boss, grounded in some unsubstantiated conclusions but based more on her instinctual mother-earth observations about her *jefe*.

"Totally innocent," he hurled back to her and went into his office.

"Yeah, right," she mumbled aloud to make her disapprobation known to her disappearing boss.

8

Back in the present moment, waiting to meet his next class of the new semester and academic year, Justin Sandberg's memory was suddenly sloshed to overflowing with so many personal narratives, some of which provoked the deepest pain in him. The recollection of his acquaintanceship with Eva Diaz made him ache over the passion that they had found in each other, the amazing length of many years (what? fifteen, twenty) that the relationship flourished. Eva struggled in the university trying to balance her pursuit of an education while rearing two daughters (especially as they traversed through the pubescent yeas), holding down a vast array of part time jobs (some of which would not exactly be called noble callings), struggling with paying the rent and maintaining broken down old junk heaps of cars sufficient to carry her to her various jobs and university classes, and occasionally meeting Justin of an afternoon at some motel across the border in Mexico.

Justin held a deep affection and admiration for Eva's determination and spunk. Through years of roiling eddies of vexation, Eva managed to not only complete her bachelor's degree in bilingual education but proceeded to earn her teaching certification and a master's in bilingual ed. as well. For Justin, it was more than sexual because he sincerely admired, as he discovered, that there was a solid core of a strong character amidst her goodness: determined, vigorous in her pursuit, indestructibly stubborn amidst slaughterous poverty, and victorious until her world crumbled apart.

Justin's mind wandered back and recalled of an afternoon when, having finished his classes for the day, he was sitting in this very office, his regular faculty office, in the same swivel chair, at the same desk when there was a soft knock on the same admission device, his office door.

"Come in," he politely invited, and the said device came slowly open to reveal Eva standing in the hall.

It had been several months since they had been together, and he had been thinking of giving her a call.

"Eva, I was just thinking about you."

"No you weren't." she countered.

"Honest, I was just thinking of giving you a call this week. Good to see you. What are you doing on campus?" By this time, she was a fulltime bilingual teacher and becoming well established in her profession.

"I came for a bilingual conference over in the Education Building. Thought I might drop by to say hello, in case you had forgotten who I am."

"I deserve that. Come on. Beat up on me some more."

A pause filled the room and then he became aware that something was wrong. She usually wore a smile, a calmly reposed face (in spite of her mis-applied make-up applications), and calm demeanor. He sensed that she was struggling for words, that something was tumbling beneath the surface. *Is she angry with me, have I hurt her feelings? I guess I have behaved like a bastard toward her but I have been really busy.* He debated speaking or not and finally came down on the side of testing the waters.

"How have you been?" He tried the conversational route.

"Well—" She stopped, an agonized look filling her face, took a long breath in order to speak, and then she broke like a sudden summer thunder shower and began to sob as though her soul was rent into, which it clearly was.

Guilt festered up from Justin's stomach into his chest.

"I am so sorry." Justin began, "I've been meaning to call you but I—I've just been so busy lately that—" He was, as usual, being solipsistic.

"It's—not—that—" she struggled to utter.

"What is it?"

Eva was incapacitated, deprived of speech.

Justin decided that the best thing to do would be for him to keep his mouth shut and wait.

After what seemed like another geological age, specifically the Ice Age, Eva finally lifted her head, her mascara running down her face in black rivulets.

"Do you—remember—my daughter—Jessica?" She finally found some language.

"Of course."

"She—she—she's—" and another summer shower broke.

"Did something happen to her?"

Eva nodded her head.

"What happened?"

"She—she's—gone—"

"Gone?"

Eva nodded her head in ascent.

"She left home?"

She shook her head "no."

"Whatta you mean gone?"

"Dead—" and a third summer shower released.

"Ohmygod!!!" The English professor suddenly could find no English words.

Justin decided his best policy was to wait it out again while she established rulership over herself. After what seemed like an appropriate interval, Justin dared with

"How did that happen?"

"It's—it's all—my—my fault."

"Don't do that."

"No, really—" she managed.

He waited. Then—

"Talk to me."

"I tried so hard—to—to be a good role model."

"And you have. Look at what you've achieved."

"All the while I was going to school and doing part time jobs—and trying so hard to hold everything together—they were growing up without a mother—"

"You were doing the best you could—given the circumstances."

"But not—ohhh—I tried so hard, so so so very hard—" And the deluge began again.

Justin lifted from his chair and came around to her side of his desk. He felt impotent, inadequate, a fraud, a disappointment to her after all his intellectual gab—he imagined as seen through her eyes—unable to rise to the occasion, and finally muttered,

"Let me hug you."

She stood and his arms coiled around her. He could feel her nervous system quivering, her breathing choppy with sobs, and the iron grip of tension in her body, but her body still felt sensuous in his arms and aroused nature's ancient feelings. *Enough of that,* he thought. Her body was perfumed powerfully and some of it adhered to him, for the remainder, as a reminder, of the afternoon. She sat back down while he returned to his swivel chair and plopped down, disturbed and guilty.

"You've got—work--to do?"

"No." He paused. "You want to tell me about it."

"This happened about two weeks ago. I came home from work one day—and after calling her and looking all through the house—I went to her room and she was sprawled across her bed—and she was—" It all resumed,

"I am so sorry."

"She had choked on her own vomit."

"Do they know--?"

"Yes. The autopsy showed that she had massive amounts of drugs and alcohol in her system. Enough to kill an elephant."

"Oh dear—"

"While I was trying to be a good role model, what they really needed was me at home."

"Don't—"

"Somehow, unknown to me, they had gotten into drugs—dropped out of school—and living pretty much on the streets during the day while I was away."

"Angie too?"

"Yes. Now I am worried about her. I am trying to get treatment for her, but I can't afford to—I need to support us. I have to work."

9

The memory of Eva's sorrow had dashed his excitement and enthusiasm of beginning a new school year with an appalled self-loathing; he decided to think of something that would engender more kindly feelings toward himself and terminate his raging, rampant guilt. He had been thinking about Norma Montoya earlier in the day before his mind had dredged up the sorrowful memory of Eva's tragedy. He wanted to dwell on the recollection of Norma as relief to his searing self-torture and eradicate the view of himself as a complete and total scoundrel, an inadmissible reality.

He picked up the strand of memory where he had left off, which was the day he had given Norma directions to his library carrel with the information that he would be there by one o'clock to do some research. He had barely opened a book or two on Shakespeare's *Hamlet* ("No! I am not Prince Hamlet, nor was meant to be; Am an attendant lord . . . /At times, indeed, almost ridiculous-- / Almost, at times, the Fool") when there was a soft tap on his carrel admission device, the door. He stood to open it and discovered Norma standing shyly there with one hand over her mouth, a signifying habit of hers, as he saw it, of her shyness. She scrunched up her shoulders as though to lessen her physical presence there, trying to be invisible as she illicitly visited a professor in his sanctuary, trying to make no disturbance nor distracting/attracting behavior.

"Come on in," he whispered. He had thought to bring another chair into his carrel in anticipation of this moment and then tutored Norma on the fact that they would have to keep their voices down. He placed the chairs side by side, patted her on the shoulders with a whispered "I am glad you came." Silence is a requirement in the library, which many students ignore, but he did not wish to attract any unnecessary attention.

"Did you get your textbooks?" the professor asked.

"Only some of them. They are very expensive," she explained.

"What are you using in your composition class?"

She dug into her bag and pulled out some notes.

"*Writing with a Purpose*, is one of them."

"Don't buy that. I have a copy you can borrow—or keep for all I care."

"Really?"

"Of course. I also have the reader Mr. Penfield uses. I'll give you that as well."

"You are so kind to me."

"It's nothing. I don't mind helping a little." Justin pretended to devalue his generosity. Free textbooks from publishers is one of the perks of the profession so his seeming generosity cost him nothing. But he did sincerely want to help her out, sensing that she came from very low economic levels, as he did many students. Whatever may be said about him, he did have a generous spirit and a natural desire to help students, which was a part of his mission.

"Thank you so much, Dr. Sandberg. I don't have a lot of money."

"When we are alone, you can call me Justin." She wide-eyed him.

Justin and Norma whispered amicably for another half-hour or so, getting to know each other and drawing closer. He had warm feelings for her and, if he could read the signs correctly, she for him.

"Well, I better let you do your work,"

"Don't go yet."

Of course, as a promising young scholar, he was expected to publish, but being chair of the department gave him a reprieve to a degree, the burden of administrative work, as everyone understood, disqualifying him from the heavy demands of time spent on scholarship and publishing. He could without guilt spend a little time his own chosen way, and he chose to move a little nigher to a tender young lady. Besides, he had already published amply for the year, well ahead of all quotas. So, the half hour turned into two hours, until, having pushed everything as far as it could go, Norma leaned in close to him and spoke with an airy rush,

"I want to tell you something."

"Ok."

"You ready for this?"

"Sure."

"I am tired of being a virgin," she sibilantly hissed to him.

"Say that again." He spoke lowly.

"I said—I am tired of being a virgin," she reiterated her message.

"That's what I thought you said."

"I am."

"Are you sure?" Justin was not in a mood for false expectations, teased or toyed with.

"Yes." She seemed a little hesitant, or perhaps scared.

"I think you should think about it some more."

"I've been thinking about it a very long time. I have even approached a couple of guys about it. Nobody would help me." He could tell that she was being completely and painfully candid.

"Probably didn't want to make a commitment."

"There is no commitment."

"You know I'm married."

"Is that a problem?"

Her question hung in the small airspace of his faculty carrel for *a desert of eternity* before he mumbled, "Not for me. Is it for you?"

"No," was her muted reply.

A line from *Romeo and Juliet,* for some strange reason, came to his mind when Sampson (Shakespeare has such a great sense of humor, especially with names) said,"

> *I will cut off their heads.*
> *Gregory: The heads of the maids?*
> *Sampson: Ay, the heads of the maids, or their maidenheads.*
> *Take it in what sense thou wilt.*
> *Gregory: They must take it in sense that feel it.*
> *Sampson brags, 'tis known I am a pretty piece of flesh…*
> *Draw thy tool!*

Justin relished the Bard's puns. And his thoughts returned to maidenheads.

They stood and embraced, and then he gave her a probing kiss, as did she, whereupon she departed after they made arrangements for their tryst, and he officiously returned to his official duties in the Chair's office, pulled *Writing With a Purpose* and the companion reader off his bookshelf, while relishing what was to transpire in the near future.

10

"Hi, my name is Eugene Betters," a slender, tallish, fortyish-looking man was standing in Justin's office doorway with his hand extended. Justin had already gathered up his books and class folder and was moving toward his door to exit his sacrarium when he was greeted there by this newcomer, slightly hunched with a smirk and a loping walk.

"Hi. My name is Justin Sandberg," and extended his hand as well.

"Yeah, I know. I just read your name on the door. Thought I would come down and introduce myself."

"Uh, look, uh, are you going to be around for a while?" Justin stalled him.

"Sure."

"I have a class right now, but I'll be back in about an hour. You want to come down then—and chat a little?"

"Yeah. I'm the new guy in Philosophy and I just saw you in the hall and figured that a good-looking guy like you could give me the scoop on--uh—you know—the chicks—and babes--and all that kind of stuff."

"Come on down in about an hour. I'll be here."

"Will do," as Betters walked back up the hall to his office, Justin sped down the stairs and off to class. *There is something about that guy that makes me extremely uneasy. Something about his attitude,* Justin thought on his way to his classroom, *calling women, chicks and babes, I don't think I like that.* From the outset, Justin felt instinctively that something was not quite right, maybe a little too flip, sardonic, cynical, strained nonchalance, maybe slithering, whatever, and thought "We are the hollow men / Our dried voices. . . Are quiet and meaningless / As wind in dry grass" echoed in his head but let it pass as he turned his mind to his debut in his approaching class, the American Drama, beginning with Eugene O'Neill and Susan Glaspell and descending all the way down to the present, a proud, stimulating, entrancing journey which Justin took once a year in this particular class. The course was fully subscribed and the classroom bulging, as his courses tended to be, a silent satisfaction which Justin kept to himself. So, Justin addressed his class, after traveling through the ritual of checking the roster and reviewing the syllabus for the semester, "where was Abraham Lincoln when he was assassinated in 1865, what was he doing at that moment?" Justin hauled the collective class members out of their new shyness and timidity.

"The theatre?" a meek voice questioned itself located on the front row.

"Right. Actually he was sitting in the balcony of the Ford Theatre in D. C. And what was the name of the play he was watching?"

This brought a roar of silence and startled looks of deadpanned faces as the mid-age professor scanned the expressions of his imprisoned acolytes. He assumed he had their attention by this point, perhaps wrongly, and resumed. "Actually, it was a play titled *Our American Cousin*." He allowed this to dangle in the air for a brief span of time and continued with his little quiz game. "So what does this title tell you about, let's say, first of all, the author of the play?" He got no response. Everyone, including the professor, was a stranger, and uncertainty, as well as reluctance, escorted the moment.

One hand finally came up. "Does it mean that the playwright is not an American?"

"Bingo!" said the would-be hip professor. "Now, if he is calling us his 'American Cousin,' what would possibly be his country of origin?"

"Canadian?" tentatively offered one meek voice.

"Good guess—but not quite right."

"British?" came another hesitant mumble.

"Right again. What this tells us is that during much of the nineteenth century, a strong American theatre had not yet developed out of our native soil, although there was some, and so the Brits sailed into New York, performed first in that harbor city (laying the foundation for modern Broadway) and then toured all across the country and back again, stuffed their pockets with American dollars, and sailed back to England, repeatedly throughout the nineteenth century. It took us awhile to develop a native theatre. The other pertinent question, which I do not expect you to know the answer to, is, what kind of play was *Our American Cousin?*"

No one took the worm.

"It was a melodrama. The dominant type of theatre in the nineteenth century, not only in the US but all across Europe." He scanned again. "Anyone know what characterizes a melodrama?"

At this point, the energetic professor flipped on the video board to show a clip of *The Perils of Pauline,* after which he let the students dissect melodrama, identifying characteristics such as over-acting, multiple episodes, sentimentality, and concluding with "the good guys versus the bad guys, the guys in the white hats versus the guys in the black hats, villains and heroes." The new professor, Eugene Betters, suddenly came to his mind. *Let that go,* he admonished himself. *There are no villains.*

"Can you think of any modern equivalents of melodrama?" he challenged them.

"How about *Star Wars*" a hesitant voice asked.

"Absolutely. Very good."

"Cowboy Westerns?"

"Cops and Robbers?"

"You bet. In fact, I think you could safely say that most of the junk coming out of Hollywood and on TV are melodramas. What's wrong with reducing life down to good guys versus bad guys?" he shot it out into the stratosphere again.

"Would you say that that is just not the way life is? In fact, Shaw said that the bad guys might be the good guys and vice versa," Herr Professor concluded as the bell rang, ending everyone's misery, except the professor who had a passion for his profession and luxuriated in his sense of self-fulfillment, not self-aggrandizement. He allowed the full throttle of these sensations as he trudged back to his office with feelings of reward.

Back in his office, his chancel, as he sometimes called it, Justin landed his books and folders neatly on the bookshelf behind his swivel chair, plopped down on his seat of learning, pulled out the morning paper and sought out the crossword puzzle section, folded to the right page, pulled out his leaded weapon, and began to assault the word game, one of his favorite modes of relaxation, always involving language. He finished filling a few "Across" lines when he heard a voice at his door with, "can I come in?"

"Sure, sure, come on in," and, annoyed, surrendered his pencil and paper to the top of his desk. "What's up?" Justin hurled to the lanky figure occupying the doorway.

"Not much," Eugene Betters volleyed back as he slipped to the chair in front of Justin's desk. Sandberg examined him closer this time and guardedly offered his hospitality. Betters seemed to be about six feet two inches in height with dark tousled hair (slightly receding), lanky in form, slightly stooped, as slender homo sapiens sometimes tended to be (as though permanently ducking overhead dangers), dark eyes, and, Sandberg noted, what seemed to be a frozen smirk, or sneer, about his mouth. Betters lumbered into the chair and crossed his legs in a womanly fashion as though apologizing for filling up too much space. He wore worn jeans, a gaudy shirt (apparently an attempt at chartreuse), and rotting sneakers. Justin withheld judgement, but he noted, in his own mind, a lack of professionalism as opposed to his own Ivy League dress, blue blazer, khaki slacks, button-down, light-blue dress shirt, and university-colors tie.

"Did you just arrive here in town?" Sandberg started safely.

"Two nights ago," Betters dribbled back to him.

"Where'd you come from?"

"Austin." Betters's eyes seemed to constantly dance around the room as though he were wary, on alert, assessing, defensive, scavenging, hiding maybe, maybe paranoid?

"What were you doing in Austin?"

"Teaching." He never looked Justin in the eye during the whole stay.

"UT?"

"Nay. I got my doctorate from UT. I was in the Austin Community College system for the last five years. Looking for a job. I was ready to say 'fuck'em, fuck the whole profession, fuck'em all,' I said. I'll drive a fucking taxi. I was about to do that when I got an offer from this fuckin place." Justin, not to be judgmental, pondered the impoverishment of his language, or the paucity of its adjectives and verbs.

"Do you talk like that in class?"

"When I fuckin feel like it." The thought, *I wonder how long he'll last here,* hurled like a dart through Justin's cranial territory.

"So within the field of philosophy, what's your specialty, what is your philosophical position?"

"Existentialism. Postmodernism. Deconstructionism. Moral Relativism . . ." Betters intended to journey down this trail some distance but was barricaded with:

"Yeah, I get it." Justin, with his undergraduate major in Philosophy, was quite conversant with the realms of abstract thought and even summoned up his feelings of shock upon his first encounters with ideas that were quite unfamiliar to him, such as Postmodern Philosophy. *Figures,* he thought to himself. Justin had been weened on Southern Baptist dogma, including the **fact** that the earth is six thousand years old, the story of Genesis is a literal account of the first seven days of the universe, that every word of the Bible is verbatim-ly true (metaphorical interpretations of the Holy Scriptures being heresy), that Jesus is God's Son (how is it possible for God to have a Son, especially since "God is a spirit," so says Jesus in the book of *John*?), that there is a Heaven and a Hell (as Johnathan Edwards declares in his sermon "Sinners in the Hands of an Angry God" that we are like a spider dangling on a spider web over a burning fire in which we shall be consumed), that one gets into Heaven by immersion in water ("and once saved, always saved"), that the woman is subservient to the man (Eve's fault there of course and that women, and children, should be seen but not heard), that the man is the head of the household and the only one who is allowed to speak in church—AND that Humanism is a deceitful conspiracy of the Devil. Justin marveled at the contrast between the teachings of his youth and that of Postmodernism in which there is no ultimate truth, that humans are alone in the universe, that the only thing that matters is the present existence, that there are no moral principles in life, that ethics is based on whatever works in the present situation (Situational Ethics), that the Age of Enlightenment, as well as Reason itself, is to be ignored, that God is a myth, and that basically one is free to do whatever one wishes to do, as long as one does not get caught by the law. Such ideas shattered his foundation but he rebuilt it by deciding that he was not going to be a Baptist minister after all and that literature sourced him with all the answers he needed. Postmodernism always seemed a little extreme to him (to justify self-indulgence), that nothing it stood for could be proved, and did not allow for the possibility that there might be something beyond the physical universe, which he felt was a possibility. *Since we know nothing anyway, we may as well embrace that which is most congenial to our disposition,* so thought Justin.

"What's your specialty—in the grand world of literature?" Betters bounced the conversational ball off the floor back to him.

"Well, generally speaking, dramatic literature—Shakespeare, Shaw, O'Neill, American and British drama, that kind of thing." Justin wanted to prove that he could be civil.

"The pay stinks here, don't you think," Betters changed gears.

"Well, I've been here long enough for mine to go up a little."

"I haven't gotten a paycheck yet and I'm broke. Let me tell you what I did," the Philosophy professor, for some unknown reason, was in a confessional mood.

"Go for it."

"I went to the University Bookstore, the Engineering section actually—"

"Ok"

"Engineering textbooks are expensive, costing five or six hundred dollars each. So I took an engineering text that was priced at $625, wrapped it inside the New York Times which I had bought, tucked it under my arm, and walked out with it."

"You're kidding!"

"Nope. Then I posted a notice on the bulletin board that I had it for sale at half price, along with my phone number. Three hundred bucks." It was revoltingly clear that Betters was proud of himself.

"You didn't"

"I gotta eat, man," he added with a self-righteous smirk.

"Situational ethics, hunh?

"You got it man," the philosopher seemed unfazed by what he was admitting, proof in Justin's mind of the unlicensed but intensely justified behavior of a modernist

Justin sat in stony silence, uncertain as to how to respond but knowing that confrontation would accomplish nothing. He made a u-turn and decided that he would get more out of the relationship by listening, studying, and observing Betters than by challenging him. He did not want to sound judgmental or simple-minded and generously thought about what he had admonished his class with: *there are no villains and no heroes, no good guys and bad guys. People are just people.* He was awash in doubt about his own creed.

"What I really wanted to ask you—" Eugene Betters hesitated.

"Yes?"

"Do you fuck your students?"

"What?!!" the English professor took a foot off his desk, sat forward, and landed both feet on the floor.

"Do you fuck your students?" Betters had a diabolical grin on his face.

"Are you kidding me?"

"Of course not. What's the big deal?" the philosopher continued in pretended innocence.

"Hey man, I've got mouths to feed. I can't afford to jeopardize that."

"Where's the harm?" Betters continued with his game of naivete.

"It's not about moral principles," Justin advocated the pragmatic dimension of his thinking, "it's about the high risk of losing your job?"

"Why? We used to do it all the time—every semester, in fact—at Austin Community College." *Is he putting me on, or what's his game?* Justin mulled.

Eugene Betters elaborated in a lengthy narrative about the seduction games that, supposedly, were waged at ACC and then terminated his saga with,

"Well, I gotta go meet my first class—check out the babes—see if there are any prospects in it," Betters said as he lifted himself from the chair and sauntered toward the door. "I'll let you know how it goes."

"Yeah. Please do," Justin inaudibly replied.

"Let's have a drink some time."

"Yeah, sure," Justin's response met the philosopher's backside as his guest ambled away.

There are no bad guys and good guys. Everybody has a saving grace. Justin interrupted his conscious flow and added, *I hope he's good to his mother.* Justin was also alert to the irony of his own advice to the philosophy professor, but, over the years, he had tried to replace his youthful indiscretions with maturity and commonsense. It was also painfully ironical that he had been reminiscing on this, the first day of classes of a new academic year, about his unwise behavior in his earlier days. There is a commonality in all things and the universe is one.

"Let's see now: 10 Across, "Lover of Daphnis." Uhh, oh yeah, "Chloe." Justin picked up his pencil and attacked the Crossword puzzle of the day with vigor.

11

Justin had one more class remaining for the day and continued his first class-day celebration with reflections of various kinds, all descending on him from a past crowded, and clouded, with memories (the crossword puzzle had been completed and put aside within minutes). He recollected the fact that Norma dropped out of the university after her first year, but, since she was no longer a student, they continued off and on over many years to remain in touch. He saw her get married and have a son, observed the son grow up, watched her through a divorce, and come out on the other side a single woman again. Life remained a battle for her as she waged war with a wide world of worries and work. She was a real estate agent, a store clerk, a factory worker, a door-to-door salesperson, a waitress, a truck stop worker, a file clerk, ad infinitum while she witnessed him go through two marriages and two divorces, due in part no doubt to his infidelities, sire five children, putting them all through college, and come out on the other side a freed man. And yet, over a period of some thirty years, they reveled in reunions and rendezvous replete with rowdy respites.

Relationships have to be stoked, pampered, prodded, or poked, otherwise inertia may set in. After Justin's second divorce, he moved through a series of encounters with disappointing outcomes, but he always kept calling Norma when there was a hiatus in his pursuits, and she always seemed compliant. They agreed during one phone call to meet for a drink.

"Hi," was Norma's opening timid invocation as she walked up behind him in the Rathskeller while he became aware of her in the mirror behind the bar. He turned on his bar stool to welcome her, squeezed her hand, and enfolded her in his arms.

"You look delicious," were his first words.

"And you haven't changed one bit," she said as she ascended the stool beside him. It had been a number of months since last fellowshipping with her. He did notice that her black hair was beginning to show some strains of white flecks in it and that her youthful skin had slightly succumbed to the years, with a minor crease here and there and a slightly darker hue. In his mind, she was still the college freshman he first knew and as comfortable as an old lounge chair.

"How have you been?" Justin opened their rendezvous.

"Ok."

"What are you drinking?' he asked her.

"What are you having?

"Chardonnay,"

"That sounds good."

Justin sidled his stool closer to hers and put his hand on her thigh.

"Your body is always so warm. I've missed seeing you."

"You're sweet."

"So tell me what's new," he said, seeking the cozy shelter inside the events of her life, getting as close to her as he could through talk.

"I've gone back to real estate, for one thing," she invited him in.

"Are you still living in the Mission Valley?"

"Yes."

"Alone?'

She kept him outside with her silence and then, after an interminable amount of time, she held up her hand.

"What?'

"Look at my index finger—I can't bend it." Tears now accompanied her gesture.

"What happened?"

"He broke it," she whispered. She took out a tissue and dabbed at her eyes and face. "I can't bend it."

"Who?"

"This guy I'm living with," as she put both hands now to her face in a gesture of shame.

"I'm going to kill the sonuvabitch," Justin clenched his jaw muscles. "Who is this guy, tell me something about him."

"He's a truck driver. I met him when I was working at the truck stop out on I-10."

"Do you like him?"

"He'll do for right now." Justin detected a note of resignation, nay, even will-lessness and fatalism.

"How did he break your finger?"

"We had a fight."

"Does he hit you?"

Justin waited languidly for more. He felt her pain and her need to hide, seething that anyone would dare abuse such a sweet human being as Norma was. *Incomprehensible,* he mumbled.

Finally, he encouraged her with, "Norma?" softly and tenderly.

"Yes."

"Yes, what?"

"Once in a while."

"Oh Norma, Norma, precious, precious Norma. You deserve so much better."

"No. I guess I deserve it."

"Never!!! Nobody deserves brutality."

"Can we go to your place. I need some tenderness."

"Well, my son is now living with me—"

"Oh."

"Tell you what—we can go to my office."

"On campus?"

"Sure." Justin put some money on the bar and stood. "Come on. Let's go."

In his office, his sacred place of work and worship, with Shakespeare's portrait staring down at him and Robert Frost sitting on the bookshelf, in the dark, on the soft carpet, they had an amazing encounter, she so receiving, eager, and accommodating, he so filled with the sweetest of feelings for her. It was the last time he ever saw her. Whenever thoughts of her introduced themselves into his consciousness, he always suffered the sharpest pangs, along with the gentlest feelings for her and worried that somehow he might have been responsible for her rudderless life.

His thoughts returned to the present moment, sitting in the very same office, staring at the very same carpet.

12

His mind was still meandering and then halted on the recollection that he and Eva, over a period of time, saw less and less of each other, she very much into her demanding public school employment, he occupied with researching, writing, publishing, teaching, and occasionally socializing. He remembered that after several years had passed, they by chance filled briefly the same space with a short exchange which became a searingly, indelibly sad moment in Justin's life. It so happened that it was upon the occasion of the beginning of another new academic year, the last days of summer and the commencement of an impending fall desert pleasantness, the glorious, in his mind, interlude of the year. It also transpired by chance that he happened to be in the Humanities Building, a building which he seldom habituated, to attend a committee meeting during the first week of the new semester (it was also a building often used for conferences). His mind was being entertained by the business of the committee meeting he had just survived, rather dissatisfied and bored with what he had just experienced, and was rambling aimlessly down the hall, observing in the far distance a rather obese lady coming in his direction, a figure he hardly noticed. With his eyes basically scouring the floor in contemplation, he heard a female voice say, "Dr. Sandberg." He swept his sight from the floor and up into the face of the lady who had just drawn parallel to him and the owner of the voice which had spoken. He flunked recognizing her and stared dumbly at her. Encountering former students after many years was not an uncommon event for him, over the years, and so did not enlarge the importance of the moment, trying solely to recall the face, class, year, anything to start the floodtide of memory.

"Don't you recognize me?" the lady queried.

"You look familiar, that's for sure. I'm trying to recall—"

"Really? Have I changed that much?" the voice wanted to know in a shock of disappointment and seeming humiliation at the thought that she was so unimportant to him.

"Give me a hint."

"Unbelievable," the lips muttered.

Dr. Sandberg mulled over the voice and then examined the face severely and whispered, "oh my god."

"Eva Diaz," she icily articulated.

Diplomacy, tact, decency, thoughtfulness, were Justin's thoughts, *whatever I do I shall not mention her weight.*

Justin observed that she had aged, furrowed, fraught, exhausted, spent, tired, weary, which the ways and weight of the world had worn on her. She had always been so cheery, smiley, sunny, friendly, and receptive. She now seemed withdrawn, distant, defensive, detached, deeply depressed and defeated. *What in the world has aged her so much?*

"What are you doing here?"

"Attending a bilingual conference. Down the hall there," she pointed in the direction she had come from.

"I'm sorry I didn—"

"It's ok. I know I've changed," she gave him some territory to stand on.

"Have you been sick?"

"In a way, I suppose, yes," she offered.

"Do you have a minute?"

"I guess," she struggled a reply.

"Look, there's an empty classroom right here. Let's go in here so we can sit down and visit for a moment." Justin opened the windowed door while Eva heaved herself forward after which he pulled two desk chairs together, facing each other and offered, "have a seat."

"Look, I know I have been negligent—not calling you—I'm so sorry."

"It's ok," she protected him.

"I have been really busy, and I know you have too, but we used to have some grand old times together. Or at least I did."

"Unhunh."

"Would you like to get together again some time?"

"No."

"I understand—"

"No you don't!" She was emphatic. He had never before seen this in her, an iron girder beneath the normally soft tissue of her nature, and wondered, in addition to her physical alteration, what trauma had occurred in her life that had spiraled her in a subterranean direction. He thought she would be eager to get together again, as he consulted with his male ego.

"That's all behind me now. I am finished with it." She was staring at the floor, speaking softly and sorrowfully. "In fact, I am finished with life," she added.

"Don't talk like that."

"I feel nothing any more. I am dead inside—and I'd just as soon be dead on the outside as well. Life has no meaning for me," she added balefully forlorn.

Justin was again at a loss for words, the English professor again unable to find the appropriate English words. Shakespeare could not rescue him in the aching present occasion, at least not anything he could think of on the fly.

"Eva." He waited for her to remove her glances from the floor. "Talk to me."

Clearly, the depth of her pain was unfathomable. She appeared to be in some kind of stupor, zombie-like, ghostly, pale, stone-faced, diamond hard. Justin wondered briefly if she was even aware of his presence. He waited for her to gather herself and wished now he had not pursued this little visit. Guilt crept in on little paws into his whole being. He did not know whether to push her forward or give her a hand to help her out of her chair so that she could leave without having to say anything more. When there is painful, deadly silence, time seems interminable, cruel, punishing, relentless, or so it seemed to Justin at the moment. She remained transfixed. Finally, Justin, out of compassion softly and slowly offered,

"Eva. Look. It's ok. I'm sorry I said anything," and he stood up. "I don't wish to pursue anything if it is so torturous for you. Maybe I should leave." She remained seated. He sat back down.

"Is there anything I can do?'

She barely shook her head hesitantly and remained dumb.

"Are you still grieving over Jessica?"

She kept her face transfixed down on her chest and gave no response, until, with her face still parallel to the floor, she uttered the unutterable, "Angie's dead too."

"Tell me it's not true."

Justin was totally unable to find himself somewhere in all the madness, fury, and injustice of it all.

"Nobody deserves this," was the most he could erect on his end.

Having finally been able to let loose with words, she found more, looked up, and was able to proceed in the only way that gave her bare comfort, "It's all my fault, all, all, all, all my fault."

"How do you figure that?"

"Just like with Jessica—when they were growing up I was trying to go to school to set an example for them, and, with no money, I had to work as much as I could to put food on the table and pay the rent. And all the while they needed me at home more than they needed for me to be going to school."

"How did she die?"

A very long breath and then an exhalation.

"OD-ed."

"When was this?"

"I am finished with life. I am out of here. I cannot face life with this burden and this sorrow that lies so deep inside of me. I can't even look at myself in the mirror. I trudge through the day just going through the motions. Life is totally meaningless to me now and I do not want to go on living."

"You have a lot to live for."

"If you're talking about fucking, forget that. I'm finished with that too. There is no pleasure in anything anymore. I just want out."

"You've got your career still, and students to help, and you have so much to offer—"

"It's all worthless, I'm telling you. I may as well be dead—"

"Don't—"

"In fact, I wish I was."

"—say that—"

Silence encrusted the moment. Then her eyes lifted up to him.

"You know I own a gun." She was still locked onto his eyes.

"Please get some help."

"Can't afford it."

"The school has counselors. They can help you."

"It's none of their business. In fact, it's nobody's business but mine. And I am going to take care of it. I have to get going—not that I have anywhere to go—or anyone to go home to." She de-chaired.

"I wish I could help you."

"All you want to do is fuck me," were her last words as she vanished out the door and into the hall.

"That's not tr—" and she was gone, and so was the memory as he returned to the present moment in his office, standing in a tidewater of shame.

Justin thought of himself as a reasonably smart person, a compassionate, caring person, and a good guy, but suddenly his last memory of Eva offered him a different view of himself, and it ran counter to everything he had ever thought about himself. This was reinforced by his sudden feeling that he did not know anything, that he ultimately had not known what to do in order to help Eva, although clearly she needed help, and he felt completely stupid, idiotic, dumbfounded, helpless, ignorant—in short, a jackass. And he was in no mood to face a semester of fresh, eager faces. He was not sure he could really confront them and pull it off that he was the most brilliant, charming professor in the university. It would take some powerful self-deception, but thirty years of experience would be on his side in the campaign.

He was finished with his last class, and the launch day of the new semester saluted him unscathed and with a sharp appetite for the work ahead, except for the last memory of Eva. He avoided reading the obituary column for some time afterwards. He was still lolling in the present moment in his office when he suddenly became aware of a red light circling around the walls of his office and bookshelves, piercing through his front window. Curiosity impelled him out of his swivel chair, around his desk, and to the window, where he saw far off to his left a police car, the source of the emanating red glow, parked at the bottom of the ramp which descended from the third floor of the Fine Arts Building wherein was housed the Departments of Art, Music, and Theatre. He was driven by his curiosity to learn what was happening. The squad car then killed its flashing red light, and an officer exited from the driver's side, apparently waiting for someone while squinting at the top of the ramp. Justin was transfixed and became cemented to the idea of discovering what was happening. After a brief moment in time, Justin saw three figures emerging from the landing in the middle of the building at the top of the smooth cement ramp, at first slightly unable to discern who or what these figures signified. As they began their descent of the ramp, it became better established that the two figures on each side of the middle figure were police officers holding the middle person by the arms. A little farther down the slope, it became increasingly clear that the middle man had handcuffs on each wrist, linked together in front of him. Justin was able to surmise that the person in the middle was rather tall and lanky, maybe six foot two or three, with a bald head, glasses, and casual dress and who, it was easily surmised, could be impersonating a college professor. *I wonder who it could be,* were Justin's prime thoughts, and then a flash of recognition hit him square in his consciousness, "oh my god, it's James Knowlton from the Theatre Department," he said instinctively and startled himself. "What the--?!?" was his incredulous response. He watched as the officers put Knowlton in the back seat of the squad car, still shackled, heard the engine jump on, saw the car separate and ease away from the ramp and curb, and passed right beneath his window, red lights again now circulating and examining the late afternoon scenery.

"What the hell was that all about," Justin spoke aloud to himself as he settled back into his desk chair. And then he thought about James Knowlton, a faculty member in the Theatre Department whose specialty was, of all things, lighting. That's right, lighting, stage lighting, as in theatre, plays, shows, dramas, interior, exterior, dark, morning, noon— whatever the plays called for, he could conjure it up. Talk about over-specializing. In fact, it did begin to test the department's resources which had begun to put pressure on him to broaden his offerings to students, to be of greater utilitarian value to the program, which led him one humbling day to Justin's office. Justin remembered it well.

"Justin, can I have a minute of your time," Knowlton queried as he stood on the threshold of Justin's office, right through the admitting device.

"Sure, come on in," Justin extended, reluctantly, an invitation, being a little tentative about his offer, not knowing what motive brought Knowlton to his office. Justin was an avid university theatre attendant, knew many of the faculty therein, often took his own students to see shows, donated some financial support, and was known around the theatre department. He knew also that Knowlton was something of a loud mouth bully with a gigantic ego, which he never hesitated to display, a know-it-all jackass, and always on stage, as he perceived himself.

"Have a seat," he offered to Knowlton. "What's up."

"I'll get to the point," he began. "The department wants me to be able to offer courses in subjects other than lighting design so I suggested that maybe I could teach a little theatre history and the dramatic text. I know your specialty is dramatic literature, so I thought maybe you might could give me a few pointers. I mean, I know a lot about it already but I thought you might give me a little different angle on things."

The meeting was relatively short and frustrated Justin somewhat, for everything that Justin suggested, Knowlton's response was, "well, I know that already" or "yeah, I've read that already" or "I'm already familiar with that," ad infinitum. Justin suggested some anthologies, some standard critical works, and the main points of a brief outline of theatre history, and some of the classic works of the theatre which should be included, including Oscar Brockett's classic *History of the Theatre*. Invariably, Knowlton spoke with a deeply resonant, dramatic voice (artificially deepened it seemed to Justin), tried to sound pontifical and authoritative on everything, and seldom listened to Justin and constantly interrupted him. Justin thought about Bottom in Shakespeare's *Midsummer Night's Dream* or Dogberry in *Much Ado About Nothing* or Jacques in *As You Like It* and the common thread that ties them altogether: they are uproariously funny characters because they are so stupid and what makes them so stupid is that they think they know everything already and establish themselves as jackasses, which Bottom literally becomes, converted into the head of an ass (*again, love the Bard's sense of humor*). In fact, Shakespeare was a genius at depicting that kind of comic character, earlier in his career, and often gives Justin the opportunity in class to elaborate on the fact that what makes a person ignorant, as happens at times, is when one thinks one knows everything already and always has one's mouth open instead of his ears ("give every man thine ear, but few thy voice"). Justin also enjoyed invoking Karl Jung's wise words about "the emotion of learning is—humility," the wise attitude being, "I don't know anything, teach me."

The meeting mercifully ended and Justin remained in his chair after Knowlton's departure and analyzed the experience. *There is something very strange about that guy, in addition to being an extremely insecure, nay even, frightened individual.* Justin smiled as he amused himself with the idle thought, *I wonder if he suffers from an undersized male equipment,* followed by, *he's probably not even very good at lighting design.*

Justin returned to the present moment with the gnawing urge of wanting to know what Knowlton was being arrested for, and then completed the thought and adjourned his committee meeting's agenda with the determination, "I think I'll wander over to the Theatre Department and see what I can find out. It's driving me batty. It's not five o'clock yet. The department office should still be open."

13

The Theatre Department's receptionist was attempting to look busy at her desk when Dr. Sandberg materialized before her. The Theatre Department occupied one-third of the Fine Arts Building shared with Music and Art. The main theatre was a state of the art affair, with a horseshoe-shaped seating arrangement around a stage that could be either thrust or proscenium with ample overhead stage room for all kinds of configurations, elaborations, and settings, and the faculty was moderately strong with, like every department, a couple of deadweights here and there and definitely some strengths. The president of the university attended one performance and was visibly rankled that the attendance was so small. Her judgement was, "we're paying all this money to reach so few people." She said zilch about the quality of the performance or the play itself, and probably did not even notice either. At another theatre gala performance, the theatre was capacity at opening curtain (and the president was pleased), and empty for the curtain after the intermission (the president being among the missing). Presidents keep a keen eye on two things, community image and financial squandering.

"Hi Lisa," Justin greeted her with his best charmer smile.

"Dr. Sandberg. What are you doing in this neck of the woods?' was her clichéd attempt at being clever.

"Oh not much. Is Dr. Morales around?" was his question for the receptionist, Jose Morales being the Theatre Department's Chair.

"No, he's not right now. You might try the theatre downstairs," was her helpful offering.

"Let me ask you something, Lisa." He pulled her attention away from the fingernail she was adorning. "I just saw Professor Knowlton being led out of the building by a couple of policemen and put in a squad car—with handcuffs on. What's going on?"

She looked up at him with an uncertain look on her face and was clearly struggling with how to answer the question. After a brief moment, she put her head down to return to her fingernail painting and answered him softly.

"I'm sorry Dr. Sandberg, I'm not allowed to talk about it."

"I see. You say Dr. Morales might be in the theatre?"

"I think so," was her uncomplicated answer as he turned to exit through the door. "Dr. Sandburg." He stopped. "If you want an answer to your question, you might want to talk to Mr. Green."

"Hunhunh. Thank you, Lisa. He's probably in the theatre as well, right."

"Yes."

Gregory Green, a theatre technician and staff member without faculty status, was a specialist in set design and theatre technology. Justin had heard that there was some sandpaper between Green and Knowlton, even though Justin did not know the source of the friction, but he was aware that they were both plagued by an egregiously enlarged sense of self.

As Justin entered the darkened auditorium of the main theatre, he ascertained that there were some students down on the stage working on a set and so drifted down to the stages edge with the question, "Is Mr. Green around?"

One student looked up from his task, whatever it was he was building, and answered, "He's in his office."

"And that would be—" Justin's finger was without direction in the air.

"Go through that door on your left and down the passage way. His office is down at the end." Justin complied with the directions and found Green's office.

"Greg?" Justin was standing in the open doorway, this being the season of portals, to Green's office, another soliciting entry to another adventure into the realm of possibilities and establishing a definite motif of open portals and singular doors for the semester thus far.

"What the--? Are you lost or something?" It seemed to Justin also that everybody in the Theatre Department was trying to be a comedian.

"You got a minute?"

"Just barely," Green grunted, "come on in." *Temperamental artist,* Justin thought to himself.

"Thanks," was Justin's retort as he strode casually to the chair in front of Green's desk.

"What's up?"

"I just saw the strangest sight—Jim Knowlton being escorted in handcuffs by police to a squad car. What's that all about?"

"**That goddamn fuckin sonuvabitch!!!**" was Green's soft response in extravagant decibels. *Not a cautiously measured response.*

Wow, I think I've hit on the mother lode here, Justin surmised.

"Please feel free to speak your mind," Justin grinned.

"I hate the bastard's guts."

"Obviously," Justin quietly managed.

"He's on his way to jail and I put him there."

"You did? What's the charge against him?" Justin questioned.

"Child pornography," was Green's simple and illuminating but cryptic answer.

"Humph. Tell me what happened." Justin wanted to appear sympathetic in order to encourage him.

"That stupid bastard has fucked up more of my sets than you can imagine. He's a stupid idiot who thinks he knows everything when he don't know nothing."

"But that doesn't—"

"Wait a minute. Let me tell you what happened. We were working on this set that you saw on stage just now for the next show. I told him I wanted to see his lighting design so that I could make adjustments to my set design. He said it was in his office on his desk, so he gave me the key to his office to go get it, like I'm his errand-boy, you know. Which I did. When I got inside his office, I found his lighting design on his desk. And then, something caught my eye over on the corner of his desk. So I took a closer look and there was this picture of a little girl—naked—so I picked it up and underneath it was a whole stack of such pictures—naked children—hundreds and hundreds of them. They looked like they had been downloaded off the internet. So I went back to my office and called the campus police. I still had his key so I let them into his office and then the campus police called the city police. End of story."

"Boy," said Justin, "he is in deep shit now. He'll probably lose his job as well, in addition to spending time."

"I hope so. I found out the damn bastard voted against my salary raise. That'll teach him. And I don't care who knows. I did the right thing. I gotta get to my set now."

"Sorry to take up your time Greg. My curiosity got the better of me."

"No problem."

Justin signatured off with "I'm looking forward to your next show."

"Take a close look at the set when you see it."

"Right.

14

On his way back to his office, Justin began to ponder what had just transpired and carried on a conversation with himself. *Boy, Greg Green is one angry person. I'm not sure I could do that to a colleague,* he thought as he trudged along the colorful landscaping of mixed desert flora in front of his building as he veered up the sidewalk. And then he thought, *But Knowlton, who must be some type of sicko, is definitely in the wrong here. I mean, innocent children! Are you kidding me?* And then he thought of his own grandchildren and turned into a purple rage. *He's getting what he deserves, but where was his brain when he gave Greg his office key? Some people become so inured to their own behavior they lose all ethical perspective, if they ever had any. And,* he thought, *actions have consequences, and we are our own destiny.* And then Richard Franklin, also in the Philosophy Department, came to mind, *caught watching adult porn on a school computer and almost lost his job over it. His excuse was that he was doing research for his Ethics Class. Yeah, right. Man, we are a public institution and should work to deserve the public trust. Maybe politicians should also remind themselves of that.*

By the end point of his meditative peregrinations Justin was positioned upright at his desk back in his Holy of Holies, ready to conclude his first day, eventful as it was, of the new semester. The end of everyday always aroused in him the sensation of satisfaction, and today was no exception, the feeling that he was doing something meaningful; whether it meant anything to anybody else or not did not matter. It was what he did. He had met all his classes, and assessed them, and considered that the horizon at the end of the semester would be a golden one, the students alert, eager, bright (being mostly English majors), and respectful. Justin enjoyed reflecting: *most of my students are Hispanic and a joy to teach. Many of them are the first in their family to go to college, most are bilingual equally adept at either English or Spanish. How I envy that, try as I may to conquer Spanish. They come majorly from blue collar families (hardworking, decent folks), grateful to be at the university. They are the flowering forth and fruitful harvest of their ancestors' dreams who struggled, roiled, toiled, and labored mightily in farmers' fields, picking tomatoes in the dust, to reach the precious soil in which a dream could be planted, nourished, and harvested.* He thought about his own son who had attended a private university in Dallas and his buddies on whom an educational opportunity was a waste, treating education with dismissive indifference and interested only in partying, drinking, courting, socializing, and getting laid—arrogant, haughty, lazy, unambitious, and boastful of their families' country clubs and Jaguars, their affluence and influence, their greed and gluttony. *Give me my humble and hungry students any day. They will be successes while the young men at his son's private university will spend their lives living off their families' money, drinking, drugging, golfing, hobbying, vacationing, and being unfaithful to their spouses and to life.* Justin dwelt in his memory for a while longer. *How this border university has changed over the years, the early days composed of a student body which was so obviously poor as compared to today's students, the children and grandchildren of those earlier paupers eating bologna sandwiches and chili rellenos (meatless of course) brought from home, and today's students driving new pickups or SUV's as compared to their ancestors' broken down jalopies, if they owned a car at all.* Thus ended Justin's reflections. And his day.

15

The semester roared to the middle of itself, with Justin attaining the rhythm and routine of his diurnal passages, when one day he circumlocuted into the same space in the hall with Gene Betters, the new Philosophy professor, who was also hitting his stride in hitting on the pulchritudinous elements in his classes, as Gene liked to boast to Justin about his out-of-class, extracurricular gamboling, probably because he knew how much student fraternization riled Justin to an acidic reaction.

"'Sup?" the sardonic Betters asked from behind his dark sunglasses.

"Hey, man," Justin teased him, "you've been in town for only a couple of weeks and you're already on the front page of the local rag."

"Damn tootin'" Betters spoke arrogantly and greasely. "Gotta stand for what's right."

"What do you have against the circus?" Justin frowned.

"Are you kidding me? Do you have any idea how they treat their animals?" came the rhetorical query.

"I imagine they are pretty well fed and taken care of," Justin bit the bait.

"Shi-et!"

"You know something I don't know?" Justin pretended ignorance, which he genuinely was since the circus was not an object of his meditations, contemplation, cogitation, nor waking-hours consciousness, except when he had taken his little tots there.

"You bet I do. I've studied it very carefully. Believe you me, they treat them like—er—animals, I mean, like shit. They starve them, beat them, cage them, torture them, brutalize them, punish them for their misbehavior, and every conceivable thing you can think of. As well as exploiting them for their own profit."

"And you got your students to join your protest?" Justin warily pushed a little further out of concern for academic standards. "How does this relate to your classes?"

"I teach about animal rights in all my classes"

"That's not what's listed in the course description. What does that have to do with philosophy?'"

"Ethics, my man, ethics. Animals have rights too you know."

"Don't you think humans are more important than animals, who have no consciousness?"

"How do you know?"

"I haven't seen a Cocker Spaniel reading a book lately," Justin challenged him.

"Have you seen one fetch a ball and begged to be petted?"

"I'm curious: how do you get your students involved in a demonstration?" Justin was very concerned about the coercion and manipulation of students for personal, subjective reasons.

"It's strictly voluntary. Although, to tell you the truth, I do offer them extra credit for joining in protests against animal abuse. It's strictly on the up and up, but there's nothing wrong with giving students a little extra credit for going beyond the call of duty, is it, within the subject matter?" It seemed to Justin that Betters was completely oblivious to the implications of his pedagogical methodology.

"I wouldn't do it."

"Say, whatta you doing this coming Saturday night?"

"I haven't made any plans yet—"

"Listen, some of my students are having this big bash down in the lower valley, wherever that is, and asked me to come. You wanna come?"

"Ohhh, I don't know. I don't think socializing with students is a wise idea—especially where there is drinking and all hell breaking lose."

"Ahhh, don't be a pussy. It'll be fun. Besides I need help finding my way to the lower valley."

"I'll think about it."

"Besides, there's this chick I wanna check out—see if I can put some moves on her." Again, Betters seemed totally oblivious to matters of ethical conduct, and it worried Justin an infinitesimal quantity, but not enough to stay him from considering the party, even against his better judgement. But he was curious.

"Why don't you come to my place at about sixish and I'll drive," was his ungenerous offer.

"I didn't say I would--," said Justin as he looked at the address Betters had written down. He shrugged his shoulders in resignation.

16

Harold Bradley, who was standing in Justin's magical doorway into his sanctuary as Justin was packing his book bag preparing to soon be homeward bound, was a senior colleague of Justin's whom he had known for years. The sight of Bradley, who appeared to be swaying slightly with purposeless, uncooperative hands, disturbed Justin. A lightning bolt of memory flicked through Justin's mind at the sight of Bradley, the remembrance of a conference which they had attempted to attend together several years back. They traveled together, Bradley's wife having driven them to the airport, as she had on other occasions. Justin's wife had placed a bottle of Bourbon in his suitcase as a surprise (this was in the days before airport security inspections), so that when Justin was settled into his motel room in Colorado Springs on a Friday afternoon, the conference being hosted by the Air Force Academy, he sat down to relax before the buses were to take them to the Officer's Club for the opening night banquet, guest speaker, and business session, all presided over by the president of the association, Harold Bradley, and poured himself a drink, exhaling a breath of relaxation. Soon, however, his placidity was ruffled by a bang on his hotel room's door (*one among a passel of portals in his present life*) which he disheartenedly opened, wishing to be alone with his own thoughts (Bradley, who was something of a "character," had already occupied Justin's listening space completely on the plane). Justin rolled his eyes regarding the visitation.

They chatted aimlessly for a while, including Bradley's story of how he began the semester's class meeting by asking all the young ladies to cross their legs, whereupon he continued, "And now that the gates of hell are closed, we'll think about Chaucer." Justin smiled.

"Whatta you drinking?" Bradley roughly asked.

"A little bourbon." Bradley's eyes reacted with a "yum." "Mind if I have a drop?"

"Are you sure?" Justin was aware of Bradley's alcoholism, although he had not existentially interacted with it.

"Sure. I'll just have a little to wet my whistle."

Bradley received the offering with thanks and a quivering hand and made his glass empty in one swallow then looked at Justin with a face that said "just a tiny bit more?"

He's an adult, what can I say, Justin diplomatically gave a little latitude.

"I'll buy you a drink, don't worry."

"I'm not worried. Drink all you want," which he felt might be a hazardous thing to say.

17

After a brief bus ride, during which Bradley was heard relishing a drink with lip-smacking and diversionary chat, they arrived at the Officer's Club on the campus of the Academy. Bradley barely had his feet on the ground when those same feet bore him directly to the bar in the Officer's Club, which was adjacent to the conference's banquet hall, where he encountered several officers on the faculty of the academy. Harold had apparently been an Air Force officer in the reserves at some point which led, in the present milieu, immediately to companionship, camaraderie, and a lot of alcohol, from which it was impossible for Justin to extract Bradley to attend the conference's banquet, which Bradley, being in charge of the evening's dinner session, was supposed to preside over. Justin stayed with Bradley to supervise him and absorb his outlandish, but entertaining fables, for which he had a real gift, funny, witty, and incredulous, increasingly as the hours sprinted pass. What seemed to Justin as a relatively short period of time, it soon became evident (who counts time on such occasions) that the banquet hall was empty, the banquet having proceeded and concluded without its leader (apparently under the aegis of the Vice-President), and Justin and his comrade-in-arms were without transportation back to the motel, until a female colleague discovered them still in the bar and informed them that she had a rental car, during which ride back to the hotel, Justin was utterly demoralized and dejected by his companion's drunken ramblings.

At the hotel breakfast table the following morning, a meeting which had been arranged upon their "goo'nights" the evening before, it inadvertently emerged that Bradley had called a taxi after Justin left him the night before, which took the professor to an after-hours subterranean hole somewhere in Colorado Springs, where he proceeded to drink the night away. At breakfast, Justin noticed his colleague slipping a folded bill of some denomination to the waiter while delivering a whispered message to him, after which the waiter brought him a coffee cup filled to the brim with a brown liquid, which was clearly not coffee. It also grew evident that the dear professor had no power nor inclination nor desire to stop. Meanwhile, Justin abandoned him to the fatal three sisters, the Moira (Clotho the Spinner, Lachesis the Allotter, and Atropos the Inflexible,) or, else, the Naiards, *the Rulers of life,* or perhaps, more appropriately, to Dionysius, the god of wine, whichever, so that he, Justin, could attend conference sessions and deliver his own inane, as he saw it, contribution to the Sahara of scholarship, for which he was amply rewarded on his faculty evaluations. Justin continued to be present at a number of different conference sessions throughout the Saturday and tried to obliterate the thought of how Bradley was spending, or consuming, his day. During the day, he welded himself to some old conference acquaintances from other universities in the Rocky Mountain region, socialized for a while and then ate dinner with them, fighting will all his strength of will to free his mind of thoughts of his old buddy Bradley and his activities and whereabouts.

18

The conference for Justin had been a grisly gruesome nightmare, scarred with embarrassment and guilt (he felt it to be his fault that Bradley had fallen off the wagon and into hog defecation), a shock to his nervous system (he had never had an experience with a full-fledged, diseased, thoroughbred, unadulterated alcoholic before), and abject humiliation (his university received a devastating body-blow to its reputation because of the dereliction of the president of the conference from which it would take years for his university to rehabilitate its reputation at this particular conference). What Bradley had done on Saturday night, Justin had no idea, did not care to know, and dreaded the plane ride home, which expectedly became an extension of the unendurable nature of the conference itself. Bradley had somehow managed to get to the airport with his luggage intact but not his personhood. Bradley had always been known as an impeccably neat, coordinated, and smart dresser, always with suits, ties, and starched white shirts, formal-looking black dress shoes and silk socks, a jaunty hat, the model of conservatism (suddenly Justin's brain was brightly flooded with the insight that Bradley's perfectionistic exterior was one of his control devices, assault weapons with which he was battling his private, insidious civil war with his demons). At the airport, Bradley looked as though he had been sucked into a 747 jet engine and then expelled into the waiting area at their gate, frumpled, crumpled, and rumpled. Justin was surprised that his companion did not order drinks on the plane, but then he became attuned to the fact that Bradley barely possessed consciousness, that he was drooling with saliva from his mouth, and his purplish, weighty eyelids would not stay open. *Surely he has reached his saturation point and he'll be ready to sleep it off and meet his classes on Monday morning.* Justin was unaware of the horrific reality of the circumstances which lay ahead and little did he know the subject of his concern.

Mrs. Bradley was scheduled to meet them at their home airport to transport the two of them to the Bradley household on Arizona Street from which Justin's wife would come to fetch him home. After the plane landed, Justin was unsure whether Bradley would be able to walk up the concourse to the escalators and gave him as much assistance as he could. Thankfully, on the escalator, Bradley was able to hold on to the moving banister and brace himself on the descending steps (*thank god he doesn't have to negotiate regular steps*) without showing much sign of disability. Justin looked down at the bottom of the escalator to the welcoming-arrivals area and saw Mrs. Bradley with the brightest, sunniest, jubilant face of welcome he had ever seen. Her joy and anticipation was a remarkable, heart-warming vision—until they reached the bottom of the escalator and Bradley tried to negotiate the escalator's forward momentum with the stationary floor, and Justin caught him just in time to break his fall to the floor. It was Mrs. Bradley's worst, unimaginable nightmare come true, and all her hopes, best wishes, welcome-homes, and happy homecomings sprawled at her feet. Justin lifted him up for her to receive her conquering hero.

Mrs. Bradley, a very reserved, dignified, elegant, soft-spoken, dower, and conservative lady, red-facedly, with veins popping in her neck and temples, screamed to Justin, "HOW THE FUCK DID THIS HAPPEN!?!

Justin scrunched upward his shoulder blades to almost touching his ears, "I was not with him most of the time," which was technically true but not the whole story. Justin wavered in uncertainty as to how much he should reveal, but did offer that it seemed to have begun on Friday night at the officers club at the Air Force Academy when he fell in with some Air Force officers with whom he had a sudden rapport and common-ground "war" stories—not to mention the buying of each other drinks. Justin redacted the part about his wife having placed a bottle of bourbon in his suitcase and felt a spasm of guilt shake his body.

19

The Bradley's navigated through the streets of Mountain Pass in a Lincoln Continental the size of an aircraft carrier. Bradley always seemed to have more money than an ordinary college professor would normally have in the bank, but Justin did know that Bradley's brother owned a Ford dealership somewhere on the dusty, wind-pained plains of Oklahoma. After a tussle about who would drive, Mrs. Bradley triumphed, even though she was smaller than Bradley, but she won by being the owner of better common sense at the moment. Bradley sat in the passenger seat in the front while Justin occupied the whole of the backseat and gave thanks that Bradley himself was not driving, even though he was giving detailed and drunken instructions to his wife about how things were supposed to be done (Justin had ridden once to a conference in Albuquerque with Bradley at the steerage and, for two-hundred-and-fifty miles, the helmsman had patted the accelerator with his foot with neck-cracking regularity, speeding up and slowing down, the entire trip and Justin swore to never ride with him again). Mrs. Bradley escorted them on that occasion. During the trip to their house, Bradley gave an endlessly glowing report about what a wonderful conference it was and how much he had learned and about all the wonderful colleagues he had met until his wife asked the fatal question: "how did your presiding over the conference go and all your planning?" Bradley responded with an evasive grunt and was soon snoring. Justin withered into himself.

The threesome entered the Bradley's doll house living room, graced by a classic Duncan-Fife brocaded couch, a Duncan-Fife oval, mahogany coffee table in front of the couch, two winged stuffed easy chairs, as they were referred to, one colonial, high-back rocker, and a colorless wall-to-wall carpet. The exterior of the house, which Justin had seen in the daylight on other occasions, was southwestern adobe, practical for the desert but totally disharmonic and anachronistic with the interior furnishings. Clearly and without a quiver of doubt, Mrs. Bradley had lovingly and expensively dedicated her soul to an effort to keep her wandering, and sometimes drunken, mate at home, but, without liquor in the house to entice him to stay there, the odds were aligned against her.

Once in the house, Justin asked Mrs. Bradley if he could use their phone to call his wife to retrieve him, which he promptly did (wanting to get out of a coiled imbroglio *inmediate*) and which wait-time then provided him with about a twenty minute hiatus to observe the inner workings of an acutely stress-laden, screaming, surreal scenario. Mrs. Bradley, as assessed by the referee Justin, won the match by virtue of her sobriety while Professor Bradley remained handicapped by the rules violation of inebriation, ceding all the points to her scoreboard.

His colleague Harold dissolved somewhere into the small internecine labyrinth of the Bradley's modest house while Justin attempted cordiality with Virginia, as she invited Justin to call her by her first name, and attempted to alleviate the ragged edges of her distress. Justin had always thought of himself as a reasonably adequate conversationalist but in the present circumstances could barely come up with, "so how has the weather since we've been gone?'

"Wretched," was her reply, but she was obviously not talking about the climate. She turned on the TV to ameliorate the nerve pain of the present moment.

"My wife should be here pretty soon," was Justin's other feeble offer to rescue a flailing conversation.

After a few of these drowning moments, Harold entered into the quaint living room from the small hall, holding unsteadily to the wall.

"WHAT ARE YOU DOING?!?! was Virginia's screaming interrogation which she speared at her husband.

Bradley had changed clothes. No longer was he in his rumpled and crumped suit and tie but dressed in casual, battered slacks, a long-sleeved sports shirt (a gaudy plaid), and tasseled, over-the-heel loafers, all very uncharacteristic of him. It was obviously a time-honored ritual in the relationship and the household.

"I am going to Mexico," was his simple declaration.

"No you are not," was her countermand.

"Just try to stop me." The look in Bradley's eye communicated the fact that her life may be at stake if she should try to stop him. He was on the phone summoning a taxi.

Justin, like everyone on the English Department faculty, had heard the rumor that Bradley had a little bit of a drinking problem, which Bradley made a fruitless effort to manage, but it was like something that existed on some remote cloud somewhere in a theoretical universe or maybe a fictional distant planet of gossip. It had no reality except as it existed in one's naive imagination. Not only had Justin never encountered anything like the hideous reality of this trip, he had never lived through a moment like this, there in the Victorian Bradley living room, even harking back to his college fraternity drinking days. It surpassed by an immeasurable furlong anything he had ever encountered.

"Jose's on duty right now, he'll take care of me" was the information Bradley consoled with, implying a familiarity with a standing custom, common routine, and ancient ritual.

"Oh, Harold, please don't do this." Tears were now in her eyes and distress covered her visage. "You know what's going to happen—"

"I'm gonna go have shome fun," his English professor's articulation was disintegrating into the present deteriorated condition.

"You're going to disappear for a couple of weeks and then finally show up full of guilt and worrying about your job. I hope they fire you."

It often astounded Justin that Bradley could vanish for periods of time while colleagues, including Justin himself, tried to cover his classes without his suffering consequences. Justin surmised that the fact that Bradley had an international reputation as a Chaucerian scholar spared him the guillotine. It was **not** that the older departmental scholars, as well as the administration, were not aware of his once-or-twice-a-semester abracabra vanishing acts or that they did not, those closest to him, try to counsel him or persuade him to seek help. During his arid spells, Harold Bradley was the most charming, agreeable, likeable, knowledgeable and cooperative person imaginable and swore religiously that he would never drink another drop. And every time, he sounded sincere, truthful, honest, convincing, guilt-tortured, and God-fearing. His native brilliance often served his deception effectively.

A car horn squawked from the street, Bradley clumped toward the door, turned to speak to Virginia and Justin, battled for a moment or so for language, slapped on the most agonizing face Justin had ever seen, swept it all off with the wave of his hand through the air, and slammed the door after him for dramatic effect, which basically said "Fuck all you people who do not understand me."

Justin had to wait for his own wife's arrival to retrieve him home after a gruesome weekend and an agonizingly torturous moment with Mrs. Bradley. He and she sat in the silence of grief and sorrow in the precious living room, both full of heart break and disappointment.

"Do you know what he is going to do, where he's going?" Justin was concerned about Harold's safety, since obviously he was in no condition to care for himself. Justin was unaware of this creature's nocturnal habits, haunts, habitations, and hibernations.

"Ohyeah," was Virginia's rapid retort.

"Really?'

"Ohyeah. There's a bar in Juarez called *Ay Carumba,* which is owned by a man and his wife. They even have their kids in the bar, or thereabouts. Harold has been going there for years, they know him very well—he is probably one of their main means of financial support—and they seem to be good people. He goes there and gets as soused as he wants to and they take care of him. They even have a small room in the back where he can go and sleep safely while waiting for his next drink. He'll stay there until he's finally had enough—a week or two—drinking and drinking—and bullshitting--and then he'll call Jose who'll get him safely back across the border."

"Does he know that he needs help?"

"Psshh. Not according to him. He is totally oblivious. He is in total denial. 'Oh, I have it totally under control, cause I have long periods of sobriety.'" Virginia tried to mimic his male testosterone voice. "He, of all things, thinks that it is perfectly normal behavior—'everybody has a little bit of a problem' he says and dismisses it."

"Wow," was Justin's juvenile response. "Has it always been like this in your relationship?'

'You know, he was the most brilliant PhD student at NYU in his day. He came from a little Texas town—Commerce—in east Texas—"

"I know the place. East Texas State is there."

"Right. That's where he did his undergraduate degree." She supplied. "I think he always felt a little inferior because of his intellectually impoverished background, especially among the Harvard and Yale grads he was competing with at NYU. He was always trying to prove himself. He worked so hard—while nourishing this hole in his soul." Virginia paused, took a deep breath, and sighed so deeply that it made Justin ache unbearably. The mystery that she had lived most of her life with was still incomprehensible to her, it seemed to Justin.

"I know this is none of my business, but he seems to always have plenty of money—for a college professor. I mean, I just worry about your wellbeing," Justin diplomatically broached the subject.

"Well, simple story: when his brother was first starting out in the automobile business, and pretty much broke, Harold took out a loan to help him get started and his brother gave him a share of the business. Subsequently, Oliver developed a very successful dealership in Oklahoma and Harold has a share of the business from which he draws regular dividends."

She was interrupted by a horn blast.

"My wife," he said.

20

The entire historical scenario cannoned through Justin's memory magazine loader in the abbreviated time it took Harold Bradley to take several unsteady steps into Justin's office.

"Whatsup?" Justin greeted him with all the casualness and nonchalance he could enlist, trying to ignore the seeming condition Bradley was in.

"Hey, my man, just wanted to thank you for covering my classes when I had the flu." *FLU, yeah, right*, thought Justin. "Got a minute?"

"Sure."

"Enough time to meet for a drink? I wanna treat you for the favor you did me. I never forget my debts." Bradley was not drunk, Justin judged, but it appeared as though he might have had one or two or else was still recovering from a binge.

"You think that's a good idea—you know—" Justin's politeness prevented him from finishing his accusatory sentence structure.

"I really need to talk to you—**badly.**" Justin felt compassion for Harold but did not want to be an abettor. "Pleeeaaassse," Bradley added with emotional emphasis. "I need somebody to talk to."

"Ok." There was no way Justin was going to turn his back on someone who was so desperately in need of help, or who just needed a receptive, non-judgmental ear.

"I'll meet you at the College Inn. Can you drive yourself? I'll probably want to go home from there."

"Sure." Bradley had a child's look of gratitude who had just been given a lollipop.

The College Inn was only several blocks from the campus, but Justin was not very comfortable patronizing the place because it was a popular hangout for students, those who were old enough to drink, which meant mostly upper classmen and graduate students, which was the primary population in his literature classes. When Justin gave permission to these reservations, he always thought of himself as a real jerk, or maybe elitist, or maybe a nerd, but he knew in his heart that that was not the origin of his feelings. Experience had taught him that fraternizing with students can get professors in trouble, as he had seen happen to various faculty over the years, and he never wanted to jeopardize his position, not out of any moral scruples (the same as with philandering with female students) but just as a matter of discretion and Ben Franklin pragmatism. Moreover, he had seen instances of students taking advantage of professors who befriended them, especially students who were always looking for an edge or a special favor. *Dangerous pathways,* he thought.

It was Happy Hour, officially, at the College Inn, which meant that the place was vibrant with young drinkers, and Justin was drenched with a crescendo of multitudinous voices, horse laughter, ear-splitting music, and raised shouts as he entered the door and scanned for a place for two, which he found at the far end of the bar.

A football game was on the television, probably a re-run from the previous weekend, the current season being submerged in college football fetishism, or neurosis, a time of year which Justin silently admitted conjured up his own mid-teen tribal liturgies (he had not been a literary scholar all his life), mainly in memory of his pallid playing career. Justin did not often come, as mentioned, to this habitat, but every time he had been there, there was one middling-young man who was always present, as though he lived there, which he did not. Justin had chatted with him on occasion and discovered that he was the descendent of a wealthy Mexican family who had made a fortune in a Ford dealership (yes, even, or especially, in Mexico), breweries, and miscellaneous businesses. The young man, Jaime, pretended to be a student, for how long only God knows, was addicted to footballs, both American and European, which he avidly watched in this particular bar eternally and knew the names of all the players, team histories, standings, ad infinitum, and always with a drink in his hand. Justin's main thought was *what a waste.* The guy was not even interesting to talk to because his range of information was so scant but he was always warm to "Dr. Sandberg."

After he was situated at the far end of the bar, Justin soon discerned Harold's silhouette in the entrance doorway against the bright setting sun and beckoned him to his location.

"Have you ordered?' were Harold's first words as he ascended onto the adjoining stool.

"Waiting for you."

"Good, I'm paying. As a way of thanking you for covering my ass," Harold repeated the gratitude he had uttered earlier.

"Chardonnay," Justin said.

"I'll have a triple scotch on the rocks." Harold gave his order to the refreshingly pretty co-ed impersonating a bartender. Justin scanned his colleague's profile without turning his head to him.

Is that wise? Justin wondered to himself but dared not say a word lest he cast a pall over their imminent confessional dialogue. *I do want to be able to help him if I can* as he bespoke his motivation silently to himself.

Harold Bradley was maybe five years older than Justin, was a prolifically published scholar in a wide variety of fields, including Chaucer, Shakespeare, Edgar Allen Poe, Ambrose Bierce (the American Civil War writer who went to Mexico, crossing at Mountain Pass, in search of Pancho Villa, and disappeared, an occurrence which originally brought Harold to the border where he too became interested in Bierce's search), and Pancho Villa about whom he published a vast number of studies. Today, Harold was dressed in an impeccably tailored suit accompanied by a subtle, expensive-looking tie escorted by a silk handkerchief in the vest pocket of his coat. His steely hair was combed straight back, his rimless glasses made him look erudite, and his shuffling walk and hunched shoulders testified to his lack of exercise and his life perusing books and scholarly sources. He was all cerebral, except for his weakness for the bottle, bars, booze, and broads, in spite of his loyalty to Virginia (he was a little bit of a scoundrel). Justin enjoyed his zaniness, gift for storytelling, his humor, and his iconoclastic attitude toward the establishment, especially the academic establishment, starting with the Chair of the department, the Dean of the college, the Provost, and, yes, even the President of the University.

"How are your classes," Harold became the lead-off batter in the conversation.

"Full. A lot of my former students, all English majors whom I know to be very bright. Should be an enjoyable semester," Justin filled him in. "And yours?"

"My classes just barely make enrollment these days. I guess I'm too demanding," Harold justified his undersubscribed classes, but Justin, keeping his own counsel, knew about Bradley's reputation as a professor who constantly wanders off the subject and rambles on for an entire class meeting about whatever is on his mind, whether it be Pancho Villa, UFO's, or wild stories about his youth, none of which have anything to do with the course he is teaching. English majors agreed that they profited very little from his classes, even though he was thoroughly entertaining, which a few students seemed to enjoy. He was also known as an easy "A." His compensatory quality was his fiery passion for ideas and information.

"I want to ask you something: did you really tell all the female students in your class to cross their legs at the first class meeting?"

"Who told you that?" Bradley asked.

"There are no secrets around this place." Justin did not want to remind him that he, Bradley, was Justin's source for the story.

"Unfortunately. Which brings me to my subject: apparently someone has informed the administration that I have a habit of going on binges and missing classes for long periods of time," Bradley elaborated.

"Nooooo." Justin hoped that Bradley missed the sardonic tone in his voice.

"Yes. I said that to the ladies. I thought it was funny. Nobody can take a joke," he mused.

"It's very misogynistic. I wouldn't want a professor saying it to my dau--" Justin stopped himself, not wanting to go too far, and back pedaled. "But it is funny—'now that the gates of hell are closed,' haha."

"Have you said anything to anyone about my absences from classes," Bradley came to the point, knowing that Justin had delivered him from dereliction by covering some of his classes.

"Never." Justin plundered his memory to ascertain whether he was telling the truth. "Ole Kim Smith, the busybody, saw me teaching your class once and asked me about it. I told her you had the flu and I was just stepping up to the plate for you—as we all do when needed."

"When was this?" Bradley was pryingly probing for details.

"Last spring."

"Bitch! She's probably the source," Harold mumbled.

"The source for what?"

"I was called into the Provost office last week." Bradley had already drained his glass and was signaling the young lady's eyes which caused her to form an apparition in front of them. "Let's have another round of the same."

Justin offered a weak objection with, "hey, I'm driving. Have to take it easy."

"Two glasses of wine won't do anything for you. I'll call a cab if I have to. So, the Provost asked me about my absences from class. I explained to him that I struggled with the flu all last spring."

"He countered with "it's been going on longer than last spring, according to my sources.' I told him somebody is prevaricating."

Justin counterpunched with silence, for he knew that Bradley's binge pattern had been present throughout his career, originating in a distant past, and Justin often wondered, to himself, how he had managed to maintain his juggling act.

"He asked me if I was about ready to retire, bastard!"

"You're not, are you," Justin was on Harold's side because he still admired him as a scholar and a friend. *We all have our flaws,* was Justin's silent justification.

"Hell no I'm not! Prick!"

"And then--?"

"He said he wants me to give it serious thought."

"And then--?"

"I said, 'I just did, and I'm not ready to retire and FUCK YOU.' And I stood up, ready to bolt from his office."

"And then--? I hate to repeat myself. Keep going." Justin wanted more of the re-enactment.

"The fucking Provost said: 'just a minute Harold.' And stared at me in silence for the longest time and then he said, 'we can make you.' Can you imagine the wormy Provost threatening me, a world re-known Chaucerian and him a total loser of an administrator in a podunk university." Harold was in his pontificating mode.

"I said, 'the hell you can. I've got tenure!' And he said—"

"Tenure can be broken," Justin interjected to finish the sentence.

"How do you know what he said?" Harold raised an eyebrow to Justin.

"I've heard him say it before. He's always threatening the faculty, trying to whip them into line with his vague threats," Justin explained.

"And I said, 'on what grounds?'" Bradley tried to finish his end of the story but Justin was stealing his encore.

"'Moral turpitude—dereliction of duty—it's in the Regent's Rules.' It's an old song with him. He has sung it many times at various faculty meetings—to make us behave and respect him—like that'll be the day," Justin continued with his analytical elucidation and interjections.

"Really?' Harold was suddenly intimidated. "Can they do that?"

"They can." Justin paused for dramatic effect and to take a sip of wine. "But they won't."

"No?" Harold poured the whole triple shot of Scotch down his throat for emphasis and comfort.

"They'd have to have a hearing, maybe go to court, offer evidence against you, go through a long drawn-out process--. They don't want a lot of bad publicity—and believe me, it would be in every news media in the country. They are horrified at the prospect of the degrading aftershock of such a negative ordeal."

"Just threats?' was Harold's desperate and pathetic ray of hope.

"Idle threats. Believe me. You think you can drive?"

"No problem." Justin did not believe him but did not want to insult him by doubting him.

"I think I'll have another."

"You will call a cab, right," Justin sought assurance for Harold's safety.

"Sure."

21

The weeks turned into mid-semester, and Justin was at full sprint, having finished some of Shakespeare's comedies before turning to two of Shakespeare's tragedies, *Hamlet* and *Othello,* by late October (the two undergraduate courses in Shakespeare divided his four tragedies—along with a few comedies, history plays, and some late romances—evenly between the two courses so that all the students could be equally exposed to Shakespeare's variety). *Hamlet* had, as always, been inspiring, and the students responded enthusiastically to the play's power, greatness, and mesmerizing magnetism, having spent four weeks on this one play, which was well worth the attention and time, and arrived at the concluding scene.

Dr. Sandberg was in his milieu and operating at maximum intensity of his ecstasy. "The final scene is one of the most powerful moments in the play: four bodies, including Hamlet's, are lying about when Fortinbras, who will be the next king of Denmark, enters and asks, '*where is this sight,*' to which question, Horatio, Hamlet's closest friend and one of the few survivors, asks, '*What is it you would see?*' and then he adds a most profound line, '*If aught of woe or wonder, cease your search.*' What Horatio means is that if one wants to see something that is both awful and awesome, look no further. It is a succinct summary of life itself for what is life if not full of tears and laughter, of sorrow and happiness, of sadness and gladness, of woe and wonder; it is what makes life so amazing, and it is also a brief description of Shakespeare's greatest play itself," and then reverently and reluctantly laying it aside, they transitioned to the next tragedy.

The first class on *Othello* was all about taking the reading quiz, introducing background information, sources, and well-known critical responses and other helpful assistance to prepare them for mining into its unique greatness. By the second class meeting, the class was assuming the task of analyzing and understanding the principle characters, Othello, the guest General and commander of the Venetian military; his wife, the daughter of a Venetian senator, Desdemona; and Othello's ensign (the banner bearer), Iago. Justin was dedicated to the Socratic method of teaching, which is basically asking questions (instead of yapping at the students) for the purpose of causing the students to rely on their own intelligence, perceptions, and insights—encouraging them to think independently and self-reliantly (instead of spooning information down their throats like infant pablum). An in-depth discussion grew out of Justin's first question about the kind of relationship Othello and Desdemona had and then gliding on to a probing interaction about the kinds of person each is. Sparks flew out of a very heated debate which produced some uncanny observations and sturdy disagreements. Justin was in Elysian Fields, proud of the tumultuous tempest he had created in forcing them to take up a position and defend it, with evidence from the text. *Bright students,* Justin thought, *I am so proud of them. But things are going too smoothly,* Justin stewed, for at the bottom of his mental awareness was always the nagging issue of race in the play, which in the American southwest is hardly ever an issue because of the diverse nature of the population of his university. And then it happened.

Almost everyone in the class had had an opportunity to speak her/his mind, except for one student who remained strangely disengaged, one Otis Brown who had sat quietly observing the debate, turning his head hither and yon to look at various students as they offered up their variegated opinions, with something of a dismayed look on his face.

"Otis," Justin turned to him, "you seem to be attentively intrigued by this discussion. Do you have any thoughts on the matter?" Justin preferred not to call on students individually by name for fear of intimidating and/or pressuring them into something they wish not to do but this one student had a rather agonized visage which aroused Justin's curiosity.

"Yes, Dr. Sandberg," Otis began, "I do have a couple of questions."

"Fire away."

"First of all, Othello is referred to in the *dramatis personae*—"

"Persons of the play."

"Yes. (beat) Referred to as a Moor."

"That is generally a reference to one's religion, that is, Muslim. Specifically it refers to the Muslims around the Mediterranean sea, Sicily, Sardinia, Corsica, Malta, and the occupants of Spain for seven hundred years before the middle ages. Later it applied more loosely to Arabs in general."

"I see. So—they are from Africa."

"Well, sort of."

"There is a passage here—let me see if I can find it—[fingering his pages]—yes, here it is. Iago tells Desdemona's father—"

"Brabantio."

"Yes. [reading] 'an old black ram is tupping your white ewe.' What does that mean?" Otis looked up inquiringly.

"Tupping—it's a euphemism for "making love.""

"But "black ram" and "white ewe—" Otis returned the volley.

"Oh. That. It's a reference to Othello and Desdemona."

"Why does it use the words "black" and "white?" Otis pressed on.

"Well, it's poetic license—"

"Meaning--?" Otis hung on.

"Well, it's hyperbole. Poetic exaggeration—like saying a basketball player is as tall as a skyscraper. Its overstatement—for effect and emphasis. But not necessarily literally true."

"Not necessarily literally true?" Otis sought clarification.

"No, not necessarily a factual statement."

"If it's not a fact, why say it?"

Justin visualized his fingers around Otis's throat and tightening his grip.

"Ok. Moving on. In another passage, Roderigo envies Othello with, "what a fortune does the *thick lips* [stressing loudly] own," if Othello can carry this off. Otis looks up at the professor: 'Thick lips?'

"Lots of people have thick lips. So what?"

"Again. Let me find the passage—[flipping pages]." Justin could see that Otis had bookmarked a number of pages and had done his due diligence. "All right. Desdemona's father says to Othello that she ran from *his* guardianship of her 'to the *sooty* bosom Of such a *thing* as thou.' What does "sooty" mean? [pause] I'll tell you what it means. In the south, we have an old expression, "as black as soot—the inside of a chimney or stove pipe. It's an overt reference to the color black." Otis was swelling into the moment.

"Totally irrelevant."

"And—I don't have to look this up—but in another place Othello is referred to as an 'Ethiope,'" meaning he is from Ethiopia which is in eastern Africa, the heart of the continent." Otis seemed to retire his case.

"Again, it is not a literal statement, hyperbole. BUT, that is not what the play is about—not what it is about at all."

"So, Othello is a black dude and Desdemona is a white chick, right?

Otis seemed very smug, and Justin for the first time detected a hint of a southern accent, mainly because Otis had seldom spoken in class, but Otis was into sharpened rhetoric at this juncture.

"Italian. But, yes, Caucasian. What does this have to do with anything?"

"I'll tell you what it is about. It's about miscegenation! The mixing of the races, which is blatantly against God's divine purpose." Otis, who had launched to his feet for his climactic moment, descended emphatically into his seat.

"Do you not realize that Othello is a very noble, ethical human being, and Iago, the white dude as you would call him, is the incarnation of evil—and *bigotry*. Do you not get that as the main point of the play?"

And then the bell buzzed.

"Otis," Justin called out to young Mr. Brown, "could I see you for a minute?" The class stood as one, gathered up its books, and mobbed the exit door.

"What's up," Otis stood in front of his professor's podium.

"Otis. I am a very fair-minded, objective, non-judgmental, tolerant professor, but one thing I will not allow in my classroom is bigotry, prejudice, and racial comments. We're all just human beings."

"And I will not allow my religious beliefs to be trampled on." Otis did not back off nor was he intimidated.

The semester just got longer and less pleasant.

"Where are you from?"

"The region I come from has nothing to do with it. It's all about my sacred beliefs and the religion I grew up in," Otis became guarded.

"What religion is that?"

"The Church of the Good Shepherd," he rejoined.

"Never heard of it."

"My father founded it—based on the teachings of the Bible. He's the minister," Otis clarified.

Even longer than I thought.

"Ah, I see."

"He also will be very interested in what happened in class today—your teaching miscegenation—"

"No! That's not—" Justin stopped. *Why argue with him.* "See you on Wednesday."

Otis paraded out of the classroom, like a Drum Major at the head of the college band.

22

Justin let the Otis Brown episode pass into history, assuming that the whole matter had climaxed, and proceeded with his life, which included joining Betters for the student bash he had been invited to. Justin acceded to Betters's offer in violation of his nobler—and saner—self, AND his better judgement. Since Betters was unfamiliar with the city, it was agreed that Justin would fetch Betters at his apartment and provide the steerage. Betters's apartment complex was outside the city, in New Mexico actually, fixed along an undulating, cushy green golf fairway, which was one of Lee Trevizo's joint business enterprises, the course in ironical contrast to the lean desert threatening it, and the dust of which Trevizo soon shook from the soles of his feet never to return after been scammed by some local *business* partners. It was late October and the desert was on fire, which only someone like Justin could discern and appreciate, with nature's annual pageantry of foliage, flowers, and flora, this being Justin's beloved of all seasons in the desert. The air was exhilarating, the sky an azure canopy, and the mild temperature Edenic, Paradise, Utopia, Elysian Fields, the River Styx, Afterlife, or Heaven, if you will—the reward for the Blessed Ones.

The door was opened to Justin by Betters after Justin rapped.

"Come on in," Betters offered, "can I get you a drink?'

"I'm ok for right now. I've got a large bottle in the car for the fiesta, knowing students don't have a lot of money."

"Have a seat." Betters was trying to be hospitable and convince Justin that he was not some type of neurotic psychopath which is how Betters assumed Justin perceived him. Justin surveyed the entangled room.

"Uh—where?"

"Right there," Betters pointed to a rather large, flat piece of unidentifiable furniture.

"Is that your bed?"

"Actually it's a couch but I keep it open like that, ready for action at a moment's notice," Betters smirked in his most lascivious voice and gave Justin a knowing, diabolical grin.

The object, whatever it was, was covered with a soiled-looking sheet, which Justin moved toward and started to assume a sitting pose on it when he stopped.

"What the hell are all these spots all over it."

"Can't you guess." Betters snaked out his answer.

"I mean, thousands of them. I haven't a clue."

"Come stains," Betters smugly and matter-of-factly answered.

"Holy shit." Justin noticed himself adopting Betters's vocabulary. "Are these just since you've been here?'

"Some of them. I actually brought it with me from Austin as a memento." It was clear that Betters took a professional warped pride in his seductive maneuvers.

"Have you ever thought about washing it?"

"Why would I?" Betters was sipping, what appeared to Justin to be, a bourbon and water.

"Well, for one thing, sanitation."

"Come is germ free."

"Students?" Justin looked up at his host, relieved that he had declined his invitation to sit down.

"Some of 'em." Betters's tone was persistently and triumphantly disdainful.

Justin wrangled against the impulse to be judgmental and condemnatory, a tussle in which he seemed thus far to be losing. *I am determined to give him a fair shake.* Since Justin's last divorce he had few male friends to socialize with, most of his colleagues being young married men—or gays who would not be enthusiastic about participating in Justin's single lifestyle and the exploration for women. In spite of two failed marriages, he was always receptive to the idea that he might once again find the love of his life. That is just the way nature orchestrates the music—and the show. And he remained hopeful that in Betters he had found a male companion to do some scavenging in the wilderness with and to obey the beckoning of the universe.

23

"How about a little music," Justin said as he touched the tuner of his car radio while exiting from Betters's apartment complex's parking lot. The light had dimmed outside, the hulking mountain in the middle of town hunched over ahead of them, lights began to sprinkle like grains of sugar here and there throughout the arrayed city snuggling against the prideful mountain while, to his right, the western sky was paling with pink, orange, and, just at the horizon, a skein of scarlet. The west always reverberated in Justin's soul and plucked the strings of his deeper self, and then Whitney Houston's "And I Will Always Love You" exuded from the car radio.

"Ohmygod!" Justin mumbled.

"What?" Betters responded.

"That song."

"What's wrong with it." Justin never thought of Betters, the philosopher, as one who cared much for such plebian, romantic junk as music and dancing.

"It spooks me."

"How so?" Betters exhibited a fragment of curiosity.

"It was *our* song."

"Our?" Betters pursued.

"My ex and I." Justin paused. "You know, it's difficult to think of her as my ex—yet."

"Fuck her." Betters always kept his shield up.

"Don't say that. She's the mother of my children." Pause. "It was our song when Dolly Parton recorded it in the eighties. It always spoke to the passion we had for each other." Justin let go of a long sigh. "Ohwell. The fire of youth, I guess, except that I wasn't so young."

"How long were you married," Betters uncharacteristically showed a personal interest.

"Twenty years. And two kids. Second marriage." Justin wished to peel off his pain, with "So, tell me about the girl who invited you to this fiesta—or siesta."

"She's fucking gorgeous. I'm getting some vibes from her." Betters proceeded without caution.

"Oh yeah? What kind of vibes?"

"Don't play the innocent one with me." The cynic proclaimed.

"What's her name?"

"Paloma. If I remember rightly, it's Paloma Garcia."

Dead silence burdened the interior of the car. Justin's policy was that when he knows too much, it's best to say nothing, the course he plotted for himself at the present moment in order to allow events to generate their own natural outcome, whether just or unjust, without any intervention from him. If he were Betters's true friend, he would flag him a warning, but he did not want to sound like Betters's monitor, and he felt, knowing Betters's disposition, that his words would not only alit on infertile ground but that they might engender a stubborn determination to continue his pursuit.

"Is she your student?"

"Of course," was Betters's damning response.

Justin, in spite of his disinclination to protrude where he was not invited, could not resist the temptation to issue sagacious words.

"If I were you," Justin began gingerly, "I think I might wait until I have tenure before jeopardizing my career."

Whether Betters was silent in order to snare attention or for histrionic effect, Justin could not discern, but it seemed a long interval. Justin shifted his position behind the steering wheel.

"Just a little gesture of collegiality," Justin assured him.

"I have tenure." Betters whispered.

"What?" Justin was catatonic and almost wrecked the car.

"I have tenure. I was hired with tenure. I would not have come without it." His arrogance was without edges.

"You're an associate professor?"

"That's right."

"You must have quite a resume." Justin probed.

"That I do, that I do." Smugness and self-satisfaction oozed from him.

Justin would later discover that Betters was the student of a well-known, Postmodernist philosopher, Clive Webber, at the University of Texas at Austin, and the two of them collaborated on a plethora of articles and books which had received considerable attention in the kingdom of their specialty. After Betters had been in the department at Justin's university for a while, it became clear to his Philosophy Department colleagues that Betters was no longer researching and publishing as he was before he was hired and as he was expected to continue to do, the lack of which was sufficient to incite one of his colleagues to do some furtive reconnaissance into Betters's past, which should have been done before he was hired. This Professor Small exposed a number of significant facts from an acquaintance who was also on the faculty in Austin. It seems that Professor Webber had taken a personal liking to Betters, befriended him by having drinks, chasing women, and making trips, and, above all, in order to foster Betters's career, allowing Betters's name to appear on his own publications, as though in collaboration, to make it seem as though Betters was a productive scholar. This all surfaced in due time as Betters began to alienate members of his own department. Time also revealed that Professor Webber had done most of the researching, writing, and work on these "joint" publications. But, whatever may come to pass, Betters had **PERMANENT TENURE** which was virtually impossible to revoke, whether deserving or not.

By this time, Justin had encountered the Interstate and was skirting around the towering mountain formation in the middle of the city and aimed the car in a southeasterly direction, moving beyond the peopled areas and into a more pastoral scape and finally taking an exit that pushed them even more southerly and toward the river and the Mexican border. Betters had given Justin the address before starting out after which Justin consulted a city map; he was now confident about where they were. They discovered themselves as being in urban/farm country, a place in transition from what had been a countryside of vast cotton acreage to a landscape suffering from an outbreak of dwellings some distances from each other. They turned onto an undulating dirt road which carted them some yardage from the paved road which had received them and brought them there.

The house loomed alone amidst cottonwood trees, creosote bushes, and desert grasses and rose above the river behind it. Justin opened his door and was immediately rocked by the raucous roar emanating from the adobe abode. He thought he could sense the presence of alcohol in the air and thought, *I'm not so sure that this is a good idea. But my role is just to be an observer. Con cuidado,* he warned himself, *be careful.*

They knocked on the door, a useless exercise, and let themselves in after becoming aware that they could not be heard above the bellowing young people.

As Justin stepped into the room to encounter a madly chaotic scene, the first image that flipped into his head, which matched the vision before him, was the triptych by Hieronymous Bosch entitled *The Garden of Earthly Delights,* a painting crowded with hundreds of nude figures of men and women (not that anyone in the room had their clothes off, yet, but, judging by their present behavior, Justin calculated that it would not be long before it happened), strange animals and creatures, unidentifiable objects, weird vegetation and structures, bizarre and unclassifiable poses and actions by the people, and absurd situations. In the left panel of Bosch's painting, it is a relatively green and tranquil depiction with God, as a very young man, joining together Adam and Eve (*The Garden of Eden*) while the panel on the right is an extremely dark, violent, brutal portrayal of *The Last Judgement.* In between the two panels is a much larger panel dramatizing all the wickedness, sinfulness, corruption, misbehavior, and debauchery that the human species is capable of. It is a very sensuous depiction but with a determinedly meaningful and powerful moral purpose. Clearly Bosch intended the title, *The Garden of Earthly Delights,* to be fiercely, sharply, judgmentally and bitterly ironical. In Justin's mind, the painting was about exactly what he had been thinking about for some time, "actions and consequences," just as he judged the scene in front of him. Justin had a difficult time brushing Bosch's painting out of his head as he surveyed the insane scene. Over to Justin's far left, two males were holding the boy in between them by the feet and arms, swinging him back and forth in an apparent effort to mop up a drink with him which he must have spilt; on a couch in the same area, a rather large woman was lying face down in her own vomit (Justin soon learned that she was a high school English teacher); to his right, several guys were sitting round

Of Woe or Wonder

a table playing a game of "Thumper," which is a drinking game in which no one wins because everybody gets drunk; a couple was shamelessly and inappropriately engaged in some heavy "petting," on another couch with the boy's hand out of sight under the hem of her dress (it wasn't clear how far he planned to go with his hand but Justin suspected that he was only beginning).

"Let's just wonder around a little, sort of get the lay of the land," Betters proposed to Justin who responded with, "whatever." *I'd rather go home,* Justin thought.

"Get it? 'lay of the land,' as in 'get laid." Betters seemed to be in his element. Justin offered up his bottle of bourdon to Dionysius, assuming, correctly, that it would soon be consumed, on an altar/table, which seemed to be functioning as a quasi-bar and poured himself a drink into a plastic cup and held the bottle up to Betters who nodded negatively.

Betters pushed a little farther into the scene with Justin reluctantly snailing behind him. Betters began to greet some of the students, obviously some of his own, tossing out suggestive commentary as he passed from student to student until the pair found themselves entering another room where some students seemed to be trying feebly and, in some cases, unsuccessfully to dance in their buzzed condition. As they reached another doorway, Betters turned to Justin to say, "Sandberg, do you see that babe in the yellow outfit?"

"Yeah."

"Gawd, she's beautiful," Betters gushed.

"She seems awfully young."

"I'm going to make a play for her. You watch," at which point, the young lady crossed the room and entered the darkened hallway.

"This is my chance. See you later," Betters proclaimed as he tracked and trailed her down the hall.

"I don't think I'd do that if I were you." Justin's admonition never reached Betters's ears which were exiting the room. *I really hate sounding like some type of self-righteous prick.*

Justin stood for a while observing the follies of youth and was bemused by their innocent attempt at corruption. *What the heck am I doing here,* he wondered, *I have nothing in common with these kids.* It was a guarded principle of Justin's, reiterated here and elsewhere, that fraternizing with students could be a risky business, at *best*, and even if no disasters ever occurred because of it, he felt his statue, or at least his image, was diminished somewhat in the eyes of students. *Never let a student get too close to you or you'll find yourself entrapped in one way or another,* was the creed he abided by as he stood there violating his very own principle. It was not a matter of morality, of right versus wrong. Since a professor must by nature of the relationship sit in judgement on students, coziness was not advocated by those who kept their sanity about them, their senses intact, and their intelligence in order. It's like a judge becoming friends with a criminal who is on trial in his own courtroom. Immersed in these cautionary thoughts for a spell, a voice from behind him interrupted his tide of anguish and discomfort.

"Dr. Sandberg! What are you doing here?" Justin pivoted to behold the vision of Paloma Garcia standing there in a very revealing blouse and skirt. His awareness of her innocent spirit and naivete stirred within him a feeling of protectiveness and guardianship.

"I'm not sure. What are you doing here?

"Just having a little fun. Don't worry, I'm not drinking."

"I'm glad to hear that."

"Thanks for the A, by the way," she continued the conversation.

"You earned it. And we both still have our dignity and our integrity."

"I learned so much from you. It turned out to be a great semester, thanks to you," she said.

"By-the-way, I hope you don't try that strategy on Professor Betters."

"Oh, don't worry. I already know about his reputation," she added.

"And that's not why you invited him here tonight, right?"

"Actually, I didn't exactly invite him. What happened was I invited the whole class. Then he asked if he could come too and I said sure. That's all there was to it." She blinked her eyes at him and grinned.

"Good. Just be careful," Justin added in a fatherly way. "You're a nice young lady. I just don't want you to get taken advantage of."

"Don't worry. I am in control of my life—again thanks to you."

"Do you live here," Justin pointed toward the floor boards with his index finger, meaning this house.

"No. A friend of mine lives here. It's his party. He invited me and told me to bring along as many friends as I wanted to, as long as they brought their own booze. BYOB, you know. That's how students do it."

"I understand. I was a poor student myself once." Justin backed off a little, feeling a little embarrassed for Paloma and their history. "Think I'll wander around a little," Justin said as he moved on. What he really had in mind was to keep an eye on Betters and make sure he did not besmirch their profession. *He can't be trusted amidst so much fresh flesh.*

Justin was not sure whose house they were in but it had the aura of a blue collar family. The furniture was old, worn, lived-in, and bargain-basement sourced. The wall décor was bad reprints of originals, but mostly it was dominated by religious iconography, pictures of Jesus holding a lamb, Jesus sweating and bleeding on a cross, emaciated saints suffering beyond endurance, and an astounding number of crucifixions of a great variety of sizes and finishes. *Probably Catholic,* he correctly surmised based on his knowledge of the Latino culture. It seemed evident that the house was a remnant of the prior cotton field era and the workers, entirely Mexican-Americans, who enriched the Anglo landowners for generations here in what was called the Mission Valley as it distanced itself from the mountain and partnered with the river. A new generation was upon the land, and, although still financially disadvantaged, they were attending college, even if only part time while still working the land and busing tables and clerking in stores. Justin knew and admired his students. They were not of a spoiled, presumptuous, privileged, lazy, indulged class. Life was a challenge for them, but full of the joy of living, of woe and wonder.

Justin ambled toward the darkened hall, stepped inside and waited a moment for his eyes to adapt, and then, as he had anticipated, he saw a dark blob down the way which looked like two people merged into one. He inched himself silently forward, hoping not to be noticed and came within range to see dimly and hear faintly. Betters was at his slimiest best. They were both leaning against the wall, Betters's hand was rubbing her back and sides, all the way down to her hips and buttocks, and pressing her against himself as he leaned over her, she being a petite bit.

"I think you and me could have something really hot going on," Betters was whispering to her. "I can show you a few tricks that'll really turn you on." He paused. "I have deep secret techniques like no other man, especially the little boys who hang around you. We can go to my place and I'll take you home afterwards. Whatta you say?"

The young lady mumbled something inaudible to Justin's ear. By this point Betters was pressing her buttocks against his groin and was making moaning sounds.

"Does that feel good?" Justin heard him ask. "There is so much more I can show you. You just put yourself in my hands. You'll have the time of your life."

He is playing a dangerous game. I don't think the girl is of age. He's also as transparent as hell but she's so young she doesn't know any better.

"Dr. Sandberg," Betters looked up and spoke to Justin, "whatta you doing here?"

"Oh, I, uh, was just passing through—looking for the john."

"Carla, this is my friend Dr. Sandberg. He's in the English Department. Dr. Sandberg, this beautiful creature here is Carla."

Carla turned around, paused for a moment, and then stuck her hand out, "Nice to meet you," they both said simultaneously.

Justin was indeed struck by her beauty. Even in the dim light he could see that she had very light, twinkly eyes, light-colored hair down to her shoulders, extremely smooth whitish skin, and a baby face but a Venus de Milo body. She seemed a little uncomfortable and reticent, perhaps a little embarrassed at having been captured by Justin in Betters's embrace and his seductive, yet insulting, maneuvers. Justin felt empathetic because of her innocence and compromised position and wanted above all else to protect her, which he knew he was powerless to do.

"Is it ok if Carla rides back with us to my place?" Betters asked and then swiveled his head to explain to the young lady that "I rode here with Dr. Sandberg."

"Sure." Justin muttered in the affirmative.

"Carla has agreed to go back to my place with me." Betters tried to compromise her into consenting to his proposal.

"No I didn't," she weakly whispered a protest.

"It'll be ok. You can trust Dr. Sandberg. He's a straight up guy," Betters attempted to coerce her into agreement—and submission.

What a smooth asshole, Justin thought to himself.

"Whatever," Justin began to extricate himself from the discomfort of the whole encounter, "I gotta find the men's room," and moved beyond them.

"You're gonna have the time of your life," Justin heard Betters say as he neared and passed on, hearing her say, "Now wait a minute" as Justin closed the bathroom door and thought, *jail bait*.

More students thronged through the front door, as the evening ventured toward lateness, more booze was brought and consumed and spilt, more dancers appeared ineptly in the open space where furniture had been pushed aside, more shouting and swearing and screaming and tittering prevailed, and more drunkenness descended on these innocent waifs who were trying to imitate adults. Justin was bored beyond smirkiness until he finally said to Betters, now trying to dance (or was he trying to have sex?) with Carla, "you about ready to leave?"

"Only if Carla comes with us." Betters continued to rub his hips against her while pretending to be swaying to the music. "Whatta you think, Carla?"

"I don't think I should," she faintly uttered.

"Hey, you're perfectly safe with me." Justin nabbed a chunk of prevarication in Betters's voice.

"You promise you'll take me home," she wanted to be reassured.

"Absolutely. Dr. Sandberg here will vouch for my noble intentions."

Yeah right, Justin breathed to himself.

"When I wanna go?" she floated a faint resistance.

"Absolutely. Come on," Betters prevailed as he firmly guided her toward the door and sallied forth.

"Let me say goodbye to Paloma," Justin detoured as his eyes toured the room in search of her, where he finally glimpsed her and moved in her direction.

"Just wanted to say thank y—"

"Dr. Sandberg!!! Did Professor Betters just leave with that kid?" Paloma demanded.

"What kid?"

"That child he was dancing with!!" Paloma's tone was surprisingly harsh, laced with indignation, judgement and blatant condemnation.

Justin could not help but sense a touch of approbation on his part to Paloma's attitude, being nicely shocked and pleased.

"I—I—I'm not sure." Justin could not lie to a student, especially Paloma, and became evasive.

"Did you two ride together?"

"Yes." Justin was barely audible.

"She is seventeen years old! YOU can be charged with aiding and abetting statutory rape." Justin felt cold terror and numbness begin at the top of his head and filter down through his body to his toes, dancing on his spine all the way down. He struggled for language, for a defense, for an explanation, while words and thoughts had deserted him and all he could so brilliantly come up with was,

"Nooooo!" as in disbelief.

"Whatta you mean no?" she leaned on him.

"I have nothing to do with it."

"That would never stand up in a court of law." Paloma was stronger than he had ever imagined her to be and slyly felt a little pride in her rectitude. He also knew for a fact that the rest of the evening, and the rest of the weekend for that matter, was going to be one of pure anguish, one of sack cloth and ashes. Job had nothing on him when it came to suffering.

"Paloma. I tried to dissuade him, even though I did not know her age. He's an adult. I have no control over him, but I'll see if I can protect her somehow." He cast a baleful eye back over his shoulder as he made his way to the door. *This is why professors should not get too cozy with students. It is a field laden with "land mines" which can explode in one's face any second.* Justin was too worried and needled to be proud of his caution and sagaciousness; there was no comfort, no snugness, nor any victory in it.

As Justin arrived at the car, he saw Betters and Clara standing by the door waiting for him to unlock it, which he did and, while admitting Carla into the back seat, he grabbed Betters by the arm and whispered, "Gene, I need to talk to you. Let's step over here," which they did, into the dark with a yellow light emanating from the dim porch light, an anti-insect repellent light, which seemed appropriate to parry off vermin like Eugene Betters.

"What's up?" Betters asked.

"I just talked to Paloma. That girl, sitting there in the backseat of my car, is seventeen years old!"

"No shit!" was all Betters could muster.

"Paloma is a straight-up young lady. I am inclined to believe her."

"That isn't what Carla told me."

"No doubt, but I don't think you can afford to take a chance. You're talking serious jail time, man."

"Shit. There goes my evening." Betters grumbled aloud.

"Shall I drive her home now from here?"

"No. Take me to my place and I'll take her home. I want to spend a little more time with her."

"You mean in order to have some deep, philosophical conversations?"

"Fuck." Betters spun around, opened the back door, and flung himself on the back seat.

In the car, Betters stewed in heavy silence, no doubt pouting over the reality of the situation. Justin tried to make conversation with Carla but found little in common with her. Finally, Justin said straight up to her,

"Carla, how old are you?"

"Eighteen," came her velvety but weak response.

"Are you a student at the university?"

"Yes."

"What's your classification?

"My what?" which made Justin wonder if she was forging everything.

"What year are you?

"I'm a freshman" was another satiny response.

"Did you just finish high school last year?"

"Yes."

It's very plausible that she is seventeen, given the college credits they now can earn in high school, often putting extremely young teenagers in college, inappropriately before they're ready. It was his little ax to grind. Justin was analyzing and pondering the information and performing a Q&A partly to endow Betters with enlightenment and caution.

"I won't go in with you guys," Justin informed the couple as they started to disembark at Betters's apartment complex. Justin assumed that the information about Carla's age which he had disseminated to Betters was sufficient to restrain and constrain him from doing anything stupid—maybe—and felt that he was in no position to supervise a forty-something year old man and that perhaps Betters was intelligent enough to make deliberative decisions. *Surely, SURELY,* Justin thought, *he won't do anything idiotic, now he being apprised of the situation and sufficiently warned,* and said "goodnight." He was not about to make any suggestive or off-color jokes about what lay ahead for the evening.

"I hope you enjoy your discussion about Postmodernism," was Justin's only pale attempt at humor. *Fuck'im, he's on his own. I can only do so much.*

24

Justin landed on campus the following Monday morning, having spent a rather tormented Sunday beset by anguish and guilt over Carla's vulnerability and lacerating himself for not having made a stronger attempt to protect her (having grown weary of being Better's voice of reason) and not having gone inside with them at Betters's apartment. He had calculated that by informing Betters of Carla's age would be sufficient to block his plans altogether, or else face prison time. *Surely*, Justin assumed, *he is not that stupid.*

Upon his Monday morning appearance in his office building, which also housed the Philosophy Department, he found that the halls were rife with rumors about Betters's conduct on Saturday night. As with many rumors, there was rampant editorialization, speculation, imagination, and exaggeration about what had actually occurred Saturday evening, and truth was inseparable from gossip. Justin was aware of some type of hum as he made his way toward his office. He saw several little huddles of students who were all bending in to the center of a secretive cluster. Their voices were low, their faces full of secrets and conjecture, and all were fertilizing the various accounts, fictional for the most part, to abet the myth's growth and maturation into actual fact. By mid-morning, the "reality" was rampant that Professor Betters had absconded with a young, under-aged filly against her will, taken her to his place where he plied her with drinks and proceeded to have non-consensual sex with her; that he had brutally swiped her virginity; that she was no doubt pregnant by this point in time; that she had called the police to rescue her; that Professor Betters was about to be arrested at any moment by the city, or at least the campus, police; that Professor Betters was no doubt on his way to jail; that he was about to be given a ten year prison term—maybe even life. This was transmitted to Justin in his office by several of his own students who had heard all about it as far away as the adjoining classroom building. In fact, it seemed to be scourging the whole campus, and Justin tried to rectify it with the facts as best he could, although he had to admit that he had merely dropped them off at Betters's apartment and was not present as an eye-witness to, nor guardian of, the remainder of the evening.

It was not too long after Justin had settled in his office and begun to look over his notes for his first class, that a gentle knock was tapped on his door.

"Come in," he invited whoever it was, who happened to be none other than Professor David Small, the chair of the Philosophy Department, who stealthily hushed the door open.

"David," Justin spoke to the figure, "come on it."

"I won't take up to much of your time," Small began, "I know you've got a class in a few minutes."

"I do, but I'm ready for it."

"I'll cut to the chase," Professor Small mildly began. "I guess you've heard the untamed talk that is rattling the halls this morning—about Eugene and his adventuresome Saturday night."

"I've gotten wind of a little something in the air."

"I also understand that you were with Gene on Saturday night—that you were his means of transportation," David continued.

"That is also correct."

"Tell me what you know," Small requested, to which inquiry Justin responded with his own account of the facts of the situation, from his point of view, including his red signal light to Betters about the young lady's age.

"What was his reaction to that?" Small continued his interrogatory session.

"He seemed to be sobered by the knowledge and indicated that he would take the young lady home after a brief visit in his place. That was the whole upshot, from my perspective."

Silence consumed the oxygen, and everything else, in the room like a black hole until Professor Small could find words again.

"There is no doubt that the Dean—as well as the Administration—will hear about this, and there is no doubt that I shall be called in to give an account of my handling of the situation—"

"No doubt." Justin echoed and comprehended the administration's conservative and super-sensitive mindset about such matters and was acutely aware of the Administration's protective attitude of the university's reputation in the community—as well as the ethical/moral ramifications involving such issues.

"Ergo," Small continued, "I cannot simply let this slide and hope it disappears from sight. I'll have to initiate an investigation of my own so that when my phone rings and the Dean is on the transmitting end, I'll have to be armed with the facts. That'll be expected of me—or else my job—you know--."

"I understand. In all honesty, David, I have no knowledge of what happened after I dropped Eugene and the girl off at Gene's apartment. All I can relate to you is my giving Gene the information about her age—and my admonition to him—and his seeming hesitation after he learned the facts."

The Philosophy Chair sat in cold silence for what seemed to Justin an unending time. Justin knew that Small was not yet finished with his interview and waited it out.

"I've got a class in a few minutes, David. We can continue this later if you wish to."

"Just one other quick question." Small paused a small space. "Do you know if Betters—how shall I put it—uh, hits up, or should I say, dates his students?" The Chair was struggling to be delicate.

Again, Justin found himself in a very deep, dark, black hole at the bottom of which it was freezing cold, as exhibited by the pores of his skin which was covered with chill-bumps. He knew he could not prevaricate, and yet he did not want to play the role of a "rat-fink," a Mafia term he had picked up somewhere along the way in keeping with his love of language.

"I'm sorry David. I can't answer that question."

"You can't—or you refuse to?" "That puts me in a "lose-lose" situation." Justin arose and gathered up his classroom materials. "Excuse me, David, not to be unfriendly--"

"I understand. You don't want to be late for class. But—[pause]—I think I have an answer to my question."

Professor Small preceded Justin through the door, Justin came after him to secure his door, and entered the hallway, which was hissing with whispers, where he was bound for his 9:00 class during which he would still be discussing *Othello*, another subject of nagging consternation for him.

After delving deeply during the class meeting into the character of Iago, the very embodiment of evil hidden behind a warm and dangerous smile, Justin wrapped up the session with a vague assignment about Desdemona's character and the questions: "how does Desdemona's pure goodness work against her in her relationship with Othello?" After the bell, he was gathering up his materials, which he seemed to spend a lot of his time doing, when Otis Brown filed pass and then peeled off from the crowd of students and stood in front of Justin's podium.

"Professor Sandberg, when are your office hours?" Otis asked with his east Texas slur.

"They're on the syllabus, Otis."

"I just want to make sure I have it right. You're always there during your office hours?" he continued the curiosity mode.

"Always. Right now, 10:30 to 12. Then I have another class from 12 to 1:30 and then I'll be back in my office after class from 1:30 to 3:00. Then I have another class at 3:00 to 4:30 when I'll go back to my office again. Can I help you with something?"

"My daddy wanted to know when you were available. I'll let him know you'll be in your office at 1:30."

"Your daddy?"

"Unh hunh. He wants to talk to you," Otis explained.

"About what?"

"I think it's about *Othello*." Otis faltered into hesitancy.

"I'll be there." *Oh shit,* Justin thought and departed the class room.

25

Back in his office, Justin had just finished putting away his materials from his previous class and brought down from the shelf his ammunition for the next one, when he heard a voice outside his door, "Professor Sandberg!"

It's busier than an ant hill around here.

"Come in," was his impatient response.

"It's me," said Harold Bradley as he poked his face through the slightly ajar door.

"Harold," Justin heralded him, "what's up?"

"Not much," said Bradley as he welcomed himself into the chair in front of Justin's desk.

"How are things?"

"Well, I lied," Harold humbly offered.

"How so?"

"Actually, things couldn't be worse," Bradley poured forth and paused, looking Justin directly in the eye.

"Yeah?"

"I have just this minute returned from the Dean's office." Harold faltered again, obviously struggling with an emotional tug as well as with words. Justin also noticed that Harold's hands were trembling and decided to let Harold proceed at his own prompting.

"I got a call this morning when I first got to my office. It was the Dean's secretary, saying that the Dean wanted to see me asap. I told her it's my office hours and that I'd be right over, pronto."

Justin chose silence as the best cue to Bradley's confessional.

"After I was seated in front of his desk, the Dean pulled out a big file, opened it, and began to read off a list of my absences over the last five years!"

Justin still opted for letting Harold slalom at his own pace. "Somebody's been taking notes and ratting on me. I just want to know who it is." Justin sensed that Bradley's eyes were moist and noticed that his upper lip was quivering.

"Hey. Don't look at me. You know I'd never do anything like that."

"I know it's not you. It's one of these fucking female instructors around the department here. That's who it is. Some nosy bitch." Bradley was turning red in the face, his anger rising, his indignation festering, and his spirits sinking.

"What else did the Dean say?"

"I don't wanna talk about it—" Bradley bowed his head, put his hand on his forehead for a few ticks and then put his hand over his eyes. Justin let him have his waver. *This is a fused bomb and I am not going to be the one who sticks a match to it,* Justin calculated.

"Yes I do." Bradley glanced up at Justin with a look of unmitigated resignation.

"Go ahead."

"Justin," Bradley pleaded as he raised his face to him, "we're good buds, aren't we?"

"Do you even have to ask that?"

"I may need your help in the days ahead." Harold had the face of a lost child.

"How so?"

"The Dean is threatening to fire me." Bradley now, instead of red-faced, had turned to pure pale, bordering on purple, accompanied by a sickly look. Justin thought that Harold might regurgitate at any moment.

"Oh shit," Justin whispered.

"Right," was Harold's unadorned response. They sat in disquieted numbness for a brief hiatus.

"On what grounds?" Justin was eventually able to align a few words.

"He pointed out to me that over the last five years, at least once every semester I have been known to disappear for a period of time, sometimes one week, sometimes two weeks, sometimes three weeks at a time—one time for an entire month." Justin was cognizant of Harold's unique landscape as an alcoholic, that Harold was not just an everyday drinker or wastrel, but a binge drinker, that once he got on a jag, it was impossible for him to hoist himself out of it. *Memories of the conference at the Air Force Academy flew back, landed and taxed in to Justin's memory. What can I say,* he thought.

"I pointed out to him that I am an internationally known Chaucer scholar, that major, prestigious universities would pay me big bucks to be on their faculty, that I had put this little insignificant wasteland, this, this back-water university on the scholarly map. . ."

"There's no water in the desert."

". . .that I am an invaluable resource for this fucking place, that I help students and colleagues to get papers accepted at major conferences and to publish articles." Bradley recreated his response for Justin's benefit, whom Bradly had also helped in the realm of scholarship."

"What'd he say to that?"

"We're a teaching institution," Bradley mocked the Dean's voice. "Fuckin' shithead!"

"I've heard it before," Justin joined in, "but when it comes to merit evaluations and promotion, they start counting the number of books and articles you've published. It's called hypocrisy."

"Fuckin' aye it is. I also pointed out to him that I have good colleagues like yourself to cover my classes for me."

"Always."

"He tells me that I'm on probation and to watch my step."

"Did he ask about the reasons for your absences?"

"No. My parting words to him were, 'don't forget I have tenure. I'll drag this university through every court in the country if I have to.' That shut him up for fair ye well."

"I've got another class." Justin informed his guest and started gathering up his books. Harold stood and shuffled toward the door.

"Harold," Justin checked him as he reached for the door knob, and, when Bradley swiveled back, lateraled to him. "I've got your back, buddy."

"You're a real friend, Justin," and was gone.

Poor Harold, Justin meditated on their conversation as he sauntered toward his class. *He has a serious problem which he seems to keep under control for long periods of time, and then, he just—falls off the wagon.* Justin disliked descending into clichés but it seemed the best way to articulate Harold's problem. *At times he seems to have it conquered and I'm relieved for him—and then there comes this implacable, unvanquishable, searing desire to have a drink—and then—it's all over. I also worry about his health—and now his job. Can tenure protect him?* Justin wondered as he strode into his class room and greeted his students with a cheery "Good after noon, my young scholars." He always tried to uplift his students by giving them a new way of thinking about themselves. "Today, we are going to start exploring some works by George Bernard Shaw," as he lifted off into his lecture.

26

Back in his office, Dr. Sandberg was very cognizant of the fact that Otis's father was coming to pay him a visit during this office hours and left his door open while he fumbled with papers, books, and materials and imaging to himself what Otis's father would be like. *I can see him now: brash, loud, aggressive, verbal, pious phony—one of these charismatic showmen, establishing his own church and surrounded by adorers. Narcissistic, egomaniacal, self-centered, probably a pompous windbag. I shall not argue with him. Not going to waste my time and words.*

Justin opened his newspaper and once again sought out the Crossword puzzle page and became transported into the world of words, which he relished. He imagined that mathematicians sat around in their spare time dreaming up algebraic formulae, that chemistry professors were eternally mixing chemicals to produce some type of magical elixir, that engineers built highway overpasses and trestles in their spare time, and business professors idled their time putting together elephantine conglomerates. Thus with words and his delight in them: "10 across, Zeus's wife. . . . Hera. . . ." he wrote in.

"Dr. Sandburn [mispronounced]," a very soft voice beckoned from beyond his door in the hallway. Justin raised his eyes to the figure in the hall.

"Reverend Brown?"

"Yes."

Not what Justin expected at all. He was not a tall person, a little under medium height, maybe five-six or five-seven with a little protrusion in front where his waist should be. His hair was heavily greased and combed straight back, not a single hair misplaced. He worn a grey suit with the three buttons on the jacket buttoned all the way up (control?), a white dress shirt which seemed too tight around the collar with a purple tie pulled up tightly around his neck under his chin (more control?). His face was slightly reddish-purple, almost coordinating with his tie, as though his tie were choking him but otherwise the rest of his complexion was extremely white. He seemed astoundingly rigid, almost mechanical, in his movements, reflecting a tightness in his whole body and carriage. The tops of his black shoes shone with a high gloss. He seemed rather shy, timid, and self-abnegating as though at any moment he might release an avalanche of tears. He carried a Bible in his hand which he clasped to his bosom. Suddenly Justin felt extreme sympathy for him, and his first thought was *Poor guy*. The reverend remained standing in the hall, awaiting an invitation. "Come on in," Justin encouraged him and thought, *Such politeness. Is it an act or--?*

"Thank you," he responded as he moved through the door and toward the chair in front of Justin's desk with his hand stuck out which Justin accepted with a one-motion shake. Justin thought he detected just a touch of an east Texas twang.

"Have a seat," Justin invited. "It's Sandberg," he added.

"May I?" Justin was disarmed by his retiring, unimposing manner.

After exchanging a few light pleasantries, Justin opened up the weighty part of the agenda with, "So, Reverend Brown, what can I do for you?"

The Reverend Brown rose from his chair and motioned toward the door, "Before we begin, do you mind if I close this door."

"No, go ahead." *What's he up to?*

After his peregrination to the door and back, the reverend stood in front of his chair and spoke, his Bible still clutched to his chest, and remained standing. Justin was unsure what trick he had up his sleeve and was again blind-sided when the reverend said,

"If you don't mind, I'd like to start our serious discussion with a prayer, asking God for guidance in all we do."

"A prayer??"

"Yessir."

"A prayer?" Justin wanted reassurance that he had heard correctly.

"If you don't mind." The reverend lowered himself to the floor where he established the position of kneeling on one knee with his arm propped on the other thigh.

Of Woe or Wonder

"No, no. Go right ahead. Don't let me stop you." *Did that sound sarcastic?* Justin speculated.

Justin suddenly had the feeling that the reverend had stolen the advantage in the onslaught, enlisting God's help, that he had established superior control on the battlefield, and was doing what he does best, invoking God's name. In all his years of teaching, Justin had never encountered anything quite like this and felt that he was out of his depth. *I could have said 'yes, I do mind,' but why start another battle over something so trivial?*

From his kneeling position, the reverend closed his eyes, lifted his face heavenward, held the Bible over his heart, and began in a sonorous voice:

"Our Heavenly Father, we come before you now with humble hearts seeking your guidance in all we say and do and seeking always to do Thy will. Please help us to know Thy Will and to always act in accordance with Thy blessed Word. May we always be a light to the world and please you in everything we do. Please allow us to show Professor Sandburn [mispronounced] the way of thy truth in all we say and do. We ask these blessings in the name of Thy only begotten son and our Lord and Savior, Jesus Christ, who lived and died to save us from our sins, Amen."

Justin sneaked out a silent fart as he stared at the portrait of Shakespeare on the opposite wall on the bookshelf behind the preacher, hoping the toot would not malodor the office. The reverend arose from his kneeling position, straightened out his pants' leg, and seated himself while uttering "Thank you. If you don't mind I'll have a seat now."

"Of course. So. What's on your mind?" Justin was eager to get to the core of the matter without any further laggardness.

"Well, I understand that you have been teaching a play by the name of *Othello*, according to my son, in your Shakespeare class." The reverend was speaking slowly and softly, almost inaudibly and certainly not aggressively.

"That is correct. We have been on it for about two weeks now."

"I see. Now, Professor, I have been doing some research on this play, along with what my son has told me, and I believe, if I am not mistaken, that Othello is a black man. Am I correct in that assumption?"

"More than likely. Shakespeare calls him a Moor, but the descriptions of him in the text inclines one to think African."

"I see. Now. I am also given to understand that he is married to a white lady," he continued, almost whispering as though he might be overheard by some secret police.

"That is also correct. She's a Venetian, Italian, which classifies her as Caucasian."

"Now, my dear professor, do you know the word miscegenation?" Justin was having a difficult time hearing him—and keeping a stoic face to camouflage his ire.

"Of course."

"The sin of the mixing of the races." Reverend Brown looked unflinchingly at Justin with the most pious and calm tone he could conjure up.

"Sin?"

"Yes. We are dealing with God's handiwork here, which is not to be tampered with. God created all the different races, white, black, yellow, red, mahogany and put them all on separate continents to keep them apart—and then mankind started monkeying with God's creation."

"Do you believe that?"

"With all my heart, soul, mind, body and every centimeter of my being." There was no shouting or impassioned rhetoric, just a simple conviction of a belief. Brown now had his Bible open and began to read, 'And hath made of one blood all nations of men for to dwell on all the face of the earth, and hath determined the times before appointed, and the *bounds* of their habitation. Acts 17:26.' Separation of the races. Do you know the story of the Tower of Babel?" as he glanced up from the Bible in his hand.

"Yes."

"Another example of God separating the tribes—"

"Wellll, not really—"

"Oh yes. And not only that, this country had laws against miscegenation, going all the way back to before we were even a nation, seventeenth, eighteenth centuries, in keeping with ancient wisdom, until the liberal courts moved in and abolished them. It is a perversion of God's plan, just like same sex marriage is a perversion. It is all against God's natural order, the way God ordained it, and it is my sacred duty to fight for God's natural order." The reverend began to abandon his softer volume and elevate his voice up a decibel or two for emphasis.

"Do you believe what the Bible says about the creation of the races?'

"Absolutely!" He thumped his Bible.

"You realize that the Bible is not really a history book."

"Whatta you mean!" his voice slightly rising even more in defense.

"Well, it is—especially the Old Testament—a people's—the Jews'--rendition of history, an oral tradition steeped in myth and folklore."

"Myth!!!?" He rose from his chair.

"Don't be offended. Myth does not mean it's not true. Myths contain spiritual truths, but not necessarily factual truths."

"Let me tell you something, Professor. The Bible is the **divinely** inspired Word of God, and every word, every sentence, every paragraph, every comma, every period—EVERYTHING!—is literally true." The reverend lowered himself into his chair. Justin stared in silence for a few minutes. He was, of course, very conversant, having been brought up in the Southern Baptist church, with the fundamentalist's point of view, one he had long since abandoned as indefensible. He was not about to debate the point and only added the closure with,

"The greatest literature in the world, all containing eternal human truths, among which is the Bible, is told in fictional form in order to get people's interest. That's all. There is much wisdom and *veritas* in the Bible."

"I bring you God's Truth." He seemed smug about his position while Justin thought, *how insecure can one person be.* Justin then audibly whispered,

"Who made *you* God's spokesperson?"

"God."

"What???!!!"

"I was the world's greatest sinner, until God delivered his message directly to me—sort of like Paul of Tarsus.

"How so?" Justin was genuinely interested in what this prophet of God had to say.

"I had a near-death experience once. I was dead on the operating table and Jesus put his loving arms round me and I knew that I was appointed to be God's emissary. I have absolutely not one flicker of a doubt what God wanted me to do, including establishing His Church from which to deliver God's divine message. It was as clear as any real experience could be. And I am not here to be obnoxious, or difficult, or a trouble-maker, but I am totally devoted to my peaceful, divine mission—and I shall fulfill that message from God if it's the last thing I do."

Justin was surprisingly moved by the minister's sincerity, honesty, and conviction—and his obviously formidable fortitude. Justin had no reserves in his bank of experience to leverage this opponent. *He's a very simple man, maybe a little dim-witted,* Justin concluded and felt pity for him.

"So. Reverend Brown. I understand your point of view, and respect it as a genuinely held belief on your part. So what is it you want from me?"

The minister sat frozen in time for a brief moment, stood up and walked toward the door, as though to arrange his thoughts, turned, and returned to stand in front of his chair. He then looked Justin in the eye in order to convince Justin that he was speaking from his inner most, authentic being and said,

"I want you to stop teaching Shakespeare's *Othello.*"

Justin felt as though someone had slammed the top of his head with an iron sledge hammer, and a punch to the gut simultaneously, then staggered to his feet, holding on to the edge of his desk, and hissed,

"Get out of my office."

"What?" the surprised minster queried.

"You heard me—get out of my office!"

"This will never do—"

"OUT—I'm telling you, OUT"

"Professor Sandburn [mispronounced], let me tell you—"

"OUT, I said. NOW."

"I have powerful friends—

"I don't give a good goddamn what you have—"

"This is not the last of this conversation."

"I don't give a holy shit—you will not violate the most sacred principle on which a university is built."

"I would advise you to start looking for another job," was the reverend's announcement.

Justin flopped into his desk chair and sat in quietude, stared at the floor, while the reverend was still standing in front of his desk, unmoved and undeterred.

"And please don't take God's name in vain," the reverend added.

"I'd appreciate it if you wouldn't use such filthy—vile—language."

"Fuck you," Justin mumbled and then sat in silence while the reverend was uncertain what to do. He was ordered to "get out" of the office but he felt that his mission was not yet finished and continued to stare at the professor. After a painful silence, Justin spoke:

"You are the one using the vilest of language."

"Whatta you mean?" the reverend puzzled.

"Have you ever heard of academic freedom?" Justin, after gathering together his rational facilities, finally posed a reasonable question to the minister.

"I suppose so," the reverend faintly acknowledged.

"Just as you consider your church to be a sacred place, and your mission to be divinely inspired, I consider the halls of this university to be sacred also—"

"How so?"

"The purpose of a university is the quest for TRUTH, and truth can only be searched for in an open and free interchange of ideas, regardless of how objectionable some ideas may seem. There can be no suppression of ideas."

"Even blasphemous ones?"

"Yes." Justin paused for effect and then explained, "ideas that are in error will not only be tested and challenged but in the end can help to strengthen the truth."

"I already have the Truth—God's Truth." He had reverted to his calm and palliative voice.

"But your truth may not be my truth."

"There is only one Truth." Softly and self-assured again.

Justin knew that he had a real challenge on his hands and met calmness with calmness.

"Let me tell you something, Reverend Brown." Justin paused to arrange the thoughts lying on the table of his mind in order to help this gentleman understand Shakespeare's truth in *Othello*.

"*Othello* is not a play about race at all."

"It's not?" came a vague whisper.

"Of course not. It is a play about a man—the General of the Venetian army—who is a very good man, with a very kind heart—who is destroyed by his friend, Iago, who is the epitome of evil and jealousy, and who also happens to be white, with an ego which is raging out of control and who gets a thrill out of showing his superiority over others—and who also happens to be a bigot." Justin lifted his thoughts off the table and hung them out there in the air for contemplation. "I would advise you to read it with Shakespeare's real purpose—his truth—in mind."

"Why does he have to be black?" came the query.

"Well, in the first place it helps to expose and shame racial bigotry. But also, that happens to be the way it was in the source he found for his story—he's just being faithful to his source. In the end, it is totally irrelevant."

Reverend Brown, unconvinced, arose from his chair and pulled himself up to his greatest height, which wasn't much, with "I know the president personally."

"What president?"

"The president of this university?"

"So?"

"She and I are well acquainted with each other. I have her phone number and her e-mail address. You'll probably be hearing from her in the near future," as he spun around and marched toward the door.

"Do whatever you have to do."

27

And his Monday continued.

Before he was due to depart for his next class, he received another visitor, Professor David Small, the chair of the Philosophy Department.

"May I come in?" was Small's tiny voice.

Somebody please give me some peace, Justin pled.

"Of course, of course. Have a seat." Small obliged. "You know I have another class in a little while."

"This won't take long—I hope," was Small's plea for a small indulgence.

"What's up?"

"I got a phone call from the Dean, as I figured I would." Small voyaged forth.

"Oh?"

"The Dean is a very unhappy man—"

"When isn't he?"

"He's getting pressure from the Provost—who apparently is getting pressure from the President," the Chair continued to establish the background conducing to the foreground.

"What's the subject of the next sentence?"

"Eugene Betters."

"I knew it."

"Right. Apparently the campus rumors about Gene's escapade last Saturday night have reached the president. Or, should I say, she has reached it—she always has her ears to the ground—or, grounds, campus grounds, that is—"

"I know. She has her—[stops]. I was going to say spies. 'Sources' is a preferred descriptor."

"Yes. Or course, her job is to protect the University."

"I understand. Always. I am not unsympathetic to that. It's my university too."

Justin did have a touch of administrative sensibilities, not like some rebellious faculty who relished taunting the administration as much as possible, as though it were the enemy—and not the source of their paycheck.

"So what does the Dean want you to do?"

"He wants me to form a faculty committee—"

"Cool move."

"—to investigate Gene."

"Uncool."

"He wants it to be composed of all full professors—to give it clout—traction as he calls it." Small continued.

"Understandable."

"He wants it to be made up of five full professors—"

"To prevent a tie—"

"The Philosophy Department has only two full professors—so we need fulls from other departments to make up the committee." Small stopped and smiled. "We're a very small department—but very philosophical."

"I don't think I like where this is going."

"Exactly. I want you to be an outside member." Small declined to elaborate further, having said enough. Justin thought about his upcoming lecture as a way of evading the unfolding narrative and then thought of an answer.

"I might not be a good choice."

"Why not?" Small was acting like a snarling mongrel. Justin was not sure how far to carry his reluctance.

"Well—you know—I'm sorta like his only friend on the faculty—he thinks. I'm not much into betrayal. I mean, he has confided a lot of confidential stuff to me. I think I know too much about his personal views—and behavior—on things."

"So much the better. You're an eye witness." Small took the pro position in the debate.

"I have to sleep at night."

"Don't you want what's best for the university?" Small leaped immediately to the territory where he knew Justin was most vulnerable—his regard for the institution—and the profession.

Silence was like a heavy curtain draped between them, muffling Justin, Professor Small silently pulling it back.

"My instinct says no. My rational mind says yes. How much time do I have?"

"I have to chat with some other fulls, but I'd like to have the committee constituted by tomorrow," Small offered diplomatically, "so I can report back to the Dean and let him know that we are moving on it as swiftly as possible."

"What time tomorrow?"

"Ah, come-on, Justin. It's for the good of the university." Small was standing by now. "Noon."

"Ok. But that is not a yes—yet." Justin was also on his feet. "I fear it's going to be a long night."

Professor David Small was by now touching the door knob on Justin's closed office door.

"David."

Professor Small halted and peered back over his shoulder.

"Is the composition of this committee going to be made public?"

"Nobody is going to know that such a committee even exists," was Small's reassurance to his reluctant victim.

"That may make it easier."

Small was no more than halfway down the hall when Gene Betters materialized in Justin's open doorway.

"Gene."

"Was that the asshole Small that was just in here?" was Betters's first sentence.

"Yeah."

"What'd he want, cocksucker?" Betters was smirking.

"Watch it, Gene."

"What's he up to?" Betters asked.

"Not much."

"Hey. Come on. You're my friend." Betters seemed a little ashen in the face but countered it with a certain swagger and bravado. The fright in his eyes betrayed his pose.

"Well. No biggy. He's heard the rumors and is concerned, as any administrator would be."

"This place is like some fuckin,' small-ass, redneck hick town." His only defense was to belittle the university.

"Just be careful, will you?"

"I got a letter," Betters quipped as he extracted a small piece of paper from his shirt pocket.

"A letter? From—?"

"Some dude."

"About--?"

"Just listen." Betters was staring at the paper in his hand. ""Dear Professor Slimeball—'

"Not a good start."

"' I am aware of your reputation for hitting up on your female students, and, as far as I am concerned, I don't really give a shit about that. However, you have now imposed yourself on the wrong co-ed, Ana Ayala, who happens to be my girlfriend of many years. She has told me about all the moves you have tried to put on her and how she has resisted them, but you seem bound and determined to compromise her integrity. I am warning you in the strongest terms possible to cease and desist your behavior toward my girlfriend or I shall report you to the administration of this university—and to the police—and Ana has agreed to stand by me should I decide to do so. DO NOT COME ANYWHERE NEAR HER AGAIN OR YOUR LIFE WILL BE IN DANGER. (Signed) Javier Rodriguez.' Whatta you think of that?"

Justin studied Betters's visage for a brief interim and then replied with,

"I got a class."

"Can we talk later?" Betters seemed to have lost all his suavity and self-assurance suddenly.

"Sure."

By this point, they were in the hall outside of Justin's office. As Justin started to descend the stairs, Betters summoned him:

"Justin."

Justin stopped on the first landing and turned to look up a Gene towering at the top of the stairs.

"I ain't 'worried." Justin raised one eye brow as though to signal "oh?"

"They can't touch me: I'm tenured."

28

All through Justin's class period, thunder grumbled, lightening complained, the inky clouds hovered, and darkness engulfed the world outside his classroom windows while inside the lights habitually flickered and buzzed as Justin ventured forth into his subject unperturbed. He was not about to deprive his students of a romp with *King Lear*. In fact, the storm neatly supplied ambiance for Shakespeare's storm scene in Act Three as the demented king stands out in the storm, stripped of his clothing, yelling "Blow winds, and crack your cheeks! Rage, blow! / You cataracts and hurricanoes, spout / Till you have drenched our steeples, drowned the cocks—" A tumult of thunder rocked the room and rattled the desk-chairs, and Justin went on with "And thou, all shaking thunder, / Strike flat the thick rotundity o' th' world. . . . Rumble thy bellyful! Spit, fire! Spout, rain!" Halting there and assuming that his luck had run out. Justin considered the possibility, so well-timed as it was, that it was supernaturally inspired and acknowledged the universe as he closed the class meeting, informing his class that he had ordered the background cacophony especially for this day's class meeting and dismissed them with a smile and wide eyes on their part and a collective, "no way."

Outside, on his way back to his office building, Justin ambled through a light spray which was descending all around as he inhaled deeply. Such refreshment is a rarity in this arid land. When water blesses the desert, the millions of creosote bushes thereupon release the strangely pleasant smell of wet pavement, fresh, pungent, and spectral. He walked slowly to indulge himself in this rarity of the desert without regard to its dampness, being a refreshing alternative to the relentlessly singeing desert sun.

Justin's intention as he walked through the mist was to engage back in his office in a little meditation, supported by the pleasant tattooing of the rain on the windows, before packing up for home, only to be met at his door by a distressed-looking Harold Bradley, "distressed" hardly being an adequate instrument to convey the terror in his eyes and the trembling curl of his lips. He appeared to be about to match the weather outside the building with a tear storm of enormous proportions.

"Harold, my man, what's wrong?"

"I need to talk to you," his voice quavered while Justin unlocked his office door.

"Come on in." Justin crossed to behind his desk while putting his books and lecture notes on his bookshelf. "Have a seat" he offered while repelling his sports jacket from his body and shaking the water from it.

"Nice little rain, hunh?"

"The cows can always use a little water around these here parts on the rainch." Justin attempted to counterpunch the dismay tatooed on Bradley's face with inane humor and a Texas twang.

Justin lowered himself wearily into his desk swivel chair, exhausted from a long day of classes and other troubles, leaned back to prop his feet up on his desk, and stared at Bradley. "I'm tired" was all he could conjure up for conversational purposes. They sat in dead silence while Justin studied Bradley who was apparently frightfully damaged and obviously in edgy emotional agony. Justin waited until finally Harold found the wherewithal to open his mouth only to be ellipted by a smack of thunder somewhere close by. Bradley waited for it to wheel on by.

"How was class?" Bradley had unaccountably changed his mind.

Justin proceeded to relate the incident of the thunderous background which accompanied his presentation of the storm scene in *Lear* when his class room reconstruction was loped short with,

"I've been fired."

Justin braked in midsentence and then aimed in a new direction with,

"What'd you say?"

"I've been fired."

"No you haven't."

"Oh yes," Bradley managed as a tear began to trowel down his cheek.

"That's not possible."

"That's what I say. Here's the letter of notification," as he placed a letter-sized sheet of paper atop Justin's desk, which Justin stole a glance at without really reading it.

"Tell me what happened."

"Ok." Bradley took out his handkerchief to wipe the moisture from his cheek and then took in a deep breath. Justin noticed that Harold's hands were unsteadily moving around, trying to find a purposeful preoccupation.

"Remember how the administration has been keeping track of my absences over the last five years or so?"

Justin nodded in polite accord.

"—and I was cautioned that I was on probation—and that if I missed another class I could be dismissed—"

"Unhunh."

"Well, last week I caught a real bad case of the flu and was laid up for a whole week—"

Justin was hesitantly tempted to be impolitic and then decided to proceed with his instinct anyway, being quite familiar with Harold's record as a binge drinker/flu-catcher.

"Was it really the flu?"

Harold arose with "I don't need this!" Justin realized that Bradley was in no emotional condition to be doubted.

"Sit down, Harold. I just wanted to make sure. I'm here to help my friend anyway I can."

"Thank you," as he returned to his chair and gazed intently at Justin in order to measure his allegiance. Justin bided.

"I have a note from the doctor—as well as his prescription and a copy of my bank statement to prove that I paid for an office visit on that day."

"You might need a lawyer" was Justin's unhelpful offer.

"I have one." Harold had gained the upper hand over his internal disturbance and wore a slight smirk of "so there" on his visage.

"Then why are you so upset? You seem well-fortified to me."

"You know what it is Justin?" Bradley took hold of another deep breath.

Justin raised a quizzical eyebrow.

"It's the fact that they don't trust me." Justin felt the irony in light of Bradley's history. "I mean, I'm a grown man, a professional in every sense of the word, a responsible citizen of the academic community, with over forty years of experience, and they need proof that I'm telling the truth. Like a schoolboy. With a note from his mommy. That's what hurts." Harold's voice grew stronger as he came within view of his summation point.

"So you've had communication with them?"

"Oh yeah. They also know I have a lawyer."

"What can I do?"

"I just needed a shoulder to cry on—" he smiled, "—literally."

"Any time."

Harold seemed to be hesitating as he approached another passing thought.

"I don't guess it would be possible—" He stopped.

"What?"

"Naw. Forget it."

"No. What?"

"I don't suppose you could testify that you covered my classes for me, could you."

"Harold, that won't work. All they have to do is ask your students if I was there those days. Then I'd be caught in a lie. But you know that I'd be happy to meet your class for you anytime. All you have to do is ask—ahead of time."

Harold seemed to go into the dark inner spaces of his pinched mind to find solace and then blurted out,

"I'm not worried about losing my job—when it comes right down to it." All the features of his face altered to a collective smile.

"Of course not."

"They can't touch me. I'm tenured." He rose jubilantly up out of his chair with "thanks for listening."

Justin picked up the letter on his desk, stole a closer look at it, and realized that the purpose of the letter from the administration was to inform Bradley that it was referring the matter to a faculty committee for investigation.

Tenure can be broken, Justin deliberated, *but not without a fight and a major embarrassment to the university—and a blacklisting by the American Association of University Professors* (the protective organization of college professors)—*a death warrant to a university since nobody would want to teach at such an institution.*

Justin carefully closed his office door, book bag swinging from his shoulder and headed into the evening without a destination.

29

November 9, 1995
Dear Professor Sandberg:

The University Administration has contacted the President of the Faculty Senate in regards to a very serious charge against one of our faculty members and has turned the matter over to the deliberation of the Faculty Senate with the recommendation that I, as President of the Faculty Senate, should create a committee composed of Full Professors to investigate, deliberate, and make a recommendation to the administration concerning the charges against said professor. Thus, I am contacting you with the expectation that you will be willing to serve as one of the committee members.

I know that you understand, since this is a personnel issue, that this is a matter of the strictest confidentiality, that I cannot reveal the name of this faculty member in this written communication, and the meetings will be held under the tightest of security measures.

Please leave your message of acceptance with the secretary in the Faculty Senate Office (ext. 7755) and plan to meet with the committee on Thursday, November 15, at 3:00pm in the conference room of the Faculty

Senate Office. Thank you for accepting this important assignment.

Sincerely,
Arnold Lawing
President, Faculty Senate
College of Engineering

Justin received this hand-delivered letter on Friday afternoon, just as he was planning to join some of his colleagues for their weekly Happy Hour, leaned back in his chair to stare at the ceiling florescent lights, and thought, *Just what I need, something more to worry about and burden myself with. And, yeah, there goes the weekend as far as relaxing is concerned*, but, being a loyal academic citizen, lifted the phone, fingered in 7755, and received a voice mail to which he responded with, "This is Professor Sandberg accepting the committee assignment which Dr. Lawing has proposed to me. You can leave a message on my phone at 6266. Thank you" and hung up. *I just hope I don't know this faculty member personally* was the only wish he had at this point. He was now on two committees investigating other faculty members and was deeply distressed by the fact. *All I want to do is just teach my classes and do my research. Why do I keep losing sight of that,* he mused, picked up his phone and dialed the Faculty Senate Office again, listened to the secretary's recorded voice, opened his mouth to decline the offer, and then slowly returned the receiver to its cradle. *Damnation! Happy hour is not going to be very happy and the weekend is not going to be very weekendish—or joyful.*

November 13, 1995
Dear Professor Sandberg:

The purpose of this letter is to inform you that a formal complaint has been filed against you on behalf of students in your English 3333, Shakespeare's Major Plays. I have placed this complaint into the hands of the President of the Faculty Senate with my instructions to turn the matter over to the Faculty Senate Grievance Committee whose mandate it is to investigate all such charges against faculty members with the further instructions to make a recommendation to the administration. This administration takes all such charges with the utmost seriousness. Under such circumstances, it may behoove you to seek legal counsel. You will be contacted by the Chair of the Faculty Grievance Committee with further instructions.

Yours truly,
Donna Nunez, President University
of Texas at Mountain Pass

"Whatta you think of that?" Justin peered over his glass of Chardonnay as he folded the epistle and returned it to its paper container, an envelope with the university's seal on the outside as well as on the letter itself, making it all ponderously and weightily official.

"Do you know what that is all about?" Ellen Cohen, his English Department colleague, offered him a hook.

"I've got a pretty good hunch."

Ellen and Justin, both twice divorced, had gravitated toward each other after the breakdown of their last marriages in mutual consolation and emotional, as well as physical, comfort of each other and surprised themselves with middle age passion. They had found, they felt, the true definition of the "golden years." Justin was in his fifties and Ellen, who had decided that sex was a forgotten memory of the past, was only a couple of years younger than he, and together they experienced a liberating freedom in their unencumbered lives and let the river of ravenous desire flow. They had raised their families properly and responsibly, had met all parental and societal expectations, had attained a respectable elevation and veneration in their profession, and could enjoy themselves free from the taint of guilt, pretense, and the local press.

Ellen was on the petite order with short-cropped auburn hair, a pleasant face, big hazel eyes, an attractive mouth, nice teeth, and a Rubenesque body.

She was originally from southern California, having graduated from UCLA with a major in Spanish and a doctorate in English from the University of Arkansas. Ellen had been at UTMP only about a year when Justin, serving as chair of the department at the time, invited her to be his assistant with no hidden, or conscious, agenda other than to help her integrate into the department more easily. It was during his chairmanship that they spent numerous after-hours doing administrative chores—course assignments, class schedules, and budget strategies—after which buying her a drink at an off-campus bar seemed like an appropriate gesture of his gratitude. Many long conversations ensued which over time grew increasingly warmer and closer, ending up one night in her bedroom, a working arrangement with benefits. A commitment was confirmed on each side.

"Talk to me," she offered.

"Remember I told you about the Bible-thumping student whose father, a minister of sorts, accused me of advocating miscegenation in my class by teaching *Othello*. . . ?"

"Yes."

"I would bet my collection of Shakespeare editions on it—that it is he."

"No."

"No?"

"Nobody's that ignorant," Ellen advocated.

"Wanna bet. I met the guy. There is no limit to his ignorance. He is a self-righteous know-it-all—which is the sure path to ignorance."

"But to file a formal complaint?" she questioned.

"He sees himself as on a personal mission from God. God speaks directly to him, so he claims."

"How can you fight him?" Ellen socratically inquired.

"Tenure was created for precisely these kinds of circumstances—someone trying to interfere with classroom content! He doesn't have the chance of a snowball in Hell."

"It's just an aggravation."

"Exactly. He doesn't have an inkling about the sanctity of academic freedom and tenure to protect professors from people just like him. He is about to get his education."

30

Justin returned a positive answer to the chair, Professor Small, by noon the next day and tightened his belt, pulled up his socks, laced up his girdle, so to speak, or, better yet, "girded up his loins" (to borrow a useful quote from Job, whom God had handpicked for testing and whom Justin was beginning to feel akin to) for the first meeting which was to take place that same afternoon.

Justin was seated in the Philosophy Department's conference room awaiting the arrival of the Chair, Professor Small, and batting the chat ball with several members of the committee whom the Chair had asked to serve on an *ad hoc* advisory committee. The full professor contingent from the Philosophy Department consisted of Dr. Jake Haddock, a Christ-like, beatific, septuagenarian; Sam Howell, a rights activist who was forever protesting outside the administration building over endless causes; and Andrew Spranger, another septuagenarian and a defrocked seminarian whose point of reference was mostly from outer space ("or his own empty, inner space," judged Justin), who was married to a French lady whom he met while studying at the Vatican and who liked to season his sentences with French. In addition to Justin, the other "outside" member of the committee came from his own English Department, a wisp of a little lady with a Napoleonic, take-no-prisoners attitude and a very large voice to match the size of her ego, Professor Ruth Goldberg. "Feisty" falls far afield in defining her.

"I don't like this at all," said Jake Haddock, who was *muy catolico* (very catholic) with twelve kids and a very catholic *esposa* (they had met at Notre Dame) and a compassionate, non-judgmental soul. "I do not like sitting in judgement on my colleagues, and when it comes right down to it, I probably won't vote."

"You have to, Jake," said Ruth Goldberg, "that's why we're here. We have a duty to the university." Ruth had served several turns as an administrator and was cognizant of the need, sometimes, for tough, career-damaging decisions, "and let the chips fall where they may," was her usual refrain. *Tough dame,* was Justin's affectionate assessment of her.

"I've got to get back to my book, *tout suite,*" was Andrew Spranger's unhelpful contribution. Andrew Spranger was in the midst of a 3,000 page study of aesthetics, his specialty, with stacks of typed pages littering his office: the shelves, his desk, several chairs, and, yes, even much of the floor. Justin, at Spranger's behest, had read some of the manuscript and could not discern any meaning in any of his sentences. It was as though it was written in some unknown tongue, upon which occasion Justin knighted him, silently, with the title of "sir space cadet."

"The one thing we have to keep in mind is that he has tenure—"

"How did he get tenure so quickly?" was Goldberg's accusatory query.

"He was hired with tenure—"

"Mistake number one," was Justin's contribution.

"He came with quite a resume," was Haddock's compassionate defense.

"So be it. It's a *fait accompli* now, an existential fact," was Sam Howell's offering, "and we have to honor it." Howell was forever championing faculty rights, even when the faculty member was wrong.

"*Serieux*—" was Spranger's celestial French addition for "it's serious."

"I'm sorry?" Justin sought clarification.

"*Peu importe.*"

"If you say so," was Justin's appeasement of Spranger.

The door opened and drew everyone's eyes to it. Professor Small entered and turned to lock the door.

"We need to keep this as confidential as possible," was David Small's explanation for his action.

There followed nods and grunts of consent, agreement, and relief.

"Ok," was the chair's brilliant opening from the head of the table. "I guess we all know why we're here, but just for clarification: we have no power. The dean appointed me to form a committee of full professors which is to be an investigative body whose sole mission is to try to establish the facts and make a recommendation to the faculty senate, which may or may not be obliged to follow our recommendation."

"In which case, sounds like a waste of our time," was the rebel Howell's quip who endlessly quibbled over legalistic minutiae and administrative boondoggles.

Small stared at him in rebuke then took a deep breath. "Nevertheless," that's why we are here."

"Now we've all heard the rumors about Eugene Betters' escapade Saturday night a week ago, which may or may not be relevant here. But what is the most disturbing, and what we are to gather the facts regarding, is Betters' reputation for—molesting—no, let me change that—hitting on— no, better yet, for "dating" his own students, which is a blatant violation of everything we hold sacred in higher education." Small paused to let it percolate while Justin took a swipe at his coffee and Small continued, "Now, I've been giving this some thought about how we are –"

Suddenly there was a raucous rattling to the locked doorknob on the conference room door.

"I'm glad I locked that," was Small's feeble justification.

And then there was a frantic, boisterous, continuous banging on the door which seemed to vibrate the walls and rattle the whole room and its content, including the persons present. Each member stared at each member around the room in turn in stunned, wide-eyed silence with a look of "what the. . . ?"

What the hell is that all about?!? was Small's weak effort at authority.

"Maybe it's some type of emergency, "the kindly Jake Haddock provided a reasonable explanation. "I'll see what it's about," as he rose from his chair and shuffled toward the thundering door which he unlocked to take a peek outside. The door was rashly and violently shoved open which forced the feeble Haddock to stumble backwards before catching himself in Ruth Goldberg's lap.

"Why, Jake, I didn't know you cared," was Goldberg's icy effort at lightening the terrifying moment.

"WHAT THE FUCK IS GOING ON IN HERE???!!! Was the roar of a livid Eugene Betters as he stomped scarlet-faced and threateningly into the room.

Everyone's mouths were agape with shock. If it was Betters' intention to traumatize the members of the committee, he was legendarily successful.

"We're having a curriculum meeting," was Small's weak prevarication.

"THAT'S NOT WHAT I HEARD," said Betters in a voice that assumed everyone in the room was suffering from hearing loss.

"What did you hear?"

"I HEARD THAT YOU ARE HAVING A MEETING ABOUT ME!"

"Who told you that?" Small was being admirably successful in conjuring up a placating tone.

"I HAPPENED TO OVERHEAR A CONVERSATION I WAS NOT SUPPOSED TO OVERHEAR." His face continued on the red end of the color spectrum and the veins on his neck throbbingly protruded.

"Don't flatter yourself." Small's reply dripped with patient sarcasm.

Betters then took several steps down alongside of the conference table, stopping at Justin's chair and screamed, "JUDAS!!!"

"I haven't said a word."

Betters then returned to the head of the table and turned. "YOU ARE ALL JUDAS'S AS FAR AS I AM CONCERNED."

"Gene." It was Haddock's calm voice. "Why don't you just relax and get ahold of yourself. You're only hurting yourself."

"I JUST HAVE ONE THING TO SAY TO THIS FUCKING, STUPID COMMITTEE AND THAT IS 'I HAVE TENURE AND YOU CAN'T TOUCH ME AND IF YOU TRY, I'LL DRAG THIS FUCKING UNIVERSITY THROUGH EVERY FUCKING COURT IN THE COUNTRY.' AND MY FINAL WORD IS, YOU ARE ALL A BUNCH OF COCK-SUCKING, FUCKING, SPINELESS ASSHOLES. SEE YOU IN COURT." Betters triumphantly tromped toward the door which he, upon exiting, slammed with a thunder so loud it could be heard in the next country, which was just across the Rio Grande. Silent speechlessness throttled the group until the chair managed,

"Well, now, nevertheless, we have an assignment. I think that, today, what we need to talk about is procedure, our methodology, research sources, and so on."

Justin noticed that Small said "and so on" a lot. "We can't collect evidence until we develop a carefully organized system. Does that sound reasonable?"

"Sure's" rocketed and hissed around the table.

After the committee outlined their approach, Justin felt compelled to say a word of honest confession.

"Look, I just want you to know that being on this committee puts me in a very awkward position. When Betters first arrived on campus, he came to my office to introduce himself, and, upon discovering that I was now unmarried, assumed that he had found someone to pal around with, which I did for a while. But the more I discovered his—er, let's say—his lifestyle, the less inclined I became to encourage the "friendship."

"So you're an eye-witness, so to speak, to his conduct?" Goldberg inserted.

"Yes."

"We'll have to put you under oath, eventually," was Small's officious rejoinder.

"No. I am going to resign from this committee assignment—"

"No—you can't do that—we need you—you are a valuable source" and such like commentary buzzed rapidly around the table.

Justin held up his hand while explaining that "as I said, this really puts me in an untenable position. *However,*" he transitioned with emphasis, "before I do, I am going to tell you one thing, and only once, and that will be my contribution."

"We're listening" "go ahead," was muttered by several.

"What I am about to tell you is not gossip, not rumor, not hearsay, not second-hand, not speculation but an eye-witness report. As I said before, Betters came to my office to introduce himself when he first came on campus, during which visit we had a pleasant exchange about things in general, and then suddenly, in our very first conversation, he looked at me and said, 'Do you fuck your students?'"

Negative rumblings reverberated in unison along with a chorus of gasps and "oh my's" from the ladies.

"Of course I was stunned and let him know it, but he casually went on justifying his remark by telling me, at great length, how "they" did it all the time at Austin Community College where he was teaching before he came here."

Tongue clucking and "tsk, tsks" were common sounds in the Chair's conference room.

"The amazing thing is—after we had a rather lengthy discussion—it was clear that he did not see anything wrong with what he was telling me.

In fact, he basically exhibited a sort of smug satisfaction, or—or—pride, in his behavior—"

"Or else he was just trying to shock you."

"I don't think he saw anything shocking in what he was telling me. He seemed totally oblivious to—what should I say—the moral overtones of such an issue."

"Have you seen him actually—behaving—that way?" was the chair's question.

"Yes. And that's all I am going to say. The one thing I know for sure, is that he already has a reputation among our students—specifically the Philosophy majors."

"Really??!!" was Jake Haddock's innocently stunned response.

"If I were you guys, I think I'd begin by talking to Philosophy majors. I believe they can provide you with a wealth of information. I know some of them who have been my students, and I heard it from them."

"What have you heard?" was Goldberg's concern.

"The rest is silence." Justin stood and departed.

31

But Justin was not out of the "mouse trap" yet. He still faced two more challenges: the Faculty Senate committee investigating an unnamed professor and the Grievance Committee's examination of the grievance lodged against him by an unidentified citizen, and he was still on stand-bye for Betters's charges. Even though he had officially resigned from that committee, he had been informed that they could summon him at any time as a consultant (he just did not wish to have to vote on Betters's case). The committee had respected his dilemma and sympathized with his acquaintanceship with Betters, and the quagmire-quirk quandary it had put him in, but still wanted to be able to call on him, should the need arise. The chair of the committee secretly passed along to the dean what had transpired with Justin, and the dean chose not to tamper with the formula.

Such were Justin's ruminations while sitting in the conference room of the Faculty Senate Office on Thursday, November 15 at a few minutes before three.

"Does anyone have a clue as to what this is all about?" asked the member from the College of Nursing, Professor Betsy Day.

Justin had just finished introducing himself to the other committee members, Professor Day, Professor John Eastman from Biology and the College of Science, Professor Edwin Mason from the College of Business, Department of Accounting, and Professor Kathy Strong, History Department, College of Liberal Arts, Justin's own college, when silence ravaged the room and prompted Professor Day's question as a relief from the stolid awkwardness of the moment.

"Just what was in the letter from the Faculty Senate about some faculty member," Justin lamely offered.

"And that it is at the behest of the administration," Kathy Strong amplified.

"Guess we'll soon find out," came an timid mumble from somewhere at the end of the table.

Whereupon the door opened with Arnold Lawing, the President of the Faculty Senate, looking back over his shoulder and addressing someone in the hall with "will do," and turned his attention to his assembled committee.

"Good afternoon, folks," were Lawing's first words to the group and was greeted with a similar simultaneous reply from all.

"First, I want to thank you for agreeing to serve on this committee. I know it is not going to be a pleasant task but we are charged with a very difficult, challenging, and, frankly, delicate chore—sitting in judgement on a fellow faculty member."

Everyone's attention was pricked to concentrated unresponsiveness, awaiting the unfolding story.

"First, the reason this is not going through the Grievance Committee is this is a direct charge from the administration who will act independently based on our recommendation when we have concluded our work. The administration has the power to do that, but they do not want to proceed on this solo but in concert with, and at the recommendation of, the faculty itself—probably to avoid a lawsuit. Also, the rules of tenure state that there must be a faculty committee. And we're it."

Professor Lawing paused, his eyes meandering from member to member who each lingered without questions, and then added, "and so on." Justin stifled a grin and silently smiled inside.

"Now. Let me just give you a little historical narrative," Lawing continued. "It seems that a number of years ago, the administration got wind of the fact that a certain professor was quite delinquent in his class attendance and so decided to put—er,--an--investigator—"

"A spy," Kathy Strong clarified.

"If you want to call it that. An investigator, on his case and began to keep a record of his absences."

Justin suddenly had a queasy, freezing feeling and a premonition of what was to come.

"The administration has a moral obligation to protect and insure the integrity of the university—specifically, in this case, of the quality of instruction, of the excellence of the education that is transpiring in the classroom. I want you to understand that this is serious business, the prime mission of this institution, of what we are all about and why we are here and why the students are here. If the administration discovers that that is not happening in the case of a specific class, or professor, it has not only the right but the duty to take action—of some kind." Lawing had trained well for the moment. "And so on," he added after a pause.

"Let's get down to specifics," Professor Strong shouldered the moment forward.

"I'm coming to that. But just follow my logic. Now, if there is a class wherein the professor is absent *one-third* of the time, maximum instruction—education—is **not** happening, regardless of what happens, how brilliant he/she is, when he **is** there and regardless of how world famous he/she may be in his discipline," the Faculty Senate president continued his presentation.

"One third of the time?" arose the incredulous rhetorical response from Professor Day from Nursing.

"It's right here in black and white," Lawing added as he held up a sheet of paper. "Pass this around; it's a record of his absences." he added as he handed the document to Professor Mason from Kinesiology on his right side. "Professor Mason, would you be so kind as to take the minutes of our meeting from this point on?"

"Sure," replied Mason as he detached a pen from his shirt pocket and exposed a piece of paper from a spiral notebook.

"Thank you. Now, it seems as though this professor has a bad habit of disappearing for several weeks at a time while his students sit in his classroom waiting for him to put in an appearance. This record covers the last five years."

The evidence passed from hand to hand, which Justin chose not to look at, while the meeting slogged forward and a low whistle came from Professor Eastman as he received the paper from Mason.

"Added to this is the well-known fact that this particular professor has a drinking problem, a binge drinker if you will, and that his disappearances are accounted for by the fact that he goes on these week-long—or longer—benders."

"You are using the pronoun 'he.'" John Eastman from Biology stepped in.

"Yes."

"What department is *he* in?" Eastman asked.

"The English Department."

Bingo!! thought Justin as everyone rotated to peer at him. Justin turned the palms of his hands upward, as though begging a higher power, or at least the ceiling, and shrugged his shoulders while ice water ran up his spine to his neck. *What the hell am I going to do now,* was Justin's initial thought. *There is no way I can sit on a committee which is skewering my friend. Can I really afford to resign from a second committee? What will my colleagues—and the administration—think of me? But—on the other hand. . . .*

"Do you know this person?" was Betsy Day's bullet-like bulletin to Justin.

Justin was immersed in staggering thoughts.

"Professor Sandberg--?"

"What?" Everyone had turned to look at him.

"Do you know who this person is?" she repeated to him.

"Yes. I do." *How much can I afford to tell them?*

"The last straw—so to speak—was the fact that the administration sent a warning, in writing, admonishing him and warning him that if he missed again, action would be taken against him. And then he promptly missed a week of classes."

Professor Lawing picked up the thread where he left off.

"He had the flu," Justin inaudibly stumbled. *That wasn't much of a defense,* he thought. The dilemma for Justin was that he was keenly cognizant of the fact that his colleague was guilty as charged, that he did in fact miss a lot of classes, that he, Justin, had to cover his classes for his friend on more than one occasion, that he, Harold Bradley, had a drinking problem, which Justin had often experienced first-hand, but on the other hand Bradley had many fine qualities, above all a passion for learning and scholarship and was himself extremely learned and full of knowledge, that he offered his students intangibles that are hard to find in higher education—and above all else, he was a good friend for whom Justin had a begrudging affection for the old fart. *That's it, I've decided: I'm going to announce that I'm resigning from this committee because of a conflict of interest. I can't sit here and listen to them excoriating my friend. Besides, I have to look him in the face every day.* It was the center of Justin's moral core that relationships are sacred and are never violated under any circumstances and that betrayal went against everything he stood for.

"Who is this person," Kathy Strong eagerly queried.

"Professor Harold Bradley," came Lawing's illuminating insertion.

"I know him," Professor Strong announced. "I served on a committee with him. Seems like a nice guy."

"Totally irrelevant," said Lawing.

"What is relevant, is that—" Justin began. Everyone swung to look at him.

"What is relevant is that I cannot continue, in the face of the present circumstances, to serve—" And then he stopped.

"Yes????" came the chorus seated around the table.

Wait a minute, what am I doing?

Justin paused and silence thundered through the room while Justin assembled a new line of thinking.

Wait a minute, he reconnoitered again, *he'll have no one to defend him if I leave. I see it now. I'll stay on the committee to be his advocate.*

Justin refreshed and then began anew. "What is relevant is—and what you people have to keep in mind—is that Professor Bradley has tenure—of long standing."

Several "umm's" harmonized and then Professor Lawing gave a counter view.

". . . which can be broken."

"Not easily," Justin offered.

Heads were swiveling between Lawing and Justin as though at a tennis match.

"I am not going to read the historical documents of 1925, by the Counsel on Education, nor of 1940, by the American Association of University Professors. Let me just summarize it by saying that a tenured professor can be *quote*, "terminated for cause," for one of three reasons:

moral turpitude, incompetence, and financial exigency, that is, if the university has financial problems, which we clearly don't have here."

"Which category does he come under?" Justin eagerly pursued clarity.

"Well," Lawing began, "you figure it out: he has missed a third of his classes. That's not moral turpitude nor financial exigency."

"He is a world-re-known Chaucer scholar. I wouldn't call that incompetence."

"Being a scholar is one thing, competence in the class room is a totally separate issue. We are focused on the class room here." Justin decided that Lawing was the administration's surrogate but he would confront him anyway.

"The first prerequisite for being effective in the class room is mastery of the subject—otherwise known as knowledge—expertise—competence in one's subject matter—"

"But it doesn't do any good if you are not present." *He's got me there,* Justin mused and dropped back to prepare a counter attack. *I don't have a leg to stand on but I'll try anyway.*

"Now," Lawing turned to the other members of the committee, "let me summarize the AAUP procedures governing tenure. First, a faculty committee has to be formed, which is what we are. The administration has covered itself here. Second, the faculty member is to be informed—in writing—of the charges, which will be our next step, should we decide to go forward. Third, the faculty member *quote* 'should have the opportunity to be heard in his or her own defense' by relevant bodies. Fourth, 'the teacher should be permitted to be accompanied by an advisor of his or her own choosing who may act as counsel.' That might well be a lawyer. The professor is entitled to due process, and also a stenographic record of the hearing must be kept. Any questions?"

"Mr. Chairman, would a motion be in order at this point?" Justin decided to try to make a bold stance, even though he knew the odds were not in his favor, but he would at least be on record as having made an attempt.

"Sure."

Justin read from a statement he had hurriedly scribbled down: "I move that the charges against Professor Bradley be dropped, that this committee should be dissolved, and that no further action be taken against said professor." Justin stood and carried the piece of paper over to Professor Mason for the minutes, to whom he spoke with "I'd like for my motion to be entered in the minutes."

Silence stumped the room until Professor Day from Nursing said,

"Just for the sake of discussion, I'll second it."

"Any discussion?" the chair officiously proceeded.

Silenced dragged itself again through the room.

"Let me just say that Professor Bradley is a very fine colleague. He brings interplanetary recognition in the world of literary studies—"

"Interplanetary?" was Strong's echo.

"—he is extremely popular with our English majors—" Justin fought on.

"Because he gives all A's," was Lawing's rejoinder, "so I have heard."

Justin could not deny it. "—he is so knowledgeable in his field. And basically, he does not deserve this kind of treatment. Not at this stage in his life."

"Any further discussion?" Silence tripled itself.

"Ok. All those in favor say "aye."

"Aye," came the lonely vote from Justin.

"All those opposed, say "nay."

The "Nay's" overwhelmed Justin's lone "aye."

"The motion fails," Lawing satisfactorily noted. "The floor is now open for any further motions."

"I move," the heads turned toward John Eastman from Biology as he began the action, reading from a hastily penned note, "I move that this committee undertake a fuller investigation into the charges against said professor and that Professor Bradley be informed, in writing, that a hearing will be conducted at a future date at which time he will be able to defend himself with counsel."

"Is there a second?"

Professor Betsy Day became the seconder for a second time.

Whose side is she on? Justin wondered.

"We have a second. The floor is now open for discussion of the motion," Lawing perfunctorily proclaimed.

"Professor Lawing?" All eyes turned to Professor Sandberg. "I'd like to be excused at this point. I have another appointment at this time and I have nothing further to contribute to the discussion. I have expressed my opinion on the matter and everyone knows where I stand." Justin headed for the door with "if you will kindly excuse me."

"Professor Sandberg?"

"Yes?" Justin stopped with his hand on the door knob.

"Look. We're not cold monsters. Ok?"

"Humph," was barely audible.

"We realize that he is a colleague of yours and apparently a good friend."

"Thank you."

"But we have a real dilemma here. The administration is very displeased with Professor Bradley's performance, and they expect us to take some type of action, to make some type of recommendation for them to act on." Lawing was suddenly human again. "We can't just blow this off and you can't just leave the room and shirk your duty. Do you understand that?"

"Of course."

"I believe, being in the position here you are in, caught between being a responsible, professional faculty member on the one hand and the friend of a negligent colleague on the other, **and** being fully cognizant of the fact that he is a tenured faculty member which could open this institution to all kinds of negative publicity—across the nation—that you, perhaps in consultation with your amigo, can come up with some type of intelligent solution. Does that sound reasonable to you?"

"More than reasonable." Justin was mollified by Lawing's deliberate and balanced approach to the problem and swore to himself that he would find a way out of this dilemma. *But how?* Justin pondered as he commenced his exit.

"Professor Sandberg?" Professor Lawing delayed Justin's departure a "second" time.

"Yes?"

"There is a motion on the floor. We need your vote," the chair extended the moment.

"My vote is 'nay.' Thank you," as he exiled himself from the conference room.

32

Justin received a phone call from the chair of the Grievance Committee, Professor Munoz, informing him that a grievance had been lodged against him and that the committee was going to launch an exploratory satellite rocket. It was a friendly conversation, and Justin managed to stifle his temper. He knew in his heart that he had done nothing wrong in his class room, being extremely circumspect about the content of his courses, and was most eager to be enlightened about the specifics of the charges, although in his Super Self he had an incontrovertible hunch about what was at the core of the apple.

"Can you meet me in my office this afternoon?" came the query from Professor Munoz, who was in the Sociology Department.

"Of course. What time?"

"How does two o'clock fit your schedule" came the polite question from Oscar Munoz.

"Perfect."

"Esta bueno," concluded the conversation.

Two o'clock could not arrive rapidly enough for the eager, needled and nettled Professor Sandberg.

33

"Justin, come on in," was the ever-gracious Oscar Munoz as he greeted Justin at his office door and guided him gently into his comfortable, abundant office with cushy upholstered winged chairs. Not only were the chairs carefully coordinated with velvety orange (school colors) fabrics, but he had blue drapes (the other school color) on the windows (most offices were fortunate if they had broken venetian blinds that functioned), a tasteful coffee table in the middle, and an elegant mahogany desk with an over-sized, brown leather-covered swivel chair into which Oscar eased himself with a "care for something to drink?"

"No thank you, I'm fine." Then Justin dropped a conversation starter on Oscar's desk with, "Oscar, I want to ask you something." Oscar raised an eyebrow and his head. "Did the university provide you with your office furnishings?"

"Oh hell no. Are you kidding?! This university?"

"It's very nice."

"Thank you. No. I paid for it all myself. They even wanted to charge me for moving out all their old junk."

"The Sociology Department must pay professors more than the English Department does."

"No. It was just an indulgence on my part. I figured that since I am chair of the Grievance Committee and I would have a lot of nervous, or upset, or *aggrieved* (he smiled at his pun on "grievance committee") visitors from time to time that I ought to at least make this environment as pleasant as possible," was Oscar's sensible explanation. It also bespoke something about the sociologist's nature and sensibilities.

"You sound just like a sociologist—with your theory about the environment—a la B. F. Skinner style."

"It may have had some influence on me," Professor Munoz delivered a sly smile, paused, and then ricocheted in a new direction. "Well, let's get down to business."

"Ok."

"I just want you to know, Justin, that I invited you here to have a little informal chat with you before we start the formal process, you know, to get to know each other, allow me to hear your side of the story, let me get a feel for things, that sort of thing."

"I appreciate it, Oscar."

"Ok. So you have been charged with teaching miscegenation in your classes. What do you say to that?"

"BULLLLSHIT!!!!"

"Not according to this document," Oscar held up a small sheaf of papers.

"Can I see it?"

"No." He paused. "Not yet anyway."

"I think I have an inkling where this is coming from."

"This is a pretty serious charge we've got here," Oscar kept a stoic face matched by the noncommittal tone in his voice.

"You know I would never do anything that stupid."

"I don't know anything," Oscar kept up his non-aggressive, non-invasive, non-involved stance.

"All I teach is Shakespeare and other great writers of the English language."

"Do you teach *Othello*?"

"Of course."

"And is Othello black--?"

"Moor."

"And is he married to a white girl?"

"Italian."

"Close enough."

"Wait a minute, Oscar—"

"Yes?"

"Whose side are you on?"

"I'm not on anyone's side. My job is to be an objective investigator into the facts of the case. That's my role."

Justin gathered together his integrity, his sincerity, his genuineness, his purity of heart and mind, and his persuasive powers, as he deliberated with himself on his next compass point. "Do you know what academic freedom is?"

"Of course."

"Are you telling me that I can't teach certain plays of one of the greatest writers the human species has ever know?"

Oscar maintained his marble-like position with "I am not saying anything."

"Do you believe in the sanctity of tenure?"

"I'm not entitled to an opinion. I just want to hear your side of the story. I have already heard the other side," upon which occasion Professor Munoz proceeded to deliver a narrative detailing the identity of the aggrieved and the nature of the complaint, most of which revolved around the accusation that Professor Sandberg was advocating miscegenation in his class lectures. The complainer, who was precisely whom Justin knew it would be, in his written complaint had laid out an elaborate Biblical and theological justification for his position, founded on his argument that God, in the beginning, had created many races who each had their own separate place on the planet, distanced by large bodies of water and divided into disparate sections of the world which modern liberals had violated by bringing the races together.

"I've heard it before," was Justin's weary, sibilant, exhaled retort.

"I'm sure. The floor is all yours," Professor Munoz charitably held the palm of his right hand upward, welcoming Justin's defense, whereupon Justin proceeded to expostulate in detail the history of the situation, from his point of view, including the fact of the importance of Shakespeare in the pantheon of world literature, being, Justin concluded rhetorically, the greatest writer who has ever lived on this earth. It was a persuasive, powerful, and impassioned articulation of the "soul-felt" conviction of one Professor Justin Sandberg, concluding with the searing question, "are we to allow some psychopathic, megalomaniac, ignorant, Bible-thumping self-proclaimed messenger of God to tell us that we can't teach certain plays by the greatest playwright who ever lived?"

"Hummm," was Munoz's neutral buzz.

Justin studied Munoz's face, which was blank. Silence filled the void briefly.

"Weren't you married to a Mexican?" was Munoz's long-awaited, ponderous question.

Justin was jolted monetarily, then re-gained his equilibrium.

"Twice."

"Twice?"

"Twice. Two different wives. What does that have to do with anything?"

"Aren't you a gringo—a white bread?"

"If you feel you need to classify me—I guess that's where you'd put me."

"Where'd your ancestors come from?" Justin was struggling to figure out where Oscar was inhabiting.

"England, mostly."

"There!"

"On my father's side—"

"And you married two Mexican women."

"Mexican-Americans."

"So you practiced miscegenation in your personal life."

"Jesus God," Justin muttered as he rolled his eyes heavenward.

"—poisoning the minds of our students—unfit to teach the youth of our university." Professor Munoz was reading from the mystery document.

"I'm glad to say that puts me in the company with Socrates—who was charged with corrupting the minds of the youth."

"Yeah, and look what happened to him."

"Where did you get this information from?"

"The preacher. Apparently he has spent quite a bit of time doing research into his subject—a subject which he seems to take very seriously. He appears to be armed and ready,"

"For your information, Mexicans are Caucasians."

"That's an old classification. Take it from a Sociologist."

"Mexicans—like all of us, are *capirotadas*(a Mexican dish with a large mixture of ingredients)—everything but the kitchen sink."

"What do you know about Mexican food?"

"I have other things to eat besides grits. Besides, most Mexicans have as much European in them as anything else. So what."

"Apparently our Reverend Brown is something of a White Supremist who plans to right the world," was Munoz's guarded defense.

"Are you a racist?" was Justin's fast ball over the middle of the plate.

"You're asking someone named Oscar Munoz with brown skin if he's a racist?"

"It's all irrelevant."

"What *is* relevant?"

"What is relevant? What about academic freedom? What about the search for truth? What about freedom of speech? What about the first amendment? What about the sacredness of tenure? What about outside interference in the halls of learning? If we let some stupid-ass, religious fanatic mettle in what goes on in a university class room, we're lost for--" Justin stopped upon noticing that Munoz's eyes were closed and his breathing was measured. "Oscar?"

"Hunh?" Munoz opened his eyes and righted himself in his throne behind the desk. "I'm listening."

"What comes next?" Justin queried as he stood.

"I have already distributed copies of the written complaint to the Grievance Committee members and called a preliminary meeting for next Tuesday. We'll see what course of action they recommend and take it from there. Normally, historically, a hearing is conducted at which all parties are present to deliver their case and then we go into executive session to take action," Oscar Munoz deliberately and meticulously explained to Justin, making it all seem balanced, open, fair, and equitable.

"I'll wait till I hear from you," was Justin's effort at seeming to be mollified, which he was not.

"I'll probably call you immediately after the meeting on Tuesday. We want to move on this as quickly as possible and not drag things out," Munoz explained.

"Thanks, Oscar" as he slowly closed the door behind him and stood in the hall, feeling dejected, downcast, and disappointed. Justin had expected Munoz, as a faculty member and a colleague, to be more sympathetic to him and his cause. If anything, he ruminated, Munoz seemed to be antagonistic toward him if not downright hostile. *Maybe it's my imagination,* he thought and proceeded slowly toward the elevators, knowing that the direction he was taking was "Down."

34

"**G**ene?" Justin was standing outside of Betters' open office door, a week or so after his appearance at the Faculty Senate committee meeting. "Can we talk?"

"PRICK!! I ain't talking to you," bellowed the reply.

"Waitaminute, Gene. Give me a chance." Justin pleaded.

"Not in this lifetime!"

"I want to tell you something."

"I ain't interested!"

"I resigned from the committee—" Justin was still standing in the doorway, looking up and down the hall to ensure that no students were within loose-gossip range.

"Asshole!! Tell it to the—!" Betters stopped, leaned forward in his desk chair and paused to process this unexpected information.

"Can I come in? This is not for general consumption." Justin took a step forward indicating the vulnerability of the hallway.

"I swore I'd never speak to you again."

"Hey, listen, I've got a conscience. I don't believe in betraying my—er—my—my colleagues." Justin felt that he was gaining some ground as he took another step. The walls of Eugene Betters' office were lined with bookshelves, all of which were tumbling with the weight of thousands of ponderous books, lined two or three rows deep on every shelf with tomes cascading down to the floor and strewn in every direction of the compass and covering the carpet, which was not visible due to stacks of books everywhere. In addition to the books, boxes of papers littered every flat surface, and reams of paper covered his desk top. As on previous occasions, Justin thought about Karl Jung's principle that one's immediate environment is a reflection of one's psyche and wondered about the orderliness of Betters' mental state.

"What'd you just say?"

"I said, I resigned from the committee. After you left—after your operatic performance, which by-the-way, was very impressive: you had everybody shaking in their under wear."

"That was my purpose. I wanted to let them know that they were not dealing with some nerdy philosophy professor—that they are in for a battle and that they had better not mess with me."

Justin felt split down the middle, acutely conscious of the dilemma he was in: on the one hand, he knew that Betters was in the wrong in his "relationships" with students and that, for the good of the students, he had betrayed Betters with his testimony before the committee, and on the other hand he respected friendships, as shabby as his acquaintanceship with Betters was.

"You actually resigned from the committee?"

"I just said that."

"Because of me?"

Justin sensed in Betters' words the feeling that no one had ever taken his side in anything, that his role as social misfit—or gadfly, as he perceived philosophers to be—was threatened.

"The sole mission of this ad hoc committee was to investigate your relationship with female students. It has no other purpose. I wanted no part of it, even though it probably cost me some points with the administration."

"And you didn't tell them anything?"

"Have you been contacted?" Justin played dodge ball.

"Yes."

"And?"

"There is going to be a hearing, at which I will be present. That's all I know."

"When?"

"Tomorrow." Betters held up the procession of thoughts, then added, "I'm allowed to have counsel of my choice."

"I know."

Betters suddenly seemed to be in a far distant place for several beats.

"Gene?" Justin tried to summon him back to the present moment.

"Yeah?"

"What's happening?"

"I was thinking about this hot chick in my Ethics class. She was here in my office before you got here. I can tell she's putting moves on me. She's lusting for my body. I think I'm getting the hots for her." Betters seemed in a distant solar system again, but mostly the solar plexus.

"You're kidding, right?"

"No. What?"

"Never mind." Justin sensed that Betters was somewhere else again, and then Betters came down with,

"Would you be my counsel?"

Justin reeled under the imponderable idea by staring at the waste basket which was appropriate for such a notion. The basket looked as though it was a repository of every conceivable kind of discard, from stacks of paper, to candy wrappers, soda bottles—and a (Justin took a second look) used condom? *What the hell is that all about* and obliterated the thought.

"Gene. You need a lawyer."

"You are a respected member of the university community."

"It's out of the question. "I'm your—er—colleague. I would have no credibility in such a setting." Again, Betters seemed to be planning his means of attack while Justin awaited his return volley.

"Her name is Leticia Garcia."

"Who?"

"This girl in my class." Betters seemed impatient that Justin could not fathom his subjective world.

"Man, you need to get your mind out of your crotch," Justin feebly countered.

"Why?"

"Can't you see that that is precisely the attitude that now has you in deep shit?"

Justin suddenly realized that Betters was completely void of a social conscience, completely unaware of the impropriety of his attitude toward co-eds, and probably completely devoid of moral rectitude. Justin began to grasp the fact that Gene was a complete nihilist, a la the French philosopher Brassier. Justin arose.

"I just wanted you to know that I resigned from the committee, because I could not sit in judgement on you—just wanted to square everything up between us. That's all."

"Preciate it. I'll let you know how it goes tomorrow."

"I want to hear about it." Justin now knew the members of the committee, having served briefly with them, was aware of their attitude toward Betters, and was curious about the outcome of the battle *royale* between moral turpitude and the principle of tenure.

35

It's all piling up on me, accumulating, heavily heaping, dragging me down, loading my lobotomy, searing my soul, crushing my conscious, pressing my person, sabotaging my sleep, slaying my soul, wilding my will, tumbling my thoughts—and so it went through the night for Justin. Sleep was not sought for, rest was not required, peace was not possible, and sanity was not sustainable. He lifted his head from his pillow, searched for the floor with his bare feet, finally finding it, and arose in an aroused, nay, stimulated, mental state. He dumbly made his way through his darkened house, knowing every turn and obstacle in his path to eventually find the handle on the refrigerator door which upon opening invited a slash of light to stab his face. He pulled a bottle of Chardonnay from the refrigerator door, found a wine glass still standing on the cabinet counter, decanted a full glass, which he hoisted with the Spanish pronouncement, invitation, sacrament, and blessing of "Salud," "good health," and quaffed off half the glass without recess. He stood staring at the darkness, the half-full glass balanced in his right hand, and thinking, thinking, thinking. He then finished the remainder of the glass in one enormous gulp and reached for the refrigerator door again. *Just one more,* he thought, and repeated the ritual. He had no idea of the time of night nor cared to know, knowing only that he needed answers—and sleep, two mutually annihilating needs.

Back in bed, the wine only worsened his will. His thinking had now become blurred, untamed by rational control and engaged in irrational lurches.

His thoughts first dashed to Betters, who seemed, Justin decided, totally incapable of understanding the impropriety of his behavior with female students. Justin felt helpless, caught between a committee on one side which seemed hell bent on revoking Betters' tenure and, on the other side, Better's inability to change his ways. *Why should I inflict so much pain on my brain when I am powerless to affect either side in the debate.* But in the darkness and in the still of the night, sanity remained outside his bedroom door, in spite of his determination to find an exit. *No Exit*, he remembered Sartre's existentialist play.

And then his mind flipped to his friend Harold Bradley who, Justin knew in spite of his regard for his friend, was also liable for the charges against him. He had tried to do his duty to his friend in the committee meeting, making a motion to drop the charges and dissolve the committee, but was trampled on by the committee which was also hell bent on breaking Bradley's tenure. How could he defend his colleague when he knew full well that Harold was negligent in his class attendance? Again, he was split down the middle without any means of reconciliation of the warring armies of friendship and academic standards. *Whatever happened to my critical thinking and problem solving skills? They've never been tested like this before. I'll turn it over to my unconscious and let it become fertile with answers.*

Good, now I can go to sleep and just close my eyes, turn off the old brain, and an answer will be awaiting me at dawn—at dawn—at dawn—at—d--

And then another four alarm clanging invaded his drowsiness with the thought of Reverend Brown, and he popped straight up to a sitting position in bed. *I need to be preparing a defense of myself without worrying about Betters and Bradley. Brown doesn't have the chance of a flea in a vat of carbolic acid. But I have to prepare my defense meticulously and thoroughly. Brown—Brown—Brown—is just nuts, that's all.*

And so he thought he would peacefully drift off, only to be dragged back into the blinding sunlight of fretfulness. *Betters—moral turpitude—no question. What argument can I use to bring him salvation? Bradley—incompetence and alcoholism—no argument there. What ploy can I propose to rescue him. Brown—dumbass preacher—perllucidly deranged. Is that admissible?* The thoughts rotated through his brain like a cartridge wheel in a revolver chamber, firing deadly thought after deadly thought. *Betters—moral turpitude, Bradley—incompetence and dereliction of duty, Brown—fanatically unhinged.* Bang, bang, bang. The revolver kept firing in his head, hitting his heart with deadly accuracy with each pull of the trigger in his brain.

And so it went on through the night like a firing range until he peaked over the sheets under which he was buried in his grave of a bed after being assassinated by the firing squad of sleep-killing thoughts, until finally his conscious mind began to relax, to let loose, to drift, with no conscious control, and he lost his grip on awareness, and plunged into blankness—for a while, for how long he could not calculate and remained in spacelessness—long enough for his unconscious to set about its task of providing answers.

And then it was like a searing floodlight was switched on in his head and he sat up—once again, this time with deep satisfaction as he neared resolutions. *Okay,* he pulled his knees up in order to embrace them, *now, in Betters's case, it is clear that what is needed is some type of separation—distance, if you will—between Betters and young women, clearly the only answer. I think I've got a plan. Now in the case of Harold Bradley,* he stretched his legs out straight in front of him and bent over so as to unknot the muscles in his back, *what is needed is a sincere commitment from him to deal with his drinking problem once and forever—and I think I've got just the right answer for him—short of institutionalizing him.* Justin smiled with triumphant joy at his own brilliance and glanced out the window to see the stealthing in of an orange morning. *Brown, I can meet head on, with relish—and a little bit of research and documentation regarding academic freedom and tenure. Now to implement my plans. As soon as the world is astir, I'll call Professor Small, even though I resigned from the committee. They said they wanted to retain me as a sort of consultant, so I won't be out of order by sharing my idea with him. And then I'll call Professor Arnold Lawing from the Faculty Senate to share an alternative idea to revoking Harold's tenure. And then I'll tell Oscar Munoz that I embrace the opportunity to confront the Reverend Brown in an open hearing.* Justin flopped back on his pillow in self-satisfaction, whether warranted or not. *We'll judge by the results,* he grinned and then began to plan his trip to the shower to start his victorious day. And tranquility, peace, and placidity ran before him, finally.

36

Thursday's were a non-teaching day for Justin so he could dedicate this day to implementing his brilliant plans, while congratulating himself on his genius and relishing the excision of the mental tumor that pressed on his brain through the night. A shower, shave, and many coffees prepared him for his first phone call while awaiting a reasonable hour for early morning chats.

"David? This is Justin Sandberg," he said, responding to a morning-sounding "ello."

"I hope I didn't get you out of bed." He was reassured.

"Listen, David, I've got a brilliant solution regarding Eugene Betters's situation. I know how we can avoid a legal entanglement with him, regarding tenure, and modify his behavior with co-eds at the same time." Justin listened for a few ticks and then concurred with, "Yes, I know your committee is meeting this afternoon at 3:00. All the more reason I need to see you before your meeting. What are your office hours today?" Justin listened while Professor Small laid out his time table for the day.

"Ok. Good. How about 11:00—in your office?" He listened for confirmation and then ended it with, "All right, I'll see you then," and made an entry in his daily log.

"Yes, be assured that it is a workable, and, in all modesty, brilliant algorithm," he consoled a wavering Professor Small as he completed the call.

Justin stood erectly with his butt against the kitchen counter, which he leaned against, as he looked out of his window at the unparalleled shimmering azure dome which blessed the southwest morning while he thumbed through his little black directory of phone numbers and addresses. *Lawing, Lawing, Lawing, Law—ah here we go* and began to push buttons and poured another cup of coffee. His nervous system was definitely honing a keen edge.

"Arnold?" he again responded to a muffled mutter of a morning "ello."

"This is Justin Sandberg," he began, and continued with, "I'm fine thank you. I hope it's not too early." He hesitated for a response and then resumed with, "Look, Arnold, I'll keep this short. I know you've got to get to the office, but I just wanted to know if I could make an appointment to see you sometime today." He listened and then continued with, "yes, it is a matter of some urgency."

After politely allowing Professor Lawing to carp about his schedule for the day and re-acted to Lawing's pointed question with, "It's in regards to Professor Harold Bradley." He was a little shaken by a piece of information which Lawing handed him.

"The committee meets this afternoon—at three?!!! How come I didn't know that?"

After absorbing the explanation, Justin apologized with, "well, I didn't check my e-mail yesterday evening after class. I was pretty exhausted."

Lawing went on quite officiously while Justin diplomatically indulged Lawing's ego.

"Well, listen, Arnold, I have come up with an unbelievably viable solution to Bradley's condition and dilemma—which makes it all the more imperative that I meet with you before our committee meeting." He waited for a response.

"Absolutely guaranteed to solve the problem." Pause. "Ok, great 1:00 o'clock in your office. I'll be there. And thanks, Arnold, I appreciate your hearing me out and I know you are going to be delighted with my solution, and I am sure it will be satisfactory on all sides including yours and Bradley himself."

He then sent a text to Oscar Munoz which read, "Oscar, I will not be intimidated by the Reverend Brown. I welcome a hearing for which I shall do research and be more than well-armed. Bring'im on!"

37

Justin was at the Philosophy Department office a few minutes before eleven and quite eager to unfold his audacious plan. He chatted with Terry, the departmental secretary (a former student of his), for a brief moment until David Small's large head appeared at the Chair's door and signaled Justin with a beckoning nod while Justin released a wide yawn.

"You sleepy," was David's first question as they settled into their respective seats, Small behind his enormous desk.

"To tell you the truth, David, I didn't sleep very much—if any—last night."

"Oh?"

"I had a lot of stuff on my mind during the night, one of which is Eugene's situation."

"I don't know why that should bother you."

"That's just the way I am," Justin elucidated.

"It's pretty simple actually. We have a number of statements from Philosophy majors regarding his behavior, we'll take a vote to break his tenure, and that will be the end of it."

"I don't think so," Justin said in disagreement.

"Why not?"

"I talked to Eugene yesterday. He told me that if you try to break his tenure he will sue the university. He's really steamed. I think he'll do what he threatens to do because he's got nothing to lose." Justin remained calm and persuasive.

"It's called moral turpitude, Justin. Grounds for breaking tenure. Open and shut case. Not a problem. *Fini. Adios.* Done. What more is there to say?"

"Betters is not going to go away that easily. He's going to 'rage, rage, rage, against the dying of the light,'—Dylan Thomas."

"Aw, you poets—so out of touch. You idealists."

"Well, being a poet and idealist, I come here with a very practical, realistic solution." Justin continued down his path of practicality.

"Let's hear it."

"Ok. First, we shall tell Betters that he is not allowed to come on campus any more," Justin began.

"What?!?!'

"Now wait a minute," Justin cautioned.

"We're going to pay him for NOT coming to work—for doing nothing—for sitting at home and watching tv? I thought you said you had a brilliant plan." David Small rarely showed his feelings—especially anger—but he was clearly outraged at such an atrocious, appalling suggestion and spewed forth his resolve. "Absolutely, undeniably out of the ques—"

"Hold your horses, as we say out west." Justin was confident in the hand he held and was patient in showing his cards.

"It's unthinkable."

"I never said anything about his not teaching his classes, did I?" Justin laid one card down.

"What?"

"He'll teach his classes—"

"How's he going to do that?"

"From home." He was slowly revealing his hand.

"Home?"

"We live in an age of modern technology—you know, computers and all that," as he turned over another card.

"Yeah—"

"Have you heard of distance learning—remote teaching?" The ace this time.

"Sorta—"

"It's very simple: he'll teach all his classes on line." It was a royal flush.

Small was unsure how to respond but finally came up with, "can he do that?"

"Not a problem. It is becoming very common."

"What about the students?"

"His courses will be listed in the schedule as on-line classes. Most students have computers these days, and those who don't can go to a computer lab. We have computer labs all over campus."

"How effective can that be, I mean, in maintaining our standards and integrity."

"David. Join the modern world. It has already been proved that on-line learning is just as effective as the classroom. It's just like in the classroom: students get out of a course what they put into it."

"I hope this doesn't catch on. We'll all be out of a job."

"David. There are professors all across the country who are teaching in their pajamas," Justin argued.

"Really?"

"Absolutely."

"God help us."

"Look: I'll come to the meeting at the beginning. I have another meeting at the same hour, so I can't stay too long. I shall very succinctly lay out my plan and then leave for my other meeting. The committee members all know me; I think I have a little credibility with them. Right?"

"Maybe." Small winked.

Professor Small then wrapped himself in a long silence, pondering the possibilities, and then finally admitted, like any thoughtful administrator, "Well, at least it might spare us from having to go to court—and suffering all the negative publicity."

"I'll talk to my colleague Ruth Goldberg, explain my plan, and then ask her to make a motion to adopt my solution." Justin stood.

"We'll need a second."

"I'll take care of that," Justin offered as he sidled toward the door with a sense of satisfaction and triumph, his sleepless, restless night starting to pay dividends, he orisoned..

Justin's next urgent appointment was with Faculty Senate President Arnold Lawing. Meanwhile, he drifted toward the Faculty Lounge to idle some moments, have a vegan lunch, and, to give edge to his mental acumen, a glass of chardonnay—which soon called for a follow up for good measure. Ellen Cohen was luckily discovered half way through his lunch and provided him an eager ear. He always found great warmth in her sympathy, erudition, and intelligence, something he had missed in so many of his relations with the distaff side. Swearing her to secrecy, he shared with her his tete-a-tete with David Small, his night of torment, and his strategy for saving the besotted Harold Bradley's career.

"Why do you take on everybody else's burdens?"

"You'd think I was Jewish, no?" he smiled for her sympathy.

"You'd never pass."

"Actually, it's my born-again Christian childhood that keeps upsetting my life." His face flashed a flicker of faith.

"Washed all your sins away, hunh?"

"Close enough—for a Jew-girl." He smiled and reached for her hand. They were both without the faith of their fathers and shared their secularism.

"I admire your compassion—and your practical solutions. They might just work."

He was well-armed for his meeting with Lawing, mostly because of the buttressing of Ellen Cohen—and the second glass of chardonnay.

38

"Justin, come on in," Professor Lawing solicited as he stood beside the secretary's desk in the Faculty Senate Office. Justin had waited only a moment, just enough time to rehearse his presentation and make a few notes.

"Thanks Arnold," Justin said as he passed the secretary's desk and lobed, "afternoon, Helen. I won't keep your boss too long, I hope."

"You look tired," was Arnold's prologue.

"I haven't slept much."

"Why is that?" Arnold followed up.

"Because I'm an idiot."

"Hunh?"

"I have this character flaw of trying to solve all the world's problems—including yours."

"You think I need help?" Arnold turned both palms up heaven-ward.

"The fault, dear Brutus, is not in our stars, / But in ourselves, that we are underlings."

"I'm an engineer. You'll have to translate," Arnold inserted with a straight face.

"It means, that's just the way I am; it's my character "fault."

"Ah."

"Let's talk about Harold Bradley," Justin transferred buses.

"I don't think you want to do that," Arnold cautioned.

"Why not?"

"Well, we have been gathering the facts, doing a lot of leg work, interviewing students and faculty alike, and have uncovered some very disturbing information," Lawing expounded.

"You want to share it with me?"

"It'll all be presented at the meeting this afternoon, but I'll give you some quick bulletin points," Lawing continued down the same byway.

"Ok."

"As you know, we have a record, a log, of his attendance, and his absences. On average, every semester, he misses at least one-third of his class meetings—"

"I am aware of that."

"When he is present, he rambles endlessly about everything except the subject of the class—"

"He loves ideas and excites his students about them."

"What does Pancho Villa have to do with Chaucer?'

"He has several books on Pancho Villa."

"But that is not the subject of English 4320—"

"What else?"

"His classes have little intellectual rigor—"

"How can you prove that?"

"True/false quizzes? Give me a break."

"Sometimes they are the hardest ones."

"He is also known to tell dirty jokes and make sexist remarks about the ladies."

"It's his sense of humor."

"He's out of touch with the times, and he is very offensive. He needs to go."

"He's tenured."

"We don't need to go through that again," Lawing leaned back in his chair.

"I'm sure, if we give him a warning—"

"He has already been given warnings—several times. He ignores them."

Justin sat back in his chair and stared at the ceiling toward which Lawing's palms had turned again in supplication; Justin was obviously pondering exactly how to counterattack such devastating charges, and then began:

"Look, as far as the absences are concerned, we can solve that problem."

"Says you."

"I'll be honest. We all know that he has a drinking problem—"

"Like he can't get enough?"

"—that he goes on binges, which is the underlying factor in his absences—"

"And you're gonna fix that?"

"Yes."

"Bull shit."

"Look, Arnold, I have been doing some research—gathering information—

"Ok."

"Instead of going through the rocky, ugly, lengthy process of trying to break his tenure, there is a better solution."

"And what might that be?" Lawing propped a foot up on his desk as he leaned back in his swivel chair.

"We can put some stipulations, some requirements—some conditions of employment on him, if you will. I looked it up in the Regents Rules. He would have to meet certain criteria in order to remain employed."

"Such as?"

"Have you ever heard of Alcoholics Anonymous?"

"I—guess—I—think—I--"

"They do incredible work."

"Humph!"

"I have a friend—well, never mind. They have taken on some of the worse cases of alcoholism and changed people's lives." Justin paused to select his next road (*"two roads diverged in a yellow wood,* he thought of Frost, *"and I--/ I took the one less traveled by, / And that has made all the difference"*)—or something like that.

"Justin?"

"Sorry. It was founded by a man by the name of Bill Wilson, who was himself an incurable alcoholic. He devised a twelve step program, it's all laid out in what they call the Big Book, but its real success comes from alcoholics helping each other. I've read a lot of testimonies—some people have been dry for 20—30—40—in some cases—50 years—"

"I don't need a sermon—."

"I'll cut to the chase: we could make it a condition of his employment—in writing—that he has to attend an AA meeting at least once a week—maybe every day at the beginning—"

"How often do they meet?"

"There is a meeting somewhere every day. They are used to working with Human Resources departments all the time, in cases where attendance is mandatory."

"Humph, I had no idea--."

"Here's the thing: identities are shielded---that's why it's called Alcoholics ANONYMOUS. Nobody need ever know. Compare that to the hassle of trying to break his tenure, going to court, and all the ensuing negative publicity, the damage to this university—"

"What if he won't cooperate?"

"It's a condition of his employment. If he doesn't cooperate, then you can quietly fire his ass."

"I'll recognize you at the meeting and let you present it to the committee," Lawing conceded.

"I may be a few minutes late. I have another committee I have to stop by for a few minutes." Justin was edging toward the door.

"Don't be too late."

"Arnold." Justin twisted around to him. "Do you think you could delay the start of your meeting until 3:30?"

"I'll have my secretary send out an email. But no later."

Justin stood in the hall outside the Faculty Senate office, inhaled an impossibly deep breath, let it slowly escape, and gave out a silent "whoopee" and raised a fist in the air.

39

Justin had been functioning on adrenalin during the dual meetings but now was confronted with the reality that he was exhausted, having had virtually no sleep, and his catecholamine supply was depleted. *Can I make it through two more meetings,* he examined himself, *and keep my lights on. I just wish I could go home and go to bed. Why do I have to crucify myself over every cause. Well, for the good of the whole,* he consoled himself, *but I've got to stop trying to be a martyr and saving the world—or the university. Maybe tomorrow.* With this he loped back to his office to get his thoughts in order, which was exceedingly difficult to do, considering that his fatigue thermometer was at a personal high, or, in the words of J. Alfred Prufrock, "spread out against the sky Like a patient etherized upon a table." Eliot was one of his favorites and always came readily to mind. He also felt like "The Hollow Men," "Headpiece filled with straw. Alas!"

At a few ticks before 3:00 pm, Justin sat bantering with members of the ad hoc committee of full professors in the Philosophy Department seminar room when Dr. Small incarnated at the door, cordially greeted everyone, and made his inaugural address with "Dr. Sandberg has resigned from this committee, for personal reasons, but he asked if he could make a brief presentation to the committee, which I consented to. Since Professor Sandberg has another meeting at this hour, I am allowing him to go first after which we'll conduct our official business. I should also inform you that I, acting in accordance with university policy, have invited Professor Betters, who is already waiting outside, to appear before this committee." He acknowledged Justin with, "Professor Sandberg?"

"Thank you Dr. Small. I'll try to make this as brief as I possibly can" and then Justin embarked on his presentation, outlining in stark form the details of his plan, beginning with the premise that the best way to keep professor Betters out of contact with female students is by banning him from campus—"

"What!?" "Waitaminute!" "You can't do that!" and other such mumblings and sentiments scurried around the table while Justin paused.

Justin then took possession again by explaining that Betters could teach all his classes from home, list all his classes in the course schedule as 'on-line' classes, which would be "live" (or "synchronous", as they jargoned it) during which he could still interact with students—but, at a celibate distance—and have all the exams taken electronically, and other such details of his plan.

Everyone sat in bewildered silence while trying to summon some rational processes, and then the clouds gathered, the lightening sparked, the thunder grumbled, the torrents rained down, and the storm broke in a cacophony of voices, and Justin could sort out such complaints as "this could never work," "what if every faculty member wanted that deal," "just stay home all day?" "hey, can I have that arrangement too," "what happened to our standards," "everybody is going to want to do that," "it is the end of the university as we know it," "is this a community college or what?" and unremittingly on they roamed for a brief interval until Professor Small demanded order and protocol and then recognized Professor Howell:

"I just want everyone to know, regardless of the results of our deliberations, I vociferously, adamantly, and unequivocally oppose such an arrangement, as I sense some of you do too, judging by your remarks. Basically, it is the end of our university as we know it—everything is gone, academic standards, integrity, student/faculty relationships which are at the heart of education, and we shall set a precedent which many faculty will want for themselves. If this becomes a motion, I shall vote against it."

"Mr. Chairman," Justin said as he raised a finger for recognition.

"You're recognized."

"I have to go to another meeting but let me make a summary statement with some major points. First, we need to join the modern world, for on-line instruction has become quite widespread and common. Second, fraternizing with students of the opposite gender, strikes at the very heart of academic ethics and integrity and is a violation of every code of conduct. Third, let him speak for himself, but Betters sees nothing wrong with what he is doing. I have had endless conversations with him about this issue and he has no intention of changing his behavior. But you can ask him that yourselves. Fourth, if the only other option is to take away his tenure, that is going to lead to a major shit storm (excuse me ladies), and the one thing this university does not need is an outrageous amount of negative publicity. Also, people will want to know the reason for his dismissal but since it is a personnel matter, you can't publicly give the real reason, which will only make the university look even worse. The best policy, I feel, and I have given this a lot of thought, is to quietly make a different teaching arrangement and let everyone go their merry, unperturbed way."

"I'll fight it to the end," rumbled Professor Howell.

"Thank you for your time and attention," Justin said as he rose from his chair and unobtrusively stole toward the door. "Buenas tardes, todos." And he vanished through the portal.

He was no sooner out the door when he encountered Eugene Betters standing in the hallowed hallway. Betters was visibly disturbed.

"What the fuck are you doing in there?! I thought you resigned from this committee." Betters staggered back a step or two.

"I did."

"Is this more of your betrayal?"

"I was just trying to save your life—and your job," Justin calmly replied.

"You were?"

"Yes," Justin said as he moved on past Betters. "I have to go. I'll talk to you later."

"Professor Betters?" Dr. Small was now outside the committee-room door, summoning Betters with "Come on in."

40

Justin was achingly demolished by the blizzardly reception of his proposal concerning Betters, which seemed to him to be a rational, intelligent solution to a dangerous, nay, nuclear holocaust procedure, in dealing with Betters' tenured situation, but Justin cheered himself and re-erected his brighter spirits in anticipation of his faculty senate committee meeting, being fully confident that his solution for Bradley's situation was nothing short of brilliant. Thus, he hastened off to the next meeting with a lighter heart and a bouncier step.

Along the way, Justin's mind kept pace with his feet, both of which were at a heart-scampering velocity, as he bounded down the steps in the Philosophy building, flung the outside door away from him, made a lunatic dash across the campus toward the building which housed the Faculty Senate office, slowed his stride in the hallway as he narrowed the distance to the meeting room door, and, oh so gently, opened it with, "Sorry, I ran into a little trouble at the other meeting," and deposited himself into a seat at the table.

"We were about to start without you."

"It's been a helluva day, starting with a sleepless night. Please forgive me," Justin managed between intakes of oxygen. *Thank god I'm a jogger.*

"I was just suggesting to the committee that today's agenda consists of procedural matters, mostly. I did not invite Professor Bradley to today's meeting. He'll get his chance later. Did everybody bring your calendars with you? We'll need to establish a hearing with Professor Bradley in attendance, according to the rules," Professor Lawing monotoned on.

After a series of typical committee-like discussions involving everyone's schedules, complaints, exceptions, obligations, responsibilities, duties, paperwork, workloads, gripes, moanings, groanings, whinings, protests, quibbling, caviling, carping, nitpickings, pettifoggings, and generally trivializing, a meeting schedule was established. Then.

"Now. The reason I requested that this committee delay today's meeting—from 3:00 to 3:30—was at the request of Professor Sandberg, who had another meeting to attend—[with a sneer and looking at his watch]—*briefly*. Now," *he has a bad habit of saying 'now' a lot,* Justin noted, "we could have gone ahead and ignored his request and started without him—because we have had this meeting set for some time *now*—but Justin presented me with some information, hitherto unknown to me—which I thought was worthy the committee's attention to hear—and to consider it if the committee so desires. So, now, Dr. Sandberg, the floor is yours."

Justin arose at his end of the table and said, "Thank you Professor Lawing. If you people remember, at our first meeting, you gave me the charge to see if I could find some type of solution for this dilemma and that is what I have been working on. I have already discussed this with Professor Lawing, as he just informed you, and I have taken your charge very seriously."

Justin then severed himself from his place at the table while saying, "If you don't mind. Give me one second," Justin strode to the front of the room, crossed over to the video control panel, punched the Screen Down button, slid in a video, and hit Play. "This will only take a few minutes, but it is more persuasive than I could ever be." Justin had done his homework, had gone to the AA library of films on-line, and selected what he deemed as the most powerful and convincing one and downloaded it. Someone by the door reached for the lights and the presentation began, during which several committee members left the room. Justin was dismayed with "*how rude*" and felt the film failure falling fast around him. *I never expected this,* was his despairing thought. The film, a brief history, statement of purpose, and outline of procedures of AA, along with some personal testimonies of successes, ended shortly thereafter as the departed committee members returned to the room. .

Justin remained standing at the focal point of the room with notes in his hand. "If you will indulge me for just another moment, I'd like to present AA's preamble to you, which can say it far better than I can," and reading,

'AA is a fellowship of men and women who share their experience, strength, and hope with each other that they may solve their common problem and help others to recover from alcoholism.

The only requirement for membership is a desire to stop drinking. There are no dues or fees for AA membership; we are self-supporting through our own contributions. AA is not allied with any sect, denomination, politics, organization or institution; does not wish to engage in any controversy, neither endorses nor opposes any causes. Our primary purpose is to stay sober and help other alcoholics to achieve sobriety.'

"All I can add is that their success has been absolutely astounding. I have talked to a number of people who swear by the organization and the miracles they have worked."

"So. What is the point of all this?" Professor Mason from Business asked.

"I am coming to that."

"Let me help Justin out a little here," Professor Lawing intervened, at which point Arnold Lawing summarized for the committee the earlier conversation which he and Sandberg had had in Lawing's office, laying down in clear terms the strategy of "condition of employment," its legality, and its effectiveness in solving a problem. It seemed so clear and simple to the alternative of a defecation tempest in a battle over tenure, it seemed to Justin, while protecting his vulnerable friend.

"It appears to me, on the surface of it, that we will be setting a very bad precedent," said Professor Eastman from the College of Science's Biology Department, "as well as opening ourselves to a law suit."

"Law suit?" Justin asked.

"This is an institution of higher learning—"

"We know that," Justin emendated.

"We are not a rehab center, we are not a drug treatment facility, we are not a hospital, and we are basically stepping out of the bounds of our mission as an institution of education—"

"And research," said Justin. "This is research—one way of looking at it."

"—and if we attempt to cure somebody and fail at it, we'll make ourselves liable to legal action," Professor Eastman continued.

"I agree with John. We are out of our depth here," Professor Edwin Mason, from the College of Business, said. "We've lost our focus—we've lost our perspective—we're chasing rainbows—all this just to salvage a hopeless drunk because he has a friend on this committee who is trying to save his ass."

"Now we're getting personal," Justin jumped jarringly in, "but, yes, we in the Humanities believe that every human being is worth trying to save—unlike you people in Science and Business."

"Whoa, whoa, whoa!" Chairman Lawing contravened, "let's not let this get out of hand and deteriorate into a shouting match and name calling. We are going to follow Roberts' Rules of Order at this point and no one can speak until they are recognized. All right? *Now?* Professor Eastman," who reacted with,

"Well, I've shared my thoughts with you, a little, but let me expand. My thought is that we may be opening up a whole can of worms here, that we may be getting into treacherous territory for the simple reason that if we don't take a firm stand against a faculty member's malfeasance—"

"MALFEASANCE!?"

"Professor Sandberg! I am warning you. I don't want to have to dismiss you from the meeting," cautioned the chairman.

"—a faculty member's dereliction of duty. If we don't take an irrevocable stand against negligence, we may be setting a very bad precedent, in the first place. Our faculty may start assuming that tenure cannot be broken, regardless of their behavior and performance, which the rules are very clear about. In the first place. In the second place, we are an institution of higher learning, an educational entity. It is our moral, ethical duty, to stay focused on our mission and not get sidetracked into areas where we don't belong—where we have no business being and where we have no training or skills. Them's my thoughts," Professor Eastman concluded with purposeful bad grammar for sarcasm's sake.

"Professor Mason, I believe your hand was up."

"Yes. I would just like to endorse, in the strongest way possible, what Professor Eastman has articulated. Bottom line: we are moving into territory where we have no business being, which is out of the realm of our expertise, and that, as John says, we are setting a very bad precedent—er, example—for the rest of the faculty for misconduct. If it comes to a vote, I shall vote against it," Professor Mason said.

"*Oh crap,*" thought Justin to himself, "*this is not going the way I thought it would. It just seemed so reasonable to me. It seems as though I may be outnumbered. I am being defeated everywhere I turn today.*"

"Professor Day, from Nursing."

"I have had some exposure to—and training in—the issue of alcoholism and I know that in some cases, from my personal experience, alcoholism can be treated—and managed. I think the fact that we make his attendance at AA meetings a "condition of employment" gives us a safeguard. He doesn't cooperative, he is quietly out the ole door, goodbye, adios, farewell. Simple. No muss no fuss," Professor Day said.

"Thank you Betsy," Justin mumbled.

"Professor Sandberg, second warning," Lawing repeated his admonition. "Professor Strong, I believe you wished to be recognized."

"Yes," said Kathy Strong, from the History Department and the College of Liberal Arts, and added, "I think I come down on the side of my colleague in Liberal Arts, Professor Sandberg, and Professor Day from Nursing. Everybody deserves a second chance—"

"Second chance!!! Ha!!! Look at his record. You mean fiftieth chance," interjected Professor Eastman.

"The chair did not recognize you, Professor Eastman."

"Sorry—"

"I know Dr. Bradley to be a very nice colleague, having served on a committee with him, and, from what I gather, a brilliant literary scholar who has brought a lot of recognition to this institution."

"*Lit-er—a—tuire*" scoffed Mason from the world of free enterprise, that is, the College of Business Administration.

"Professor Mason. Order! I don't want to have to call the campus police."

"I'll vote to give him a chance. We have protection built into the proposal. What more can we hope for. And besides, it beats going through the wrangling—to use a wild west term—of trying to revoke his tenure," Kathy Strong summed up.

"Professor Sandberg."

"Well, I have already presented all the content and conditions of my proposal. I just want to say at this point, thank you to those who support my proposal. I believe with all my heart that you are doing the right thing. I believe that people in this life can be salvaged. I continue to be an optimist about the potential of human beings. Thank you."

"All right. Now," Chairman Lawing began, "I have been listening to all the arguments and opinions expressed on both sides here this afternoon, and I have made an executive decision. We are not going to take a vote this afternoon. Instead, I am going to invite Professor Bradley to our next meeting, give him a chance to say his piece—see what he has to say, how he defends himself—and then unfold the Alcoholics Anonymous proposal to him and see how he reacts to it. As some of you say, give him a chance. If he balks at the proposal, then we have his answer and the case is closed. If he is receptive, then we can take it from there." Lawing's eyes reconnoitered the faces around the table while he paused.

"That sounds fair to me," Justin said.

"I am opposed to the whole idea, but I am willing to go that far—to give him a voice," Professor Eastman said.

A chorus of agreement vocalized around the room.

"Two stalemates in one day," Justin thought, not yet knowing the outcome of the first meeting. *"Professors can be so golldurn contrary and obstinate. This is the last time I am losing sleep over what is none of my business.*

Yeah right."

Professor Justin Sandberg snailed his way back to his office (thinking of Jacque's Seven Ages of Man speech in *As You Like It* and "the whining schoolboy with his satchel and shining morning face creeping like snail unwillingly to school"), wearily opened his office door, opened his desk drawer, opened his laptop, opened his email, and opened a missive from Oscar Munoz:

> As you know, we have had a difficult time scheduling a meeting of our Grievance Committee because of the busy schedule of the filer, being the minister of a church. I apologize for this late notification, but the complaintant has contacted me to let us know that he can be available

tomorrow afternoon at 3:00pm. Please make every effort to clear your schedule and make yourself available for this critical meeting, which shall be held in the conference room next to my office Room 313. Please let me know ASAP if this is a problem for any of you. It is extremely important for everyone to be present. And please RSVP, asap.

Sincerely,
Oscar Munoz
Professor of Sociology
Chair, Faculty Senate Grievance Committee"

"Crap!! Another sleepless night. I'm really having a bad run right now," Justin ruminated as he placed his fingers on the keyboard, did as he was requested,

and closed with, "I assume you want me to be present."

"To hell with it. I'm going to go have a drink so that I'll really be in bad shape tomorrow—and I won't give a shit." Pause. "Ellen, this is Justin," as he spoke into his cell phone, "could you meet me for a drink? [pause] Yes, right now. [pause] I'll tell you all about it. I need some TLC right now. Ok, Fifteen minutes, the Garden Inn." He contemplated empty space momentarily then gathered himself, and his possessions, up.

41

"Good afternoon, everybody," Oscar Munoz began. "I first want to thank you for working this meeting into your busy schedules at the last minute. I apologize for such short notice, but I figure we have postponed this long enough and since the complainant finally found a place in his busy schedule where he could fit us in, I figured—if you'll pardon my cliché—we needed to strike while the iron was hot. So. Here we are. Since this is our first meeting, I think an appropriate way to begin would be to go around the table and let each member of the committee introduce him/herself, name, academic affiliation, social security number, haha, and so on. Starting over here to my right."

"Uh, yes. I am James Skinner from the Department of Psychology, College of Liberal Arts and a Full Professor," the first one said.

"All right. Thanks for helping us out James," said Munoz. "Next."

"Yes. I am Helen Huff from the Physical Therapy program in the College of Health Sciences and a Full Professor—and happy to announce that we have just received approval for our PhD program in Physical Therapy. Thank you."

"Thank you Helen. Congratulations on your program. Next."

"Good afternoon. My name is Allen McClure from the Department of Civil Engineering in the College of Engineering. I am a Full Professor."

"Thank you Allen. Reverent Brown, we'll skip you for right now and introduce you at the appropriate time. Next."

"Hi. My name is Carlos Figueroa. I am a Full Professor in the Department of Accounting in the College of Business Administration. Buenas tardes todos."

"And, Justin, we'll skip you for right now, saving you for later. We're just introducing the members of the committee for now. And last, but certainly not least—"

"Yes. My name is Diane Dewey, my specialty is Early Childhood Development and I am a Full Professor in the College of Education. So watch your language."

"Thank you Diane. And, again, thanks to all of you for being so accommodating at the last minute. All right. Let's get down to business. As you all know, a member of our community has come to the Grievance Committee to file a complaint against one of our faculty members, Dr. Justin Sandberg. According to the Systems bylaws, the filer has the right to appear before this committee in order to amplify and elaborate on his complaint. Also, again, according to the bylaws, the subject of the complaint has a right to appear before the committee to defend himself, with counsel, if he so desires. So, that's where we are."

"The filer of the grievance is Reverend Otis Brown the minister of [looking at his notes]—er—the Church of the Good Shepherd—which he is also the founder of. He received his undergraduate degree from Bob Jones University in Greenville, South Carolina and did graduate work in theology at Liberty University in Lynchburg Virginia—an on-line program, that is—Champions for Christ, I think it's called. Is that right?"

"Amen, brother."

"So. Reverend Brown. The floor is yours."

"Thank you Brother. D' you mind if I come to the front of the room."

"Not all," Oscar complied.

As he cantered toward the front of the room, he continued by saying, "I'm use t' standin in front of a congregation—so I can look everybody in the eye. That's jest my style—or habit, you might say, bein' a preacher. If you'll excuse me," he said piously and quietly, almost whispering. *"I've seen this act before,* Justin reminisced, *"What a phony."* The Reverend Brown was wearing a black suit, a white dress shirt, a subdued tie of uncertain color, black polished shoes, and carrying a black Bible close to his chest. *Must be in mourning for his life,* Justin thought. Reverend Brown whirled to confront his audience.

"Before I begin, I would like to call on Gawd fur his guid'nce fur all of us'n durin this critical moment," he began with his sanctimonious voice.

"What are you talking about," Oscar intervened from his chair at the head of the table.

"A prayer. To—you know—Gawd—fur his divine assistance."

"No," was Professor Munoz's authoritative and abrupt response.

"What? Why not?" he whined.

"This is a state institution."

"So?"

"You've never heard of the separation of church and state?" chairman Munoz clarified, "a fundamental principle of our American constitution."

"No wonder this country is goin' to hell in a handbasket. Howsomever, you cain't take my trust in the Lord away from me—"

"No ones--"

"—nor stop me from prayin on my own," whereupon the Reverend Brown veiled his eyes with one hand, turned his face heavenward, worked his lips in a silent, pathetic paean (*mumbo jumbo,* thought Justin), then said "amen," and scouted the faces staring at him. "I jest want to say first that I am deeply, sincerely, genu-winely concerned about the corruption of our youth, one of my main missions in life. That is my sole motivation for bein' here. I owe it to my Lord and Savior Jesus Christ to do everythaing in my power to keep society from goin' astray, to keep us from fallin' into the depths of rottenness and keep us out of the clutches of Satan, which society seems hell bent on doin'. I read my Bible, not only daily but hourly, I am in constant prayer to God, and I keep my mind focused on the purity of a rich spiritual life—and on heaven and my eternal reward."

"Reverend?" the chair cautioned, "spare us the sermon."

"No, no. I say these thangs to establish my credentials, so that you will know about my Godly life and my heavenly aspirations in order to sit in judgement on someone laike Professor Sandbun and so you will know how truly **sincere** I am. AND, if I suspect there is a person who matriculates with our youth (*he doesn't even know what the word matriculates means,* thought Justin), and corruptin' our youth, it is my Godly, sanctioned mission to root out that evil."

I think everyone can see that he is a sick human being and a cuckcoo."

At this point, Reverend Brown gave a summary, from his perspective, of the events regarding Shakespeare's *Othello* and his charge against

Sandberg of miscegenation, and the Biblical basis for his argument, going back to creation, the Tower of Babel, the creation of the races, and other Biblical citations. But he was not finished, oh no. He then began an attack on Justin Sandberg.

"Mr. Chairman, with your permission I would like to direct some questions to Professor Sandberg, just to clarify the picture a little more completely."

"All right."

"Professor Sandberg, I believe that I am correct in sayin' that you don't go to church—that you are not a religious person—that you are—er—in all likelihood—a atheist?"

"No. You cannot say that."

"You believe in a Supreme Bein?" Brown asked.

"Yes." Brown's eyes widened. "His name is William Shakespeare."

This evoked a gentle smirk from several around the table.

"This is not a jokin' matter!" The reverend practiced a severe face, smacked his left palm with his right fist, and continued, "Do you ever read the Bible."

"I grew up on the Bible." Everyone turned to look at him, *"and all his men looked at each other with a wild surmise—silent, upon a peak in Darien,"* Justin called Keats to mind. "I spent my boyhood in the Southern Baptist church."

The reverend Brown was flummoxed and looked at his notes and then up to his audience.

"How many times have you been married and divorced?"

"None of your fucking business!!" came Justin's inflamed retort.

"And were both of your wives Mexicans?" Brown continued.

"Mr. Chairman—" Justin invoked Professor Munoz, "are you going to allow this?"

"Reverend Brown—"

"A clear case of miscegenation. I hope everyone can see that I am establishin' Mr. Sandberg's moral code, based on his personal life and conduct. It is vita'ly import'nt." He sifted through several scraps of paper and then spoke directly to Professor Sandberg, "did you have a student by the name of Eva Diaz?"

Justin froze. *Where the fuck is he going with this."*

"Yes or no. Very simple."

"Yes I did," Justin softly spoke in order to gain control of his rage.

"And did you have intimacy with her?"

"Dr. Munoz—"

"I think we'd like an answer to the question," Oscar said to Justin. "That is a serious accusation."

"Not while she was my student," Justin spoke even more firmly soft, "no."

"And did you know a student at UTMP by the name of—let's see—uh, yeah—Norma Montoya?"

"Yes."

"And were you intimate with her?" Reverend Brown had put on his reading glasses and was peering over the top of them.

"She was never my student—and no, not while she was a student at the university," Justin truthfully clarified.

"Have you ever been known to attend wild student parties where there was heavy drinking and lewd, obscene behavior?" Reverend Brown continued on his jolly way.

Silence filled the void.

"Professor Sandberg?"

"I was coerced into attending one—once. But I had no alcohol and left early." *Man, he has really been digging.*

"But you wuz there."

"I've explained it already," Justin whispered.

"Let's see now, aw yes, here we go. Do you know a professor by the name of Eugene Betters in the Philosophy Department?"

"Yes."

"Have you ever socialized with him?"

"On occasion."

"And is he a professor who is known to—er—what am I lookin for here—er—date—or as we say—hit—on his female students?"

"What does that have to do with me?"

"A man is known by the company he keeps and *he* is known, among the students here, as someone who—er—exploits his female students. Yes?" Justin stared at the floor without blinking. "And have you every socialized with a professor in the English Department by the name of Harold Bradley?"

"We have shared a few drinks."

"And do you drink a lot?"

"Mr. Chairman—?"

"Well, your friend, Dr. Bradley, is a known alcoholic who misses many of his classes because he is drunk. The students all know this about him. Are you with him when he binge drinks?"

"Never."

He pleated his notes and submitted them to his inside coat pocket.

"Ladies and gentlemen, I think you can see what I am getting out with this interrogation. It is clear that Professor Sandberg brings to the classroom—and our innocent students—a pattern of questionable behavior—so that when he teaches a play like *Othello*, filled with filthy sin as it is, he clearly has no qualms about teaching a play whure a black man is having intercourse with a white girl. Make out of *that* what you will. Now, the question is, why have I gone to all this trouble, did all this research, wasted my valuable time away from my flock? What is it that I am seeking? At the very least, for Professor Sandberg to stop teaching this immoral play. At best, to let a professor like Professor Justin Sandberg go. He does not belong in a position where he can corrupt our youth. Thank you for your time and attention."

"*Surely these well-educated faculty members are not buying this bullshit,*" Justin thought to himself. "*And how do I address something so inanely stupid?*"

"Professor Sandberg," Professor Munoz turned to Justin, "do you have anything you'd like to say? Be our guest."

"Well," Justin stood up at his place at the table. "I too think better on my feet—being a college professor, but not a preacher. I hardly know where to begin, but as a generalization, I would say that I have never heard such a gross misrepresentation and distortion of the facts. I should like to say first, that I have been a professor at my beloved institution for over forty years, and in all these years, there has never been one iota of a complaint or hint or question about my moral conduct. NEVER!!! I have been guided by certain inviolable principles. Here, let me tell you what my career long philosophy has always been, from the first time I ever stepped into a college classroom as the professor. [He enumerates on his fingers.]

One: NEVER touch a student! Period; Two, never close my office door with a student inside; Three, never accept a gift, favor, money or anything from a student or his/her family (although there have been any number of offers); Four; never socialize, fraternize, share a drink, or anything socially with a student in any way, shape, or form. AND, I have never violated any of these principles. And I have never become involved with a student who was in my class, NEVER!! Those are the principles on which I have built my career, and I have faithfully abided by them for forty years. And you can ask anyone who knows me, that I am a person of my word. Everything else that has been presented here this afternoon are mere gross misrepresentations, distortions, exaggerations, and plain prevarications. I am not going to lower myself to answering baseless assertions. That is all I have to say. Thank you." And he sat down, and then stood back up. "Oh, one other thing, after over four hundred years of scrutiny, analysis, examination, study, discussion, ad infinitum, Shakespeare is not on trial here. Anyone who knows Shakespeare knows that he is a very moral playwright and that *Othello,* a story of a very good man who is destroyed by his wicked friend, is a very moral play featuring two very good people, Othello and his wife Desdemona, whose very goodness actually works against them in the plot, part of the Bard's ironical point. What the play is really about is the character of Iago, who seems on the surface to be a very good person (he reiterates "good" while looking at the reverend) who is actually evil incarnate and goes about to destroy his friend Othello out of sheer jealousy. Shakespeare's main point is that people may appear to be good while hiding a wicked heart. Any other reading of the play is just plain ignorance, stupidity, and bigotry. Thank you." Justin smugly and disgustedly declined into his seat, and then sliced a cursory glance at the reverend who, Justin could have sworn, was of a very light shade of white. *Asshole!* said Justin silently.

"Well." Dr. Munoz exhaled, fluttering his lips. "Thank you Dr. Sandberg. And—thank you Reverend Brown. Now. I think at this point we should excuse our two visitors while we go into executive session. Unless, anyone, has anything else they wish to ask the witnesses or say for the public record?" Munoz awaited a response and then expired, "all right. Thank you to our two witnesses. You don't need to wait around outside. I'll be in touch tomorrow with both of you," upon which utterance, Munoz arose and proceeded to open the door for the visitors who withdrew into the hall. Outside, the Reverend offered his hand to Justin, to which offer Justin said, "Fuck you," and strolled away.

As fast as Justin had galloped to this meeting before hand, as slowly now he sauntered back to his office, where he unhurriedly deposited himself into his desk chair and mused about the week he had just brought to a terminal point.

"*Damn!!*" was the only word he could think of to describe his week and his feelings. "*I thought it was going to be a great week when it first started off—and it turns out to be one of the worse weeks of my life. I need some stroking,*" consoled himself as he reached for his phone. "Ellen," and spoke her name. "Where are you? [beat] Home? Hey, could I join you. [beat] Thanks. I'll pick up a couple of bottles of vino. [beat] Great! I'll see you shortly," and disconnected from her. "Boyohboy! Just what I need to take my mind off of everything," and he began to quietly sing "All My Loving. . . Close your eyes and I'll kiss you. / Tomorrow I'll miss you. / Remember I'll always be true. / And the while I'm away I'll write home every day. / And I'll send all my loving to you . . . All my loving. . . something, something. . . Darling I'll be true" as he closed his office door and thought of Ellen's cushy warm little body. "The perfect antidote. I'll bury myself in her caring spirit."

42

Justin consulted with his messages on his office phone and his cell all Friday evening (much to Ellen's annoyance), all day Saturday, all day Sunday and extending into Sunday evening and received nothing from Oscar Munoz, Chair of the Grievance Committee, who had promised that he would be in touch after the members scattered from their conclusive meeting. There are those people who, on the expectation of pressing news, have the ability to dismiss it from their conscious bank and proceed with other business, other activities, or their lives, as though nothing was at stake, nothing was at issue, nothing in the whole universe mattered. Justin Sandberg was not among those types. As cool as he tried to be, as indifferent as he pretended to be, as nonchalant as he seemed to be, there was in his breast and head a raging, tortuous, agonizing conflagration of expectation, doubt, and anxiety. It was a weekend of a living hell, hades, purgatory, and all the burning pits and agonies of Dante's *Inferno* with the searing tagline of "abandon hope all ye who enter here." Justin was a remarkably bright person, smart, well-educated, learned, knowledgeable, scholarly, articulate, with Shakespeare always right below the surface of his mind; none of these powerful attributes came to his rescue but indeed exacerbated his torment because of an overactive mind. The weekend was a chapter to be forgotten in the Book of Life, except for the moments when he clung to Ellen, psychologically and physically.

As the semester was spending itself into mid-to-late November, the Director of the show, a man by the name of Omfa (OMF), otherwise known as Old Man Fate (or if you like, a woman by the name of Owfa, (OWF), otherwise known as Old Woman Fate) was mysteriously and secretively putting on an extravagant dramatic show, with lots of light and sound cues, costumes, and live actors, i.e., human beings. Only He/

She held the script, there to give the cue when needed and when one had forgotten the lines. Justin knew some of the actors/characters, and how they played their parts, but he was in the dark, as in an unlighted theatre, and had not a clue as to what the plot line was. It is a strange sensation to be a part of a drama in which one knows one's lines, the conflicts, the plot, the characters, the setting, the dialogue, the situation, the crisis, the climax (so to speak), and, god forbid, the themes. But ineluctable Destiny was working things out, and Justin surrendered himself with *Que sera, sera,* stopped torturing himself and went on with his daily bread of teaching his classes, doing research, dedicating himself to his perusals, and seeking oblivion in the charms of Ellen.

43

While Justin peregrinated through his days and nights, unbeknownst to him counter forces were accumulating, starting with an innocuous phone call from the Chair of the Philosophy Department, Dr. David Small, to professor Eugene Betters, Associate, Tenured Professor in the Philosophy Department:

"Eugene? This is David Small."

"Yeah." Betters was curt and guarded.

"Gene, I need to talk to you. Are you busy right now?"

"I can get unbusy in a hurry," Betters suspiciously and warily responded.

"Can you come up to my office right now?"

"I'll be right there," Betters spontaneously replied, slammed the phone and, one flight up from the basement where his office was, corporealed in the departmental outer office where the secretary was positioned as guardian, like the dog Cerberus again.

"He's waiting for you. Go on in," was Terri's reception to Betters.

"Have a seat." Professor Small was standing behind the chairperson's desk as he semaphored Betters with his hand.

Betters's gangly body lowered itself into a chair in front of the desk with "what the fuck's up?" Small came around from behind the desk, passed Betters's seat, causing Betters's to flinch defensively, reached for the door and closed it. Betters's eyes traced him back to the chair's chair and reiterated, "what th' fuck's up?"

"Gene. You'd be a lot better off if you didn't use that kind of language here around the office where you never know who might hear you, like students, secretaries, colleagues--"

"What the fuck!!!"

Professor Small stared in disbelief for what seemed several eons while Betters squirmed like a worm on a fish hook with expanding hostility and defensiveness. What Professor Small was finally processing was the lifting of the veil and the rising realization that Eugene Betters really did not have any social acumen, awareness, relatedness, empathy, compassion, graces, neighborliness, collegiality, breeding, civility, consideration, courtesy, decorum, etiquette—not one ethical gland nor one moral organ in his body. *The committee's recommendation is extremely wise*, Small thought.

"Before we discuss the recommendation which comes from the ad hoc committee, created by the administration to study your situation," Small explained-

"My situation?"

"Correct. The committee does have a recommendation."

"I'd like to hear it."

"Be assured you will. But let me lay down a couple of principles."

"What fuckin' principles?"

"The first thing I want you to understand, above all else, is that this is not about sex. Do you grasp that? This is not some puritanical, anti-sin, moralistic position the university is taking. There are issues which are far more important, far more reaching, far more significant, than having sex with a student."

"Yeah, yeah, I get it."

"I don't want you consigning to the university the position that we are some hick-town, narrow-minded, unsophisticated, rigid religious freaks. Ok?"

"Whatever."

"The primary purpose of this university—and the reason the state of Texas supports us, need I remind you—is the education of our youth. In other words, teaching, and for effective teaching to happen, there has to be an attitude of respect, of teachers respecting the students, and **students respecting the teachers**. And when that is gone, teaching effectiveness vanishes. Are you following me?"

"Yeah, yeah."

"When a teacher has a reputation for taking advantage of his position by hitting—if that's the word—on students, that respect is gone—along with his effectiveness as a teacher." Professor Small leaned back in his chair.

"Are you finished?"

"I'm just getting started." Betters looked at his watch. "Do you have to be somewhere?"

"I'm supposed to be working on an article for a journal."

"Right now this is more important," Small said.

"You think so?"

"Your job is on the line," Small whispered. Silence stung the air.

"Really?"

"You'll see. Ok. On top of that, there is the matter of the respect, integrity, dignity and ethical codes of our profession. In other words, there are some things you just don't do to damage the sacredness of your professional duties and integrity."

"Sacredness? Shit." Betters scoffed.

"I'm going to ignore that. Additionally, this university holds a position of trust in this community which gives us incredible support—"

"Like the football team—such as it is."

"You're really doing everything you can to make me dislike you, aren't you," Small queried.

"I don't give a shit whether you like me or not."

"We are important in this community, and ninety-five percent of our student body comes from this area." Small was constraining himself to keep from kicking Betters out of his office. "Whether you realize it or not, we have the enthusiastic support of our graduates because we have changed their lives for the better." Small stop to ponder the likelihood that he was gaining no yardage with Betters.

Betters remained stolid and stoic, in true philosophical fashion.

"Finally—"Small detected a sibilant, unvoiced "thank god"—"and this is the most important point of all; your behavior with students is ceding power to them over you."

"How so?"

"You can't see that?"

"Apparently not."

"You are putting yourself at their mercy, in terms of grades, blackmail, obligations, indebtedness, reputation—and again respect—in countless ways—" Small halted out of utter futility, and Betters squirmed again as though Small may have been making a slight indentation in Betters's armored psyche.

At this point, Small cautiously slid into a full, detailed presentation of the committee's recommendation that Betters be banned from campus and to teach all his classes on-line from home, or anywhere where there were no students present. For the first time in their meeting, or perhaps for the first time in the little time Small had known Betters, Betters blanched and seemed flummoxed, rattled, disoriented, exposed--unflip, uncool, unsophisticated, ill. Both sat immovably erect and wordless (Betters had finally put squirming aside), until Small said oh so softly, "of course the other recommendation, which I rejected, was castration." Betters snapped his head up and slowly, imperceptibly, moved his hand to his private parts with a grimace.

"Of course, you should know that I don't go along with the committee's recommendation," Small said softly.

"You don't?"

"My recommendation would be to fire your ass, especially after this meeting, which has made me come to the realization that we really don't need someone like you on our faculty."

Betters lifted his limp, languid, and lengthy body to full statue, tentatively turned his torso toward the exit, with his head bowed, stopped, and mumbled, "fuck you."

"Yeah, and fuck you," was Doctor Small's uncharacteristic and mockingly dry retort.

As Betters stormed into the hall outside the Philosophy Departmental office, Ole Man Fate, or Woman, was operative again as Justin happened to stroll by Betters, who was steaming down the hall and whom Justin hailed with a warm, "Gene, how goes it, my man?" to which Betters returned a nasty "fuck you!" and continued snorting on his solitary path.

"What the--?" was all Justin could supply to the situation in consternation and puzzlement and continued on to his class in the next building, whereupon he encountered in a parallel hallway his colleague and friend Harold Bradley, who responded to Justin's welcoming salutation with glacial silence and the coldest shoulder Justin had ever seen as Bradley turned his back on him and proceeded in quietude. With his approaching lecture pressing on his mind, Justin shrugged it off and entered his classroom with "*fuck trying to be a friend.*" Unbeknownst to Justin, Bradley had just received a notification from Professor Arnold Lawing regarding Bradley's appearance before the Faculty Senate committee, whose names were attached to the memo, including that of one Professor Justin Sandberg. In Bradley's panicked mind and totally misreading the situation, Bradley was silently accusing Justin of betrayal. Justin, as a committee member, would receive the same missive after his next class and all would become clear, sort of, as Justin eventually consoled his amigo with the awareness that his role on the committee, as Justin perceived it, was to defend his friend Bradley.

44

"I have asked Dr. Bradley to wait just a moment outside while we conduct a little business," Professor Lawing launched the Faculty Senate committee meeting with a few thoughts of his own and continued with "I thought it less awkward this way than to have him sitting here before the meeting begins with us and having to engage in idle chitchat. I explained that the format was to let him give his presentation first and then we can open up a Q and A session, if you so desire. Any questions?"

Justin's hand reached for the ceiling, and Lawing nodded his head Justin's way. "Who is going to present the AA proposal to him?"

"I'll make the initial presentation, and then if anyone wishes to make any corrections or additions, he/she will be given a chance to do so," Lawing elaborated.

"I'd like to stay out of it as much as possible, being in the same department with him, but, I know him and he is one hardheaded human being; I think it needs to be made clear that his participation in AA is a condition of employment, that he doesn't have a choice as to whether to attend meetings or not—and still have a job," Justin offered.

"We'll make that abundantly clear. Anyone else?" Professor Lawing offered time-space and then clenched with "Ok. Let's bring him in," whereupon he eased to the door and was heard to say from the hall, "Professor Bradley, would you like to come in now" and a mumbled response was heard from outside. Justin cringed and slid a little lower in his chair, hopping to be inconspicuous—to no avail.

"Dr. Bradley, you can sit here to my left, here at the head of the table, so everyone can see you. Everyone," he appraised the faces turned his way, then "this is Professor Harold Bradley from the Department of English,

College of Liberal Arts." Mumbled greetings lapped around the table and then he acknowledged Bradley sitting next to him, who seemed a little disdainful and condescending.

"Dr. Bradley, you probably don't know some of our committee members so let me start by introducing everybody. To my right here is Professor Betsy Day from the School of Nursing in the College of Health Science. Next to her is Professor John Eastman, from Biology in the College of Science. Then we have Professor Edwin Mason from the Marketing Department in the College of Business Administration. Next we have Professor Kathy Strong from the History Department in the College of Liberal Arts. I think you two know each other?"

They both muttered, "yes we do."

"And the next member, I think, needs no introduction to you—"

"No."

"But, in the spirit of equal treatment, let me present Professor Justin Sandberg from the English Department in the College of Liberal Arts. So. There. Let's get started. First off, I don't believe it's necessary to go into the details of what the issue is here. We are all familiar with the situation, so, as I mentioned to you, Dr. Bradley, I deemed it appropriate to allow you to make your presentation first, which can then be followed by a Q and A session, if necessary. Dr. Bradley?" Professor Lawing then placed himself into the seat at the head of the table, with Bradley and Day on each side of him.

"Thank you Professor Lawing." Bradley rose to his feet while everyone quizzically frowned at the uncertainty of what Bradley was going to do. He commenced with, "and thank you everyone for your time and allowing me to present my story." *"I never knew he could be so gracious,"* thought Justin. Bradley then started moving from chair to chair and placing a sheaf of paper at each person's space. *"A gentle enough beginning"* thought Justin. Bradley was presently standing at the head of the table with a journal-seeming object in his hand which he proceeded to hold up for everyone to notice.

"Ladies and gentlemen," he embarked, "what I have in my hand here is a copy of a publication titled *The Chaucer Journal*, which is published by the International Chaucer Society. This particular edition was published two years ago and opposite the title page is a full-page picture." He holds the volume aloft and moves it from left to right and then back again so that everyone could see the picture. "For those who cannot see it very clearly, this is a picture of MOI, yours truly." Some audible reactions followed.

"The reason I am featured in this particular issue is that this issue of the journal was dedicated to, [reading], "Dr. Harold Bradley of the University of Texas at Mountain Pass in recognition of his invaluable, timeless, and distinguished contributions to the area of Chaucerian Studies. His contributions over the years have been unsurpassed in the history of Chaucer scholarship worldwide, and the deepest gratitude is owed to him from the International Chaucer Society for his advancement of the study of Chaucer."

"Ladies and gentlemen, the first thing I want to point out is the recognition which I have brought to this institution, as cited in the dedication. The second thing I want to note is that this is a rare and supreme honor for a scholar in my field of expertise. And the third thing I want to note is that my cv is published with this dedication, which I have copied for each of you to have in your hand."

"Ok, I draw your attention to my resume which you have in front of you.

If you will study it closely, the first thing you will notice is that I have six books which have been published by very distinguished presses, including Harvard, Yale, Johns Hopkins, University of New Mexico, University of Texas, and so on. I should also point out that my resume has over fifty articles published by prestigious journals all around the world, and I have given hundreds of presentations of scholarly papers—and I have received numerous awards, honors, and acknowledgements from every imaginable prestigious organization. Ladies and gentlemen, do you *understand* the kind of recognition and—and—and—distinction I have brought to this insignificant, remote little university in the middle of the American southwest desert?" Bradley paused for absorption purposes, roamed the room with his retinas, and remarked, "does anyone have any questions?"

Everyone stilled.

Bradley added, "I dare say that few, if any, in this room, or in the whole university for that matter, can claim such national and international recognition in their area of expertise, as I have received," his eyes searched the faces turned to him, "and you want to fire somebody with this kind of distinction? It would create as much turmoil and—and—and--ugliness as opening Pandora's Box—or worse." Bradley seemed to have exhausted his argument and stood staring vacantly at the heavens (in supplication?) while Justin wondered *"what's happening? I noticed he didn't mention his teaching."*

Professor Lawing life-saved him with, "Thank you Professor Bradley. You may be seated," which Harold Bradley promptly complied with.

"Professor Bradley," Arnold Lawing braved on, "this committee has been struggling with how to resolve this problem—"

"What problem?" Bradley asked.

Lawing paused, then pawed his left palm with his right palm, then proceeded with "the problem of chronic absenteeism from your classes."

"Oh. That."

"Yes, and we know the underlying cause of it which is what we have been wrestling with and trying to find a solution for, short of recalling your tenure. Are you with me?"

"I've had the flu," came a hoarse response.

At this point, Dr. Lawing began an oblique, seemingly irrelevant, description, in great detail, of an organization by the name of Alcoholics Anonymous, and its effectiveness, a presentation which lasted some fifteen to twenty minutes, at the end of which Dr. Bradley said,

"I think I know where this is going."

"Yes. Let me continue," bulldozed Professor Lawing and proceeded to lay out the details of the committee's recommendation that the "terms of his employment" will be daily attendance at AA meetings for a minimum of ninety days and a continuance in the organization thereafter; Lawing ventured on with a lengthy description of the minutia involved. Everyone awaited Bradley's attitude and acceptance until he final exhaled with,

"Whew! That is going to take up a lot of my time. How am I going to have time for my scholarship?"

"It'll take up far less time that binge drinking," Lawing referenced the idea for the first time in the meeting. "What is your reaction to our proposal?" Lawing went on trying to probe Bradley's willingness to cooperate. "Do you have any questions?"

"Yes. Just one: whose stupid idea was this?"

Everyone turned to look at Professor Justin Sandberg, with eye corners, who was staring down at nothing.

"Oh," said Dr. Bradley, then slaughtered Justin with a look.

"Ok, as I said," Lawing continued, "we will open up for a Q and A, in the name of judiciousness. So." Justin noted his "*So's* again.

Chairman Lawing identified the raised hand of Professor Betsy Day from Nursing who turned to Bradley with, "Have you ever had any association with—or attendance at—AA meetings??

"I tried it once or twice a long time ago."

"They do incredible work," she gently contributed.

Professor Lawing then nodded to Kathy Strong from History who asked, "if you don't mind my asking, how close are you to retiring?" Justin knew that she was a strong, bold, and outspoken woman but this caught him by surprise as he turned reluctantly to look at Bradley who seemed to waiver between abashment and arrogance as embodied in his hesitancy.

"Actually," Bradley began, and then stopped with, "I hadn't thought about it."

"Anyone else?" Lawing flung the invitation across the table and waited. "Professor Bradley, I just want to say in conclusion that this committee—and the university—are very aware of your invaluable, remarkable contributions to the world of scholarship. We are not unmindful of it and we appreciate what you have done in that area. All right? But, I remind you, that classroom effectiveness is also a major part of our mission as a state supported, EDUCATIONAL institution."

"I bring so much to my classrooms," Bradley pleaded.

"When you are there, and stay on the subject." Truth was surrounding Bradley every way he fiddled.

Bradley burrowed his face into his hands and muttered an inarticulate sound.

"*Embarrassment? Frustration? Anger? Resentment? Despair? Disappointment?* Justin tried to speculate about what was transpiring with his friend but could not fathom it.

"I think we are about finished with you," Lawing broke in, "Just one question before you go: what is your initial reaction to the proposal? Whatta you think about it?" All heads turned to Bradley and glared inquisitively at the slumped figure at the head of the table which then seemed to look up to contemplate a fluorescent light at a forty-five degrees angle above him and then joined the present moment with,

"Could I have some time to think about it?" He suddenly seemed so aged.

"How much time do you need?" It was such a quick response that it seemed as though Lawing had already anticipated Bradley's request.

"Forty-eight hours?" Bradley spoke very softly.

"Just keep in mind what the alternative is if you reject our offer," Lawing stood and extended his hand to Bradley, which Bradley received as he awkwardly rose, "I'll give you a call in forty-eight hours," as he looked at his watch.

Justin entertained grave doubts about whether his colleague could conquer his insidious disease, as he maneuvered his car down the early dusk highway and into the encroaching darkness.

45

Justin had smugly congratulated himself for his, as he perceived it, brilliant and compassionate solutions for two friends who were assured of losing their jobs, but halfway through the process, he had begun to sense that his friends were not as persuaded of the nobility of his efforts as he was, and he did not look forward to an encounter with either of them, in consequence of which he submerged himself into his teaching, his scholarship, and Ellen, who was a mighty comfort to him and who happened to be sitting in Justin's office one day when there came a rap on his door. Justin looked at Ellen, who shrugged her shoulders and he shrugged his back at her with a loving smile.

"Pasale!" Justin called out in Spanish.

Betters poked his head in the a-jarred door and said, "does that mean come in?"

"Not to you it doesn't."

"Oops, you have company," Betters stopped and politely managed a one-step retreat.

"Gene, this is Ellen Cohen. You've heard me mention her. Ellen, this is Eugene Betters from Philosophy," Justin said.

"I'll catch you later."

"Nono. It's ok. Ellen and I are close professional friends. We share a lot together—especially professional issues," Justin said, "have a seat." Justin surmised, probably correctly, that Betters had in mind to confront Justin about the proposal which had been issued to him about the remote management of his classes and the on-line manner of instruction, and that perhaps Ellen's presence might placate, or ameliorate, Betters' display of dissatisfaction, destitution, and disruption, which he had seemingly planned to display and which it seemingly did, at first.

Betters glanced at Justin and then at Ellen, then back to Justin and then back to Ellen and began with, "Ok. If you say so. Well." He suspended everything momentarily. "I'll be honest with you, both of you since you insist, I feel like I've been fucked."

"How so?" Justin asked as Ellen politely listened and observed.

"Well, first of all, I love the classroom experience, interacting with students, creating a dialogue, generating some intellectual electricity, confronting and exchanging ideas, all that excitement, and so on, and I feel that a major component of my enjoyment and satisfaction of my career—or, profession—is being denied me—has been taken away from me."

"But—"Justin attempted to intervene.

"NO! WAIT! Let me tell you something, just as a footnote, that I have done nothing wrong. Ok? I think I have been misunderstood, maligned, misrepresented, and so on, and that I am totally innocent. Because my relationship with my students is my fucking business and nobody else's."

"Not really," Elaine quietly inserted.

"Yes, really. In fact, why do you think I went into this stupid profession in the first place? Hunh? Love of learning? Bullshit. Educating the youth? Double bullshit. Building a better society? Triple bullshit. To get rich? Quadruple bullshit. The main reason I went into this goddamn profession was so I could be around hot chicks every day—"

"Whoa," Justin exclaimed.

"Really?" Ellen could not restrain her shock at such audacity and blatant disregard for basic decency.

"LET ME CONTIUNE—without being interrupted—" Pause. "Thank you. Moreover, I feel like I am being singled out, nay, even being prejudiced against—like some type of—of—of freak around the department—some type of pariah—or—leper—and the laughingstock of the university—and it's fucking embarrassing to me—personally."

"Now Gene, think about the—"

"I AM NOT FINISHED! And on top of everything else, I feel betrayed."

"By whom?!"

"By you—that's who. Here I thought you were my friend, and you, I have come to find out, are the very person who concocted this fucking scheme to bar me from the campus."

"But don't you understand?!!! You were in danger—"

"The one person who I thought I could trust—"

"Whom."

"Whom. A regular Judas—a—a—a—asshole!"

"Hold on just a minute here." Ellen rose to her feet, not being very tall she did not have too far up to go, almost at eye level with Betters who was seated. "Let me tell you something, mister: you know what you should do? [expecting no answer to a rhetorical question], you know what you should do [repetition for emphasis], you should fall down on your knees right here on the office floor and kiss Dr. Sandberg's feet and thank him for saving your job. The only thing you should be feeling right now is heartfelt, everlasting gratitude, because were it not for Dr. Sandberg, you would be out on the street panhandling and sleeping in a homeless shelter and starving to death. Whether you recognize it or not—or admit it or not—he saved your ass. He performed the service of a true friend. Frankly, if it were up to me, I'd let them can your ass because you deserve nothing less. And speaking as a feminist, your attitude toward women is disgustingly medieval, and, and, evil—but I won't even go into that now which would be another hour's lecture." Ellen stood momentarily then dropped into her chair with "that's all I have to say."

Silence skirted the walls of Justin's office while all three remained momentarily in stunned silence.

"Well. We know how she feels." Justin smiled proudly with admiration but unsurprised at Ellen's rectitude.

"I gotta go," were Betters's words of acquiescence as he towered up and vanished through Justin's office door. Justin smiled at Ellen and Ellen stuck her tongue out at Justin.

"Good job."

46

Thanksgiving was looming somewhere over the autumn desert floor as Justin continued doing his duty to his classes with extreme diligence, attention and conscientiousness, ignoring the 'whirligig of time," when one day he received an email which stated:

> "This is to notify members of the Grievance Committee that an emergency meeting is being called for Tuesday at 3:00pm in the conference room next to my office. There are two items on the agenda: progress report of committee's deliberations and a response to Reverend Brown's request to appear before the committee again. Please RSVP ASAP.
>
> Oscar Munoz, Chair, Faculty Senate Grievance Committee
> Cc: Reverend Otis Brown; Dr. Justin Sandberg"

Dr. Sandberg continued on his material Monday moments and movements until the day was exhausted, and so was he, eagerly anticipating his "stagger day," the next day, Tuesday, being one of them, of no classes which had now been marred by the announcement of a Grievance Committee meeting. But Justin had now become impervious to the nuisance of such events and marched on with his meandering Monday until on a moon-wrapped Monday night he wrapped himself in the oblivion of motionless sleep.

At 3:00 o'clock on Tuesday afternoon, Justin tussled in his chair in the conference room abutting the office of Oscar Munoz, when another

Of Woe or Wonder

event was marred by another irritant, the arrival of one Reverend Otis Brown, who circled the table shaking hands with the members of the committee, until he came to Justin, behind whose chair he stood waiting for a salutation from Justin who never flinched, flexed, nor flicked a muscle.

"Aw-rite then," he said and then waddled around to a vacant chair, at which moment Professor Oscar Munoz entered through the open door and greeted everyone most heartily.

"Again," Dr. Munoz began, "I want to thank you for attending this meeting on such short notice. I, and the wheels of justice, appreciate it (*he's always trying to be funny*, Justin noted). The first thing I want to do is bring everyone, and especially our two combatants (*har har*), up to date on our deliberations. We have met several times, well, two to be exact, in executive sessions and have sort of mapped out our procedural strategy. We have also created some research assignments which each member of the committee is engaged in. To bring the two of you up-to-date (as he nodded to Reverend Brown and then to Sandberg), we have created a list of charges as filed by Reverend Brown, and each member of the committee has been assigned one of the charges and is researching his or her topic.. We take these charges very seriously, Reverend Brown--"

"God Bless You, brother."

"--and it is our duty to investigate each and every one of them and to arrive at the answer to the question: is this charge valid or is it not. Everyone has been out in the field, so to speak, and we should be producing answers pretty soon. So (*again*). That is where things stand as of this moment. Any questions? [pause] From either of the two of you?"

"Yes."

"Dr. Sandberg."

"Are you interviewing students?"

"Absolutely. That is one of our main sources," Oscar said as he looked off in space as though double-checking the accuracy of his answer. "Anything else?"

"Yes. In your investigating these negative charges with students, are you also soliciting opinions from students about *my* reputation for honesty, forthrightness, dedication, integrity, and effectiveness as a teacher?"

"That is part of the whole picture, yes indeed. When one does research, one does not investigate only the negative aspects of a question. In the pursuit of truth, as you know Dr. Sandberg, one seeks the whole picture, negative, positive, and neutral. The members of this committee make no pre-judgements, like all competent researchers, which they all are, and seek only objective, verifiable, inductive—TRUTH."

"How soon will you have an answer," came the twang of Otis Brown.

"When we have finished."

"But, but, but, how much time—"

"I apologize, Reverend, I was being flip. Let me just say that all the members of the committee have been working diligently—much to the neglect of their own research agendas, I might add—at gathering information, taking notes, and so on—they are all responsible citizens of the university community—trust me. I would like to speculate that during the month long winter recess, that we will have finished our work. We shall proceed as expeditiously as possible and submit our report, hopefully, to the Faculty Senate at the beginning of the spring semester."

"This will go before the entire Faculty Senate?"

"What did you think was going to happen to the results of our investigations?"

"I—"

"You attacked the career of a very respected faculty member. That is not a frivolous matter. That is a life-altering, career-destroying maneuver on your part and we shall see it through to the end—one way or another—either completely exonerated, that is not guilty, or guilty and destroyed."

Reverend Brown seemed to slip down in his chair a little and suddenly seemed quite small.

"Now, Reverent Brown, I believe that you have come up with some additional charges against Professor Sandberg? Is that correct?"

"Yessir. But now I see, considerin' what has just come to pass here, that you people are all on Professor Sandberg's side and agenst me. You people are gangin' up on me. I will not—"

"NO SIR!!! That is unequivocally not true! We are here to deal with the facts wherever they lead us!"

Justin, along with everyone else in the room, except for Oscar Munoz, marble-statued in place to prevent looking at the Reverend Brown who, everyone assumed, must be slightly humiliated by Munoz's aggressive response and suppression of the reverend. Silence permeated the moment, and then Professor Munoz proceeded with,

"Now, Reverend Brown, we convened this special meeting at your request with the caveat that you have additional information, as I just indicated. Is that correct?"

"Yes *sir*, that is absolutely correct. May I," as he pointed toward the front and proceeded there, talking and walking simultaneously, "I have been doing some more diggin', interviewin', and—and—and—gatherin' information and have come up with information which, I thank, would be of great interest to this committee—as you continue your investigation. Now, I don't seek to harm nobody—not another soul, but on the other hand I have a moral responsibility to speak up when I find something that is wrong and rotten, specially when it is somebody who touches the lives of young people on a daily basis. Because what I have found is deeply, deeply, **deeply, profoundly** disturbin' and I know that the university would want to know about this—and will eventually thank me for the service I have done to this community and the young people in it. So. If I may," picking up his briefcase, opening it, and extracting a rather large sheaf of papers, "what I have here, as you will—"

BANG! BANG! BANG! BANG! BANG! BANG! wildly thumped the door.

Brown ceased, the committee members slyly side-wised at each other, and Munoz stood with,

"Let me see what this is. Excuse us just a moment, Reverend Brown," by which time Oscar had opened the door to divulge three police officers bunched outside the doorway.

"May I help you," Munoz was heard to ask as the committee members craned their necks in every tortuous position to steal a glance.

"Yessir. We apologize for interrupting whatever business you people are tending to but this is a matter of some urgency. May we come inside? We don't like to do business out in a hallway with gawkers looking on."

"Yes, yes, come on in," Oscar said in his most genial tone. Most people, who are responsible citizens, have learned that politeness and cooperation are the most fertile and least barren maneuvers when facing the law.

The committee members held possession of very dumbfounded, perplexed, and flabbergasted facial expressions while Justin observed that there were two campus police officers and one city policeman—"*This must be serious business; it couldn't possibly involve me, could it?*" Justin mused.

"Good afternoon," the lead officer began, "my name is Sergeant Lopez of the UTMP Campus Police, this is my associate on the campus police unit, Corporal Chavez, and the third officer here is Sergeant Perez from the Mountain Pass city police department. Again, we apologize for intruding like this but when it comes to police work the motto is *carpe diem*—"

"What?!!!" Justin loudly could not restrain himself. "Do you know what *Carpe diem* means?"

"Yessir. Seize the day. I have a degree from this fine institution of higher learning, Criminal Justice," Sergeant Lopez said. He had already won his audience.

"In police work, it is all in the timing, sirs, and ma'ams, and when the opportunity presents itself, whatever the circumstances may be, you have to—(he looked at Professor Sandberg)—"seize the moment."

"Day," said Justin.

"Yes, day. Whatever the circumstances may be—as on the present occasion," Sergeant Lopez justified.

"What can we help you with, Sergeant Lopez?" Dr. Munoz graciously asked.

"Yes. Do you have here among you, one Reverend Otis Brown?"

Disbelief paralyzed the room, iced it, froze it, embalmed it.

Professor Munoz temporized, truly uncertain as to what to do, and gave a weak, "why do you ask?"

Sergeant Lopez, recognizing the strategy of non-commital-ness and avoidance of self-implication, bypassed the Chair with, "does anyone here answer to that name?"

Most heads were bowed in non-involvement and detachment, until a trembling voice answered, "yes."

"Ah! Good," said Sergeant Lopez, recognizing the source of the answer, and strode to the side of Brown standing at the head of the table.

"Mr. Otis Brown. You are under arrest," Sergeant Lopez officially pronounced. "You have the right to remain silent, anything you say can beheld against you, and you have the right to legal counsel. Hands behind your back, sir," and as quickly as skill and habit would allow it, Corporal Chavez had snapped the handcuffs to both wrists and Sergeant Lopez continued with "let's go."

"Where are you taking him?" Oscar Munoz inquired.

"The county jail."

"May I—may I—bring my papers," was Brown's weakened query.

"We'll send someone for them later. Let's go," and Lopez marched toward the door with his—suspect—in tow.

"Officer Lopez?" Professor Munoz attempted an intervention.

"Yessir?" came Lopez's response as he halted his pace.

"May I—may I—(*seems to be catching*, thought Justin)—ask what the charges are," Oscar shyly asked.

"Not until he has been officially booked. Sorry. We're out of here, let's go" and the four disappeared out the door and down the hall while the committee sat in pure, unadulterated, stunned quietude and total dumbfoundedness. It was a moment that would register itself forever in the permanent memory of everyone present, but especially Justin—and in the recesses of the University of Texas at Mountain Pass.

"Professor Sandberg?" Justin raised his eyes to Munoz who asked "did you blow the whistle on him?"

"Not I."

"I've never dealt with anything like this before. I don't think there is a precedent, but I would say that it looks like you are off the hook--for right now, if there is no one here to charge you." Professor Munoz's, as well as the committee's, *raison d'etre* just walked out the door, or should one say was suspended, or better yet, arrested in mid-performance.

No one knew how to proceed, nor knew what the protocol was, nor knew what to say, nor how to act (should we just sit here, stand up, make a motion, take a vote, walk out the door like the accuser did); do *Roberts' Rules of Order* cover this unexpected eventuality, does a report have to be made to the Faculty Senate, is a motion to adjourn in order; everything was in the interrogative, speculative mode.

"So."(*again*, Justin registered Munoz's habit). "Not knowing what else to do, I think we can adjourn, temporarily at least, until I've had a chance to consult with the president and executive board of the Faculty Senate.

So. (*again*) Just stay tuned until I can find some answers. This meeting is adjourned."

Justin sauntered oh so slowly and tentatively, snailing back across the campus, his head thrust forward and downward in deep deliberation and contemplation, actually talking softly aloud to himself: "That is the most bizarre thing I've ever experienced," finding only feeble words with which to wonder and wander, in spite of being a college English professor. "Sometimes words just aren't up to the task," as he meandered on his way and then he thought about OMF (or OWF), "especially when Old Man Fate intrudes his power into people's business," and again he thought about the feeling of being in a drama in which he does not know his lines nor have a copy of the script.

Justin, the type of person who believes in controlling his own destiny, makes a valiant effort at all times to be in charge of his existence and every move on a regular basis, suddenly felt the fatal, falling feeling of unfathomableness in the hands of fate.

47

"Justin! I need to talk to you," came the hoarse voice which leaped from his office phone into his ear. Justin was still sitting in his office rehabilitating from the electric shock of the arrest of Reverend Brown when his office phone nabbed him with Harold Bradley rasping on the other end.

"Are you on campus?" Justin wanted to know.

"No," Bradley answered.

"Well—what--?"

"Can we meet somewhere?" Bradley throated on.

"Where?"

"The College Inn?" Bradley suggested.

"Is that a good idea?"

"Why?"

"Well, uh, never mind," Justin dared not venture to suggest anything indelicate at this point about his drinking problem.

"What? You think I might get drunk?"

"Give me a chance to pack up my stuff. I'll meet you there in twenty minutes," Justin said reluctantly as he moved the receiver through space toward the phone's base and sat in consternation. *How am I going to help this guy if he can't help himself?* Justin bundled up his necessities, trudged to his car, and pondered that very pertinent question as he drove musingly to the appointed place.

"Let's find a quiet corner," Justin said to Bradley as he approached him sitting at the bar, and they were soon settled in a conversational location at a table at the back of the room.

"Well," Justin feebly began—

"You fuckin sonofabitching, assholing, cocksucking, twofaced, slimball, scum-of-the-earth, shitass, turdface, piece of vomit and pathetic excuse of a human being? What the fuck have you done to me?!!!" Bradley was a deep shade of crimson.

Justin deciphered, decoded, disentangled, disengaged, and defaulted from speech and accurately read the subtext.

"I hate your goddamn, fucking, good-for-nothing, pretty-boy guts."

Justin decided to sit this dance out.

"What the fuck have you done to me?!!!"

"You said that already," Justin tranquilly offered.

"Yes, I did, and I'll say it a thousand more frigging times until I have an answer. You have ruined my career, ruined my life, ruined my marriage, ruined my happiness, ruined my reputation, ruined my respectability, ruined my—my—my—aw fuck!—ruined everything."

"Your marriage?"

"Virginia's not speaking to me."

"How many drinks have you had?"

"None of your goddamn fucking business!"

"I see."

"How!? How!? How!? Could you do this to me?"

"I—"

"Ah shit. Let's have a drink," and summoned, "Miss--?"

Justin instinctively knew that what was happening on the surface was not what was really happening and waited for the true subtext to emerge, which he felt that sooner or later it would. And the drinks were brought.

"Salud. Fucker," Bradley raised his glass and tinged with Justin's and added, "I love you, you cocksucker."

"That I deny," as silence prevailed, while they sipped, and then, "so—"

"Why did you do this?"

"Come on man, I am not your enemy, in your heart you know me. I was just trying to be helpful—and save your job. It's the only way I could see because—whether you realize it or not—believe me, 'they' were determined to fire your ass. Can you grasp that? I was just being a friend—"

"I know, I know." Silence lingered again.

"Come on man, do you know the seriousness of the situation? Hunh? Do you? Come on. Think about it, pal." Silence trailed. "Hunh? Come on man, we're talking no job—at this point in your life? Get it? No job!!!" Justin was uncertain as to whether he was penetrating Bradley's double bourbon density and engaged a hiatus to await an interminable time.

"Ok." Bradley expired and both suspended all motion. "So what's next?"

"Ok. Now we're talking," Justin bristled up. "Stop resisting."

Bradley melancholically and wistfully resigned himself to a reality in which all his glorious binges would be relinquished and foregone.

"Now," Justin began, "we're talking about attending some AA meetings. Right? No biggie. Right?" Justin was attempting to minimalize the arrangement as much as possible but knew that he had an unwilling, reluctant participant. *What can I do to give him the support he needs?*

"Ok. So where do we start?" Bradley peacefully conceded.

"Well, first, aren't you supposed to let Arnold Lawing know something soon—before a certain deadline?"

"The weekend didn't count. I got an email from him. He gave me until tomorrow morning," Bradley ruefully explained, "I can handle that with a phone call."

"I got the info on AA—meeting places, times, days, etcetera," Justin said, "there are a slew meetings every day."

"Ah, shit. I don't know if I can do this," Bradley said.

Justin studied Bradley closely and vaulted to the realization that his friend was in desperate need of support of all kinds. *What can I do for him?* Justin pondered while his own spirit became increasingly distressed, depressed, daunted, and defeated.

"In fact, I know I can't," Bradley continued, "I just feel like—like—like—I don't know—committing suicide or something. I got a nice revolver in my closet at home. I feel like using it and ending the whole goddamn thing. Just get rid of the whole fucking mess."

"Don't even go there." And then Justin opened his mouth and words began to come out that he had no idea of their wellspring, as though some possessing spirit had taken over his words and mouth.

"I'll tell you what we'll do—"

"Yes?"

"We'll do this together—"

"Do what?"

"The AA meetings. I'll go with you, it'll be our joint project, I'll pick you up and attend the meetings with you—get you safely home afterwards. All will be well. Whatta you think?"

Justin could not see Bradley's face very well in the darkened bar and could only sense his astonishment until the light broke from Bradley's face and seemed to light up the table.

"You'd do this for me?"

Justin paused for emphasis and then released the moment with "you watch me."

Bradley, as Justin read him, was profoundly moved, and Justin detected a sparkle in Bradley's eyes and then became cognizant of the fact that it was moisture in his eyes as the anger was replaced by a gigantic gush of gratitude.

"Are you ok?"

"Yeah. Sure. I'm fine. I've just never had anyone—"Bradley braked and broke.

"Anyone what?"

"Have faith in me—to—to—to—"and his quivering lips inhibited the termination of the expression of his thought. Justin was quite willing to wait this one out until, "you really are a friend, aren't you?" His eyes searched and then,

"Ok, buddy. We can do this. I know we can. I'll become a changed man. I'll dry out and everything will be great—never better—clear sailing ahead, as they say, happy days are here again,' right o'buddy?"

"All will be well."

"I'll drink to that." And he did.

48

By week's end, Professor Sandberg, reposing in his office after his last class of the week and making plans in his imagination with Ellen for the weekend—a good play, concert, movie, whatever—when he saw the shadow of a figure outside his office door, which door was fast becoming a symbol of all his troubles of the preceding weeks, by admitting disturbances into his life (he was contemplating offering a sacrifice to Janus, the two-faced god of doorways and entrances, after whom the month of January is named), and spoke loudly and sardonically, whoever you are, reveal yourself—unless you have a gun in which case go away."

"It's just me—and I don't have a gun," Betters answered without showing himself.

"Well, stop hiding."

"I think it's *Betters* this way."

"What?"

"This is what it's going to be like in the future around here," the voice gave back.

Justin arose from his chair and proceeded to the door with "what are you talking about?"

"I'll be seen no more—never, never, never more," Betters spoke eerily, having turned his back to Justin who was standing in his office doorway.

"'Tis. . . Some late visitor entreating entrance at my chamber door, This it is, and nothing more. . . quoth *The Raven* 'Nevermore,'" Justin cited Poe.

"That's about right. I shall henceforth be invisible—a faded memory—a great absence—a large cipher, a huge blank, a blurred erasure, zilch, nada—

"As in 'Our nada, who art in nada, nada be our nada?'"

"What's that from?"

"Hemingway's short story 'A Clean Well-lighted Place.'"

"I like it. My feelings exactly."

"Come on in—or stand here in the hall. I don't care." Justin retreated to his desk chair, sat, and then observed Betters walking backwards into his office.

"Very funny."

"My face shall never be seen no more," and remained erect with his back to Justin's desk.

"*Will* never be seen *any* more. Misuse of "shall" and a double negative." Justin fumbled with some papers on his desk while Betters ceased his performance and touched down in the chair in front of Justin's desk.

"Well, I just came by to say goodbye," Betters spoke humbly and softly.

Playacting, Justin thought.

"Where 're you going?"

"It's not where am I going, it's where am I NOT going."

"I don't know. Where are you NOT going?" Justin stayed the course.

"I am not going to be here no more, after this semester is over."

"Any more."

"So. What'd your girlfriend say about me?" Betters asked.

"Nothing. Why?"

"I could tell she didn't like me."

"She doesn't like your attitude toward women."

"Bitch."

"She is not a bitch. She is a very nice person."

"I didn't appreciate the way she confronted me—scolded me—embarrassed me—humiliated me—in front of you. I don't take that from women."

"She's a very strong person—and smart—and well-educated. The way I like 'em." Betters silently mulled it over. "And, yes, she has very stalwart opinions—especially when it comes to the treatment of women. She doesn't like them being used as doormats—as things."

"That's the way **I** like them."

"Doormats?"

"Bed mats. Soft, pliable, cooperative, accommodating, yielding, acquiescent, good in bed. You get the picture," Betters grinned his vile smirk.

"You know, Eugene, you would think, your being an educated man, PhD and all that, that you would want a woman worthy of your world of wisdom—your intellectual equal, not some undergraduate co-ed who is still growing up."

"If I want intellectual stimulation, I'll read a book. I want a different kind of stimulation from a woman," Betters concluded and stood. "Well, I guess this is it."

"*So much the betters,*" Justin smiled his friendliest goodbye grin at Betters and closed the door after his departure to meditate on this strange phenomenon.

49

The weekend with Ellen scampered by and Justin all too quickly found himself in the middle of the following week, located himself sitting in his office one afternoon, discovered himself responding to Janus the god of doorways' knock, detected himself looking into the eyes of Paloma Garcia, and established himself by greeting her with "Paloma! What a pleasant surprise! Come on in," and saw himself offering the chair in front of his desk to her with a signal from the palm of his hand, a chair all too often occupied by less welcome guests.

"Wow. How the heck are you?" Justin began the ritual of re-acquainting in undergraduate jargon.

"I'm ok, I guess." Paloma was very subdued and barely audible. Justin examined and analyzed her response, her face, and her body language.

"What's going on?"

"I don't know."

"That doesn't sound good." Silence defined the moment until Justin provided relief with "how's school going?"

"Ok, I guess."

"Aren't you about to graduate by now?" Justin asked.

"In the spring."

"Ah." An interminable pause intervened and Justin measured the parameters and ventured with, "are you ok?"

"I'm ok." Pause. "I guess."

"Not to be rude, but I think you said that already. Talk to me." Justin leaned forward.

"Ok. The reason I'm here, is, is, is, I need a reference," Paloma explained.

Of Woe or Wonder

"You know that I'd be happy to give you a reference any time—and a very strong one as well," Justin said.

"Thank you."

"Just give me the particulars—you know—the organization, or whatever it is you're applying for," Justin continued.

Paloma sat in the middle of her silence, unmoved physically but clearly roiling inside."

"Are you applying for a job?" Justin tried to be helpful.

"No."

"For graduate school?"

"No."

"So you need a reference for--?"

"Maybe I used the wrong word."

"That's ok. We all do that at times," Justin said, "try again."

"The reason I am here," she began cautiously "is—is—is—to ask you to—to—to—serve—as—as—as—uh—I guess the right word is—a character witness?"

"Why do you need a character witness?"

"Well, well, it's—it's—it's—" and then the seam popped open, a torrent of troubled tears tumbled down her cheeks, all civilized restraint collapsed, and she dissolved into a floodtide.

"Take your time. We've got all day." Justin awaited her patiently, lifted himself from his chair, managed to get to the door of Janus, and eased it closed.

"I have a rule never to close my office door with a female student inside but I think we need some privacy," Justin said as he re-crossed to his desk chair.

"Thank you," she sniffled while Justin watched, waited, and wondered about the witnessing and then dared with,

"You need a character witness—"

She nodded and sobbed.

"—is there going to be some type of trial—?" he braved on.

She managed another nod of her head.

"Anytime soon?" he evasively avoided specifics and direct confrontation with her troubles, side-stepping diplomatically around it. *When she's ready,* he thought.

She took a deep breath, steadied her inner self, finally gained possession, and charged ahead.

"Have you heard anything about what's going on in my life?" she raised her moistened, reddened eyes to him.

"No. I'm not a very active member of the grape vine society. Catch me up," Justin matched Paloma's low decibel level and grave tone.

"I—I—I—I—"

"You don't have to do this if you don't want to, you know," Justin whispered.

"Raped" she managed.

"What?!!!"

"Raped." It seemed easier the second time.

"Who?"

"Me."

Justin rose to his full height, then re-sat himself, then rose again, then sat again, then was up again, moved to his left, then moved back to his chair, sat again, jumped to his feet and reached over the top of his computer screen and rammed his fist into the wall, obviously hurting himself, and then tried to shake the pain from his fist.

"I'LL KILL THE FUCKING BASTARD, I DON'T GIVE A SHIT WHO IT IS, YOU UNDERSTAND ME??? I'LL KILL HIM," he raged on.

"Dr. Sandberg?"

He stopped and looked at her with "I'm sorry, I—I—I—[and snorted]."

"Now look who's speechless." He gave her a look of the tenderest, daughterly/fatherly compassion and slowly shook his head in plain pain and agony.

"Is the fucker in jail?"

"Out on bond."

"Humph."

Justin, being an English professor, was infrequently at a loss for words, until this moment, and he was stupefied into wordlessness.

"And there's going to be a trial?" He whispered.

"Yes."

"When?" with great softness.

"In January."

Of Woe or Wonder

"Sonuvabitch," Justin mouthed and waited. "Was it another student," he finally gained composure and language.

She shook her head no.

"Does this person have a name?"

She nodded yes.

"Do I know him--?" tentativeness, unsure which way to venture, came forth.

She shook her head no. And he wished to wait for her personhood, and then,

"I mean, I'm going to serve as a character witness for you, so sooner or later, when it goes to trial, I am going to find out who it is," Justin said.

> Paloma uttered something inaudible.
> "I'm sorry. I couldn't hear you."
> "His name is Reverend Otis Brown," she finally managed.
> Justin stared at her interminably, mouth open and eyes bulging, then he began to laugh.

"You're laughing?"

"I get it: this is a joke. Right, Paloma? You're trying to pull my leg, aren't you."

"Dr. Sandberg. Don't laugh at my trauma," Paloma pleaded.

Justin gathered a few moments together to gain his sensibilities and then came, "all I can say is that god has a very vile, perverted, *sick sense of humor.*" He paused, trying to recover from the crippling punch to his sanity, and, still conscious but incomprehensibly, offered up an oration to this mad god with, "how could this be?"

"Do you know this person?" Paloma asked. She too was open-mouthed and speechless.

"Indeed I do," Justin replied.

"How?"

"His son was in my class—"

"Otis Junior."

"Yes. It's a long story, but, bottom line, the good reverend tried to get me fired for teaching *Othello*," Justin said.

"Typical."

"How do you know him?" Justin asked, "I mean, you're like from two different universes."

"I—my family—go to his church, until—you know—it—hap—" and was unable to finish through the pain. Justin permitted some courteous silence, and then,

"It happened in church?"

"Nono."

"You don't have to talk about it," Justin said, and offered another considerate silence.

"In his car."

"Ohmygod"

"He offered me a ride home one night, and drove to the desert instead."

"No witnesses."

"Nope. Which is why I need character witnesses."

"I appreciate your asking me. I'm flattered."

Justin wondered if she had heard him because her face had no response features.

"Paloma?"

"Yes."

"Thank you."

The air was full of question marks but Justin, out of concern for Paloma, did not invoke any of them but opted instead to console her with his own relevant, softly, languidly spoken narrative.

"Let me tell you something ironical. The good Reverend Brown, as I said, filed a grievance against me with the administration for teaching miscegenation, i.e., *Othello*. You know the play about Othello and Desdemona."

"Yes." She brightened a little. Academic discussions are mutually reassuring and comfortable discussions about a shared knowledge and experience and provide powerful templates for conversations about human affairs, and Justin knew that Paloma knew the story well, for she had done well in his class and was involved in many classroom dissections of it. He knew she would understand.

"He apparently put a lot of time and energy into this project, interviewing students, lady friends, friends, acquaintances, *etcetera,* (I'll hand it to him, he was very thorough in his research) and then filed a formal grievance which was handed over to the Faculty Senate's Grievance Committee which did its own investigation (the university does not ignore complaints from the community, regardless of how frivolous or absurd they may seem) and then scheduled a hearing, at which both parties were to appear. And then—you'll never believe this—"

"Try me." She smiled her first smile of the present tense and seemed to find momentary distraction from her own horrors and to transcend her own wounds.

"At the hearing, after opening statements by the chair of the committee, the floor was yielded to the good Reverend Brown for his presentation, and just as he was "warming up the crowd" came a banging on the door which turned out to be the police, just like in a B-grade, bad, melodramatic flick—"Justin smiled the smug, satisfied smile of divine retribution.

"And then?"

"The police proceeded to arrest one Reverend Otis Brown right there in front of the whole committee, which eventually included the whole university, his whole congregation, the whole city, the Holy Trinity, and the whole universe. All of which he deserves. Everything comes full circle, in this case, thanks to the whole you—and your—your solidness as a human being which triumphs over his rottenness. Everything is driven by character."

She smiled wanly, combining pain and justice. "Something told me to not let him get away with it. And here we are."

"And 'that should teach us, there's a divinity that shapes our ends, rough hew them how we will.' *Hamlet*."

"I recognized it."

"I figured you did. It also teaches us that the whole universe is interconnected and Justice sits next to the throne of God."

49

Justin had been attending AA open meetings with Harold Bradley for two weeks, fourteen meetings thus far, when one evening as he was driving to fetch Harold to transport him to the evening's meeting, he was reflecting on the brief history of the preceding two weeks and the success they seemed to be having, even though Bradley had been quite resistant, recalcitrant, obstinate, ornery, obdurate, perverse, contrary, uncooperative, and *argumentative*—Bradley went anyway, knowing the consequences. Justin was leery but determined, satisfied but dissatisfied, smug but discontented, hopeful but despairing, trustful but distrustful, optimistic but pessimistic, supportive but ready to surrender; he was steeled to fulfilling his end of the bargain but was aware of Bradley's unhappiness. *"Hey, look, it's on me. I've got to be the strong one. He's depending on me. I can't let him down, above all I can't let myself down, and I can't let my doubts show,"* Justin thought.

He parked his car in front of the Bradley domicile, ambled up the front sidewalk, bent over to pick up the newspaper lying in the grass, looked up to pay homage to the dying sky for its November awesomeness, approached the porch and then the front door, all the while litanizing *"we are going to beat this thing, we shall overcome (sixties, he thought), just takes some time and encouragement without faltering, we shall conquer, we will be triumphant,"* and then "good evening Virginia, your evening newspaper, ma'am."

"Justin, come on in. He's almost ready," and he entered in her wake. "Justin, I just want you to know how much I appreciate what you are doing for us. I know it is not easy and that it is a sacrifice of your time and effort—when you could be doing something more fun for yourself." She reached for his hand, took it, squeezed it, and, with all the honesty one could conjure up mouthed, "thank you."

"It's nothing."

"Yes it—"

"Hey everybody." Bradley was standing in the doorway (*another Janus*, thought Justin) with what appeared to be a bottle of mouthwash in his hand, "just finishing brushing my teeth. Be right with you," and stepped back into the hall bathroom.

Justin and Virginia were a little discomfited by the awkwardness of the situation but Justin dismissed it.

"That's his third bottle today," Virginia said.

"What?!"

"That's his third bottle—"

"Nono. I heard what you said. You're talking about—"

"Mouthwash," Virginia clarified and emphasized.

"What are you saying?"

"That is the third bottle of mouthwash he has drunk today—this evening," Virginia said.

"He drinks bottles of mouthwash?!"

"Yes."

"Which is—what—about fifteen percent alcohol?"

"It is? I didn't know that."

Justin, who till now had been standing just inside the front door, negotiated his way to the nearest stuffed chair and submerged into it, unable to actualize this earth-cracking, startling piece of reality. "*Despair is a sin, according to the existentialist,*" Justin reminded himself, "*and I am sinning.*"

Justin looked at Virginia, who seemed oblivious to the ramifications of the information she had passed to him, with compassion. "Every day?"

"Not—*every* day."

"Ok folks," Harold blithely sang as he entered the living room, "I'm ready."

They uttered their goodbyes and departed.

In the car, Bradley was quite effusive and high pitched and was airborn into a monologue. (*Adrenlin or—mouthwash*)

"Hey pal, I really 'preciate all you're doin for me," Harold managed.

It was not Harold's regular tone of voice, *perhaps a little too cheery, artificially so,* Justin thought.

"Es nada," Justin rejoined.

"I mean, together we're going to lick this thing, right pal?" *and a little overly friendly.* "I mean, I'm turning over a new leaf. I am going to make a fresh start. I mean, I've made my mistakes, I've had my troubles in the past, but that is all behind me now. Right? I'm finished with that kind of life. I've got my buddy now to help me, that I can lean on and I can't let him down. No siree bob. I cannot, will not, let my old pal down. He has shown how much he cares and how much he supports me. Can't do that kind of thing anymore. You are going to see one changed man, I mean it. You just watch me."

He's trying too hard, Justin thought.

"Ok."

Justin wished Bradley would shut up, exposing himself as he was, but Bradley persisted in going on, and the remainder of the ride was buoyed by Harold's optimistic, positive, confident, hopeful, bullish, upbeat bordering on euphoric--hollow attitude. Justin realized it was the mouth wash talking, and his only response was, "we're here."

Inside the meeting hall, Bradley continued his gregarious and effusive ways, introducing himself to everyone, shaking everyone's hand, laughing at his own inane jokes, slapping people on the back, bordering on rudeness, and attracting everyone's attention who rendered him a sly, suspicious, corner of the eye quizzical look, although no one could smell alcohol. But these people are pros and are not to be fooled because *you can't con a con!*

During the meeting, several people volunteered with their stories and all went smoothly until Bradley stood at his chair, coughed loudly, turning all heads around to him, cleared his throat and said,

"Hi, I'm Harold, and I—I—I—am—uh—an— The words would not arrive to his lips as he respited.

"An alcoholic," Justin whispered loudly to him.

And Bradley sibilantly muttered, "an alcoholic." Everyone released a collectively held breath. Bradley hesitated and then said, "hello again" and smiled a baby-faced grin.

"I come from a small town in east Texas, Commerce, Texas, to be exact, part of the Bible Belt, as H. L. Mencken called it, a German from Baltimore, who did not intend the label to be a compliment. In fact, he was being sarcastic and condescending. Which I resent. And H. L. Mencken was not actually a literary giant. In fact, he was more of a hack journalist." And then he began to ramble on about Mencken and Yankees' attitudes toward the south and got completely off the subject and seemed to not even realize what his purpose was in speaking, same as occurs in his classes. And then he found his way again. "I was brought up in a very strict Southern Baptist home where we went to church almost every day of the week and five times on Sunday, and alcohol was completely verboten (a medieval English verb) in our community. It was considered a sin and anyone who drank was a drunk and going straight to hell—which just made alcohol all that much more attractive when I went off to college, where I had my first drinks. In fact, I was in a fraternity and every weekend I, along with my fraternity brothers, were completely lobotomized. College was really my downfall as well as the beginning of my life which led me into the world of scholarship. . . ."

And Harold continued to wander all over outer space, with no focus, no purpose, and no conclusion, telling jokes and anecdotes and personal narratives (which he was quite adept at), idle commentary and gossip (although mildly entertaining), after about twenty minutes of which, the chair, realizing that there was to be no damming of the floodtide, interceded with, "Harold," and Harold continued to stagger on; "Harold," a little louder this time with no effect on Harold, and then, very boisterously, "HAROLD!!!."

Harold paused, looked around and seemed startled to suddenly realize where he was and what was happening (*I guess the mouth wash effect wore off*, Justin thought), and seated himself, apparently in great consternation and humiliation at himself. He slithered in his chair after he was seated, squirmed a little, and then seemed to withdraw from the rest of the session.

In the car, silence prevailed for a short period until Harold cleared his throat, sat forward in his seat, and tapped Justin on the arm.

"Justin?"

"Yeah buddy."

"Could we—[pause]—could we—"

"What's up?"

"Could we—you know—stop—"

"Stop?"

"Yeah. You know. Stop. For just one little drinkypoo?"

Justin felt his entire being sink as an incalculable weight pressed down on him, starting at the top of his head and pressing slowly down through his whole body until it reached his toes.

"Whatta you think? Hunh?"

"No."

"Awww. Come on. Just one tiny little drinkypoo. It won't hurt anything." Harold spoke like a chastened child chastised. "Hummm??" with his most persuasive tone.

"No." Justin replicated the Great Wall of China.

"Why not? Give me one good reason," Harold whined. It was—no other word suffices—pathetic, and Justin was not unsympathetic, for he felt what Harold was going through.

"You want to know why?" Justin calmly asked, "because: one little drinkypoo leads to two little drinkypoos which leads to three little drinkypoos and before you know it, the night is drinkypooed away."

Silence again damaged the inside of the car for a brief while until Harold said,

"Stop the car!"

"WHAT!?

"Stop the car!!"

"No."

"STOP THIS GODDAMN FUCKING CAR!!!"

"No. This is why I am doing the driving. I am in charge and I am responsible for you."

"ALL RIGHT THEN, HERE GOES—" And Harold opened the passenger door to a small degree and then rasped, "if you don't stop this fucking car, I am going to jump—"

Suddenly Justin was rammed with fright, not knowing what Harold might do, and pulled the car over to the side of the street.

"Thank you," said Harold and exited from the car while Justin sat there in great dejection, desolation, discouragement, and, bordering on delirium, gathered up his dignity and drove away without looking back. Justin had a bad night when he got home, and had one drink, his first of the evening, before retiring.

Midway through his drink, his phone rang which he had been anticipating and dreading, and gave a very defeated "hello."

"Justin. This is Virginia. Where are you guys?"

Justin stood in a crosscurrent of thoughts, feelings, and attitudes: he felt guilty, it was not his fault, he took responsibility, he had tried his best to help, he had clearly failed, he just wanted to help his friend, his friend was beyond help, he remained positive throughout the whole process, he had acquiesced to a more powerful force, he was truly supportive, he was going to be blamed. He was in a quagmire with his head barely above the swampy disturbance.

"Virginia." Justin hardly knew how to begin. "I don't know how to tell you this—He heard an "ohno" and then the dial tone.

51

"Dr. Sandberg?" He was standing in his office with his phone to his ear when he heard the female voice on the other end. "Yes?"

"This is Paloma." He recognized the voice.

"Yes Paloma?"

"Have you heard the news?"

"What news?"

"Can I come see you in your office."

"Yes. Of course. What news?"

"I'll be right there. I am just in the next building," she said.

"What news?" And she was gone to silence. He slowly delivered the receiver to its place on his desk with *"wonder what that is all about. I've been working all day. I haven't heard any news."* He then moved to one of his favorite locations in the universe: his office window looking out over the campus through which he witnessed lots of life lingering outside and noted Paloma hurrying up the sidewalk toward his building. He picked up the folded newspaper on the corner of his desk and fumbled through its pages without finding anything of note. *I haven't a clue what she's talking about"*

"May I come in?" were the next words he welcomed.

"Of course. Have a seat," he invited her. She accepted his invitation and promptly seated herself, looked up at him with a terrorized look in her eyes, but she could not get comfortable as she repeatedly re-sat herself and then stood up and began to move around the room. He noted too that her hands were trembling as she kept wiping her hair away from her face which was not in her face.

"Are you ok?" was all he could offer her at the moment.

"Yes. No. Oh god! I wish I had a drink."

"Sorry."

"Give me a minute."

"Take your time." And he ceded it to her.

"You haven't heard anything?"

"Nada. I've been teaching." And waited some more. "Can I bring you a cup of water?"

"Yes. Please.'"

He picked up his community coffee cup, exited across the hall to the fountain, filled it, and return with, "wish I had something stronger for you, since you're of age, but *aqua* will have to do."

"Thank you," and she inhaled the water deeply after the quivering cup reached her lips.

"Take a deep breath," he advised. And she did, several times, very deeply as he noted her nubile breast and imaginatively slapped his own face for even noticing.

"Ok?"

"Ok." He studied her to make sure she was being truthful and then repeated,

"What news?"

"The Reverend Otis Brown—"She took another very deep breath to generate enough oxygen to create the words and another sip of water to moisten the words with.

"Yes?"

"Is—dead."

"What?"

"Dead."

"How—from what?"

"That's all I know."

"How do you know this?"

"I got an email from a girlfriend—who goes to the same church."

"But at my back I always hear
Times winged chariot hurrying near;
And yonder all before us lie
Deserts of vast eternity . . . something, something, something,
Thus, though we cannot make our sun
Stand still, yet we will make him run."

"This seems so strange. Something is—"

A ping sound was then heard from Paloma's purse as she went trolling for her phone.

"A text," was all that she could manage at this point as she opened her flip mobile phone and scanned the screen while a look of pure horror covered her face. She appeared traumatized, ashen, frozen, and then lifted her wild eyes to her professor,

"Suicide."

"At my back I always hear time's winged chariot hurrying near." And then an evil grin crossed Justin's lips as he uttered, "And all before us lie, deserts of vast eternity. Damned if I'm going to his funeral."

52

Justin's friend, Professor Harold Bradley, disappeared for several weeks while on a binge but showed up in time for the final exams and then announced his retirement after the fall semester. Professor Eugene Betters was never seen on campus again, except on occasion when he was allowed to check his mailbox. Paloma, giantess that she is, graduated at the end of the spring semester and became an exemplary high school English teacher and also found love. The Grievance Committee, by necessity, having no griever, dropped all charges against Dr. Sandberg, the Church of the Good Shepherd was deposited into the trash can of history, and *Othello* became Dr. Sandberg's favorite Shakespearean play to teach.

53

"*Othello* was Shakespeare's next tragedy after he wrote *Hamlet*. In some ways, it is a better play than *Hamlet*, which many consider to be his greatest play, if not the greatest piece of literature in the English language." Dr. Sandberg was pontificating from behind the podium at the front of the classroom several weeks into the following semester. "It tells the story of Othello, a general in the Venetian army, and his wife Desdemona, the daughter of a powerful senator of Venice."

A hand slowly appeared above the rows of student desks.

"Yessir?"

"Dr. Sandberg, It says here on the title page, *Othello, the Moor of Venice*. What's a Moor?" the young man asked.

"Let's get one thing pellucidly clear from the start: *Othello* is NOT a play about race. Ok? It is the story of a great love between a husband and his wife which is destroyed by the husband's best friend, Iago. Bottom line: it explores the nature of evil. Don't add anything extraneous to that basic fact.

"Oh, by-the-way, a Moor is a Muslin from the Mediterranean region," he interjected.

"Now, let's look at the play's many merits."

www.ingramcontent.com/pod-product-compliance
Lightning Source LLC
LaVergne TN
LVHW021700060526
838200LV00050B/2433